D0335111

The
Baker's Sister

Gracie Hart was born in Leeds and raised on the family farm in the Yorkshire Dales. She began her career as a glass engraver before raising her family. Gracie has now written several family sagas.

Gracie and her husband still live in the Yorkshire Dales and they have two children and four grandchildren.

Gracie HART

The Baker's Sister

**SIMON &
SCHUSTER**

London · New York · Sydney · Toronto · New Delhi

First published in Great Britain by Simon & Schuster UK Ltd, 2023

Copyright © Gracie Hart, 2023

The right of Gracie Hart to be identified as author
of this work has been asserted in accordance with the
Copyright, Designs and Patents Act, 1988.

1 3 5 7 9 10 8 6 4 2

Simon & Schuster UK Ltd
1st Floor
222 Gray's Inn Road
London WC1X 8HB

Simon & Schuster Australia, Sydney
Simon & Schuster India, New Delhi

www.simonandschuster.co.uk
www.simonandschuster.com.au
www.simonandschuster.co.in

A CIP catalogue record for this book
is available from the British Library

Hardback ISBN: 978-1-3985-0813-2
eBook ISBN: 978-1-3985-0814-9

This book is a work of fiction. Names, characters, places and incidents are either
a product of the author's imagination or are used fictitiously. Any resemblance
to actual people living or dead, events or locales is entirely coincidental.

Printed and Bound in the UK using 100% Renewable
Electricity at CPI Group (UK) Ltd

MIX
Paper | Supporting
responsible forestry
FSC® C171272

The
Baker's Sister

Chapter 1

Meg Fairfax sat at the table and counted the money she was about to take to the bank.

She leaned back in her chair and smiled to herself, remembering the day when she first walked into the bank on Commercial Street. She had been full of nerves and clutching the two pounds that she was to open her bank account with, all in loose change. That had been three years ago, three years of a lot of hard work and heartbreak along the way. Still, now she would have enough money there to do what she had set out to do when she was just sixteen – to buy the bakery that she was still living above, running as a manager and baker for Joe Dinsdale.

Meg looked down at the accounts book that she had kept each day, totting up each penny she made and each payment made to Joe Dinsdale, and felt satisfied. The time was right to purchase the bakery. It had gone from strength to strength thanks to her – and then she could put her fiancé out of his misery and marry him. Poor Frankie, he had been patient and had waited long enough to finally have her as his bride. They were supposed to have married over three years ago but she had delayed, wanting to prove to him and herself that she was just as good if not better than him in business.

She smiled as she drew the string on the money bag to; she was shortly to achieve both of her dreams. But Frankie also had worked hard. Both of them had needed to show that they could run their own business and that, once wed, their union would be an equal partnership. In her short life, Meg had seen too many women obeying their husbands and watching what food they ate, to keep themselves attractive for their men. That life was not for her; she wanted her independence, married or not.

Closing her accounts book she pushed back her chair and peered out of her window. It was early spring. The buds on the lilac tree in the small garden in front of number 2 York Street across from the bakery were just beginning to show after the harsh winter months. Soon the good weather would bring more people sauntering the streets and looking into her bakery's window. More reason for her to visit Joe now and make her offer to him while trade was slow after Christmas and the cold winter months had kept people in their homes.

Meg reached for her thick woollen cloak and placed the bag of money into her bag. But before she could set out on her mission to do business with her employer she needed to check that her assistant Janet had plenty to do in her absence.

'Have you mixed the scone dough and placed it into the oven, Janet?' she enquired of the young lass who was proving to be a real asset to her in the bakery. 'Customers always like our scones just as fresh as the bread first thing in the morning. I also hope that you have made the mixture half plain and half with currants? Else Mrs Whittaker will only complain if we have no fruit scones and I don't think I could put up with her complaints today, I've so much on my mind.'

Janet nodded. 'Yes, don't worry Miss Fairfax, another five minutes and they should be out of the oven – and I have made plain and fruit. Once they are out and the oven is a little cooler I'll put the sponge cakes in and then the small fancies.'

The young girl had been grateful for the opportunity to work for Meg, who had knocked on the door of Janet's home on Albert Street one day apparently out of the blue. Meg had rescued her from a life of being in service after hearing from Janet's mother how much she enjoyed baking. She'd worked at the small bakery now for six months and although Meg expected a lot from her, she was treated and paid well, both much better than she could have made being a skivvy in one of the many grand houses that were now being built in Leeds.

'That's good. I don't know how long I'll be this morning, Janet. I've business with both the bank and Mr Dinsdale. Will you be able to manage on your own?' Meg asked, knowing full well that Janet was more than capable and that the bakery was in the safe hands of the sensible level-headed girl who was proving to be a Godsend. 'And I think now is the time, Janet, that you start calling me Meg. You have been so much help to me of late.' Meg touched her friend and employee's arm lightly.

'Yes ... Meg, if you are sure. And don't worry,' Janet reassured her. 'The early morning factory rush has been and gone, George has picked up the baking for Mr Dinsdale. Customers will just come in at a steady stream now. You take your time, I know this morning is important for you.' Janet smiled and looked at the worry on Meg's face. She knew what was at stake – her employer had confided that she hoped to be the new owner upon her return. 'Good luck. I hope that you are successful.' She hesitated for a moment then added, 'You deserve to own the bakery if I'm not speaking out of turn.'

'Thank you, Janet, that means a lot.' Meg reached for her hand and squeezed it tightly then took a deep breath. 'I'll need all the luck I can get: a woman doing business in a man's world always does. Always remember we are just as clever as them, Janet, if not more so.'

Meg gave a last smile to the lass who reminded her so much of herself at that age as she closed the shop's door behind her. She looked up at the bakery sign above the door. It proclaimed that Joe Dinsdale was the owner, but hopefully on her return she would be ordering a new sign with her own name upon it to put in pride of place.

She stepped out with purpose down the street, acknowledging her neighbours and customers as her heart beat wildly at the thought of the day's business in front of her. It was a day she had dreamt of for so long that was about to come to fruition, through her hard work and thriftiness.

'Now then, Meg, I've been expecting you,' Joe Dinsdale said as she arrived. 'I've told George and the other lad not to disturb us. We want nowt with folk coming and going listening to what we are talking about this morning.' Joe – not just the owner of her bakery but also a string of grocery shops in and around Leeds – stepped back and held the door to his backroom and office open. Meg made her way past queuing customers in the busy grocery shop that everyone in that part of Leeds used. 'Are you well this morning? It'll be a big day for you today, but you don't have to worry,' Joe said matter-of-factly. 'We both know what we want and how much we can afford. You'll not find me unreasonable.'

'I'm very well, thank you, Mr Dinsdale. And you?' Meg asked as she pulled her gloves off and sat down in the chair that Joe Dinsdale offered.

'Isn't it time you started to call me Joe? After all, we both know you are equal to me in your business skills, else we wouldn't be sitting down here today discussing the sale of the bakery and shop.' Joe smiled at the lass. She had made him a small fortune with her baking. He knew that the only right thing to do was to sell her the bakery that had both turned their fortunes for the better.

'I was always told by my mother to respect my elders and not to call them by their first names,' Meg said and blushed.

'Aye, well that was back then and you hardly knew me. I

5

think after working together for nearly three years you can start calling me Joe.' He smiled and sat down in the chair next to her. 'Now, let's not beat around the bush. We both know why we are sitting together this morning. Besides, you look like a bag of nerves. I know that it's a big amount of money to be talking about for you and I'll not keep you hanging on with an answer. Did you get my solicitor's letter, and was the amount acceptable?'

Meg unfolded the solicitor's letter with all the clauses regarding the purchase of the bakery and shop within it.

'It is a lot that you are asking,' Meg pointed out. 'Will you not come down by another fifty guineas? That would leave me with some equity in my bank, something to fall back upon in case anything goes wrong?' Her hand was shaking as she looked down at the letter and the price written upon it for the bakery. She knew Joe Dinsdale had only paid a quarter of the sum he'd named to Ted Lund, the original owner.

'You'll not be short of a bob or two once you've got that fella of yours married,' Joe laughed. 'I hear he's bought another bakery in Ilkley. Surely he'll be there to help you out?'

Meg's face clouded over. 'This is nothing to do with him,' she said firmly. 'This is my bakery, you should know that he'll not be interested in it. If I marry him he will be my partner but I'll still run it as I do at the moment.' After a moment, Meg added sharply, 'Frankie has no time for the "little run-down bakery on the back streets", as he calls it.

He is too busy courting the rich and famous with his fancy patisserie.'

'Aye, that's what I maybe thought, but I had to make sure he wasn't going to be involved in the sale else I'd be asking full price,' Joe admitted. 'I was nobbut asking. Are you in agreement with supplying me still at cost price. You know I've just bought another shop on Wakefield Street? I'll be wanting baking for there as well as here and my other.'

'As long as you take into account the price of goods and what I have to pay for them,' Meg replied, knowing she wouldn't have dared speak to Joe in this way a few years ago when they first went into business together. 'I've got Janet working for me now, I've her wages to pay so there'll need to be a small charge on top of the cost price. Else I'd be losing brass.'

'And you'll still get main of your ingredients from me?' Joe confirmed.

'Aye, it works, why should I change it? George delivers and collects and is always punctual. It's in both our interests to trade with one another.'

Joe sniggered. 'It's in George's interest and all,' he told her. 'He's sweet on that new lass of yours, and she's all he's talked about lately.' Joe sat back in his chair and looked across at Meg. 'Tha knows lass, you know how to do business, you always have. Go on I'll accept a fifty less. Five fifty and it's all yours with my blessing although you have robbed me blind! You've earned every piece of brick and mortar. I just hope you can manage it all on your own.'

'Oh, I'll do that alright, Mr Dinsdale.' Meg beamed and could have hugged him.

'It's Joe now!' her now-former landlord reminded her. 'You are in business now, lass. Now make sure you've enough money in the bank and I'll get my solicitor to hand over the deeds to you once you've paid up. I knew you'd buy it from me the moment I made you the manager and I'm glad that you have. I know nowt about baking, except that I like eating it. Perhaps a little too much.' Joe patted his stomach and held his hand out to be shaken.

'Thank you, thank you . . . Joe,' she said hesitantly. 'I'm so glad that it's mine at long last.' She smiled and felt as if she could burst with the good news that the bakery was to be hers.

'Who's else could it have been lass? That bakery was made for you,' Joe told her as she made for the door.

He smiled to himself. At long last he'd put right the wrong that Ted Lund had done to the lass and he was happy for her.

A little later, Meg sat in front of the manager of the bank, feeling nervous as she wrote the cheque out for her property. She had never held a cheque book before and this was the first cheque she had ever written, never really dreaming of having that much money, let alone be signing it away to Joe Dinsdale for the purchase of his business. Her hand trembled as she wrote down the amount in numbers and then in letters, looking up at the manager as he made sure she made no mistakes.

'That's it. Now you need to sign it with your signature right there at the bottom and then we will authorize it with this stamp and it is ready to be handed over in payment of your property.' The bank manager looked across at the young woman. She had been as regular as clockwork with payments into her account and he admired her sharp mind and good head for figures. 'Now tear the cheque out and keep the rest in the book for if you need to pay for anything large in the future. Just do what you have done today, and, providing there is money in your account, we will honour the cheque.'

'Oh, I'll always have money in the bank, you can be certain of that,' Meg told the manager. 'I wouldn't dare not to have, that's how you end up in debtor's prison.'

'That's not done anymore my dear,' the manager told her, 'but, if we had to, we would declare you bankrupt and perhaps demand that you sold your property in order to pay us back.' He gave her a kindly smile. 'However, I know it will never come to that with you, unlike some of our other clients. I know you to be very astute with your business and I hope that we can be of further service to you.'

Meg rose from her chair and the manager held his hand out. She took it and shook it feeling very important; she'd never been asked to shake hands with a bank manager before. The smile didn't leave her face as she left the bank with the cheque ready to give to Joe Dinsdale's solicitor.

She was a proper businesswoman, she thought to herself. Her own boss with nobody to tell her what to do – something that she had only dreamed of in the past.

Chapter 2

Frankie Pearson sat at his desk and looked at the pile of invoices that he was about to pay. His businesses were thriving but his overheads and bills were constantly rising.

Now the owner of three patisseries, Frankie's life was filled with the running of them. He no longer baked every day in his busy bakeries; instead, he employed two pastry chefs, one from as far away as Paris, the other from London. They had to be paid along with the rest of the staff who worked in his patisseries.

He sometimes envied his fiancée, Meg. She had such a simple lifestyle, running her dilapidated bakery on the back streets, but just why she wanted to waste her hard-earned money on such an outdated business he could never understand. He shook his head as he thought about her: she'd been adamant she wouldn't marry him until she had bought the place, wanting to prove to herself and him that she could stand on her own two feet and had no need of marriage to protect and shelter her like a lot of women. She had postponed their marriage at least twice, but perhaps now she would name a date – after all, she was to sign for the bakery that morning. Looking at the clock on the mantelpiece, he realized the deal should have been struck by now.

He signed another cheque in payment of his accounts. He hoped that there was enough money in the business account to pay for it. Plenty of money came into his account, but with him dealing with the wealthier of society they took their time to pay. A patisserie bill was low down on their priorities, so sometimes it got to six months before they settled their affairs with him. However, it was not polite to be seen chasing the money owed to him, so he accepted his lot rather than lose the patronage of the great and good.

Frankie put his pen down as he heard the door being answered by Ada, his maid. He smiled as he heard Meg's voice ask where he was.

'*Ma cherie*, you sound excited,' he said, as he came out into the hallway. 'I take it the deal has been done, and now you are the owner of your own bakery?' He smiled as Meg removed her hat and gave it to his maid and with a big beam on her face came over and kissed him on the cheek.

'Yes, my bakery is now my own, I've just paid and signed for it,' Meg confirmed. 'Can you believe it, I own my own bakery? Me! Who never had a penny to my name a few years back? I'm so excited! The things that I can do now will be nobody's business.'

Meg flopped down on the chaise longue next to the window but even in her excitement she could see the worry on Frankie's face as he closed his roll-top desk, obviously not wanting her to see the pile of unpaid bills that he was wading through.

'Is everything alright?' she asked.

Frankie forced a smile, then made his way over to sit next to her. 'Everything's fine, *ma cherie*. I'm happy for you. I've just been seeing to my monthly accounts – they take some managing now that I have the accounts for three shops. So, just ignore me. You know how I am around accounts and paperwork. Unlike yourself, I find it a chore.'

'You are sure? Everything is alright, isn't it? You keep telling me all the bakeries are just as successful as one another and that you are run off your feet.' Meg's ecstatic smile faded. She knew to the last penny what she was worth but Frankie's affairs were another matter. 'I'll never have the same problems as you as my customers buy what they can afford and pay at the same time. I made it obvious from the start that I wasn't going to give anyone tick. That way there is no embarrassment for them or me. I'd not sleep of a night if people owed me a lot every month.'

Meg was a little annoyed that the glory of her big day of signing had been taken away with Frankie moidering about his accounts once again. 'I know the society that you deal with just decides that they can pay when they want,' she said trying to be understanding, even if it was a way of doing business that would never work for her.

'Yes, you have to hold your nerve but people usually pay up. It is a matter of just when!' Frankie reached for Meg's hand. 'Now, let us change the subject.' He smiled, leaned forward and kissed her lightly on the lips. 'Now, that you are a woman of property and have your own business, can we please set a date for our wedding? I've been patient and understanding seeing that the bakery meant so much to you but now I need you as my wife and I won't take any more delay.' He squeezed her hand again.

'I promised, didn't I, that once I had secured the bakery as my own, I would marry you,' Meg agreed. 'So, yes, Frankie Pearson, I will now marry you. You have waited long enough for me to decide upon a definite date and wear your wedding ring.' Meg sat back and curled up under his arm feeling secure and loved as he kissed her head. 'How about a wedding in September, just before the cold winds of autumn start and while the chrysanthemums are in bloom for the church and my bouquet?' Meg looked up at him and smiled. 'I did promise and I do love you so much. I am ready for marriage now.'

Frankie's smile lit up the room. 'I thought that you were never going to set a date with me,' he admitted. 'September it is then, my love. We will go and see the vicar as soon as possible and fix a date. I'm not going to let you change your mind this time. My wedding ring will be going on that finger of yours this time.' Frankie picked her left hand up and kissed it gently. 'Today's quite a day for you, Meg Fairfax, a business bought and a date set for your marriage. What more could you wish for?' He kissed her again.

'News from my sister, Sarah,' Meg said with a tinge of

sadness. 'Just to know that she is safe and well. It's been so long since she wrote to me and she is no longer at the address with the Hopkirks. Her letters keep getting returned.' Meg pulled her handkerchief out to blow her nose. 'I do nothing but worry about her. I know she will eventually let me know where she is. She did say the last time she wrote that after the last winter season in the music hall she might be looking for somewhere else to go. It's just not knowing where she is and if all is well.' Meg tried to smile as she looked up at Frankie.

'Your Sarah has been able to look after herself ever since I first met you. I'm sure she will be fine and will be writing to you shortly.' Frankie had had many a conversation over Meg's stubborn-headed sister and was not about to let her be a reason to put his wedding date off. He tried to take Meg's mind off the elusive Sarah, who always seemed to be courting adventure and danger. 'Now, which church are we to be married at? Saint Mary's or my local church here at Headingley? To be honest, it makes no difference to me.'

'It makes no difference to me either,' Meg told him, 'but I would perhaps prefer to be married at my local church. I know it's silly but I think my mother will be watching us from Heaven above, seeing she is laid to rest in the church-yard there.'

Frankie leaned down and kissed her again as she wiped a tear away from her eye.

'Then Saint Mary's it is. I'll see the vicar to arrange the ceremony and no doubt he will want to see you so it will be more convenient for you anyway. I've waited so long to walk down the aisle with you on my arm, I can't quite believe that we are to actually set a date for our big day. At least people can't say that we have rushed into it and that our love must be strong.'

'I know, I've made you wait, but I wanted for the time to be right for both of us and of course the time to be right for us to have children if we are blessed with them. I'm sorry.'

The clock struck one, and Meg realized that she had been away from the shop too long. 'I'll have to go. Janet will be wanting to go home, I didn't realize that was the time.'

Frankie stood up as Meg made her way to the doorway. 'Then I will visit you when I've set the date in September with the vicar in mid-week. Until then, I'll be thinking of you each and every minute, my love.'

'And I you, my dear. I can't wait to tell Janet that I am the new owner of the bakery and it will be my name that will be going up over the doorway.' Meg's grin returned as Ada brought her hat and cape.

'Surely it would be more prudent to wait until we are married to put up a new board over the doorway then it could read Pearson's Bakery? You would be part of my business then as it should be,' Frankie said.

Meg fastened her cape then turned to look firmly at him.

'No, it is my bakery, Frankie. I'll keep it in my name and run it myself. After all, it is a backstreet bakery and is nowhere near your posh standards. Horses for courses, Frankie —isn't that what you have always said? Just because I'm to marry doesn't mean I'm going to stop working.' Meg kissed him on the cheek. 'Don't worry, I can be married and run a business too. You'll not be a neglected husband and when children come along, well I'm sure we will come to some arrangement.'

'We'll see, my dear,' Frankie said and returned her kiss. That wasn't what he had planned. York Street was changing. The occupants were beginning to be more affluent, and it was the ideal place for a new patisserie, in the bakery already owned by his wife-to-be.

'Yes, we will see. But now I must go. I hope there's a carriage free on the street corner else I am going to be late for Janet.'

As she walked to the door, Meg was resolute. The bakery on York Street would have her name above the door, not Frankie's. Even though she did love him, it was hers. She had not worked so hard to buy it just to see someone else's name there. She would paint MEG'S BAKERY in bright letters, then it would be in her name, either married or single.

Meg sat back in her carriage and wished the horse and driver would go faster. It was getting near two and now they had come to a standstill as they reached the Headrow. She shouted up to the hackney cab driver to see why there were so many horses and carriages blocking their way.

'I'm sorry, ma'am, it's those bloody women again, they are marching down the Headrow with their banners and the like,' the driver shouted back down. 'They are a bloody nuisance. They want to be back home cooking dinner for their men and looking after the house. It's alright these mill lasses wanting more pay and better working conditions, but I wish I could do the same. I've all on to keep my family fed and all. The world's gone mad, women, shouting and yelling and making fools of themselves, when they should be back at home or making some money for their families.' The driver pushed the horse on a little as they reached the corner of the Headrow.

Meg sat back in her seat and smiled. Things were changing. Women were wanting more independence and she agreed with that, although she did not let her feelings be known to the carriage driver. He obviously believed that women should be still tied to the kitchen sink!

'Come and join us, sister, come and make your voice heard,' a well-dressed woman, a flowered hat on her head, pleaded with her as the driver ploughed his way forward and swore at them all. Meg didn't respond, but sat back in her seat and thought about the commitment she could feel in the eyes that had stared at her for that brief moment.

She sympathized with the movement: men did have too much say in women's lives and they weren't treated as equals. She thought about Frankie automatically thinking that once they were married her bakery would come under his ownership. She'd been right to make him wait, and now the deeds were being written in her name she would never let him own it. It would be her inheritance to their children and she would still run it with the aid of a manager. She certainly would not hand over her business to Frankie – he could barely manage to run the ones he already had, although he thought that she did not know the extent of the problems. He tried to keep his affairs to himself but she knew that he was always struggling to pay his creditors. The trouble was that he pretended to be something that he wasn't and portrayed himself to everyone as the rich successful patisserie owner when he actually depended on every penny from his rich and wealthy clientele. Once she was married to him, she would try to bring a little order to his accounts – if she was allowed.

Meg sighed as the cab driver finally turned down York Street. She smiled at her small bakery that was so loved and cared for – and would look even better, she thought, with its new sign.

'Thank you.' Meg passed payment to the cab driver and he doffed his cap to her.

'Sorry for the delay, miss. As I say, those women held us up, else I would have had you home earlier.' He grunted as he climbed up the steps of the cab and flicked the reins of his horse across its back.

Those women were brave to show their true colours, Meg thought as she saw Janet watching from within the bakery, waiting to go home. If she had the nerve she would be standing with them instead of putting her head down and not commenting.

She pushed the bakery door open and heard the shop bell jingle. The sound made her grin: she now owned the bell, the shop and the bakery. It was all hers, and nobody could take it away from her.

Janet looked on with anticipation at hopefully the good news that she was expecting to hear. 'Well! Did you do it? Is it yours?' she asked, excitement in her voice as she untied her apron strings and saw the look of happiness on her boss's face.

Meg beamed. 'I did, Janet, it is now Meg's Bakery. I still can't believe it. Every nook and cranny of this old place is *mine*. Isn't that just wonderful?'

'It is indeed, Meg. You have done ever so well since you started here. A woman to be admired, I'd say. I knew that from the minute that I came to work for you. Every day you were so determined to make the bakery pay and you have learned me so much since I came to work for you.'

'Thank you, Janet. You didn't take much training – you had a love of baking just like me when you first came to me and learning you new things was easy. I hope that you'll be working for me for many years to come. I'll need a steady hand running my business when I marry Mr Pearson.' Meg smiled. 'Not only have I bought the bakery but I've put poor Frankie out of his misery – I've agreed to marry him this autumn. He is to fix a date with the vicar this week.'

'Congratulations, I am so glad,' Janet said. 'The poor man must have asked you a million times for a date to be set only to be rebuffed.' She stepped forward and stopped for a moment before she plucked up the courage to put her arms around her employer for a reserved hug.

'Yes, but that doesn't mean that I am to let him run my bakery. It will still be mine. I've made that very plain to him, so I will still need your help. Even more so if we are lucky enough to be blessed with family.' Meg passed Janet her coat from the stand next to the bakery door and watched her put it on.

'But will Mr Pearson be happy with that? Surely you should hand it over to him?' Janet asked, perplexed at the idea of a wife doing anything other than pass the business to her husband.

'I love Frankie dearly but I will always run my own business,' Meg replied firmly. 'Besides, he has enough on his plate with his own little empire. Now, you've dallied long enough waiting for my return, Janet, go and look after that family of yours. Your mother will be missing you as she waits for the return of your brothers and sisters from school. I trust they are all well?' Janet was the oldest of six children, and although her father and mother were both at work she knew they struggled with their bills.

'Yes, thank you, poor but hearty as my mother says. Like most people.' Janet hesitated at the bakery door. 'Your friend Daisy called by when you were out. She said she would call back later this afternoon on your return. She looked worried.' Janet hesitated again before adding, 'I do feel sorry for her and the baby.' She shook her head as she closed the door behind her.

Meg watched Janet almost run down the cobbled road back home and thought about poor Daisy and the trouble she was in. Her friend, no doubt, would be back later, like she was every day after closing. Since she had been down on her luck, she was living off Meg's leftovers each day.

The tables had turned since they had first met. Now it was Meg's turn to look after her closest friend. Society had turned its back on Daisy, and abandoned her when she became an unwed mother with a baby by a respectable married man. Nothing better than a whore, she had heard whispered, but Meg knew better. Daisy had been a woman in love, let down by the man who had said he loved her but abandoned her once she was carrying his child. It was the same old story, Meg thought: men could do what they wanted but women had to know their place.

She started to clear the shelves of the unsold morning's bread and discounted it in a large woven basket next to the door. Every time she did that it reminded her of Ted Lund, the original owner, who would have sold the loaves of bread as being fresh for at least two more days and then they would have been filled with sawdust to boot.

Things really had changed since she first worked there and they were about to change again now that she owned it. She had made sure there was some money left over for improvements. One was replacing the wooden oven with gas. Her fear of gas had abated and besides, the ovens were advertised now as being much safer. The gas pipeline had been laid down York Street and it was time for her to take advantage of the resource and make life easier for her and Janet. Lighting a switch in the morning would be so much simpler than firing up the oven at an unearthly hour with coal and wood – and besides that, she could put gas lighting in every room. Then she could offer Janet her rooms to rent if she wanted peace from her family. Or dare she even imagine, her sister Sarah, returning from London one day, would actually need the rooms. Either way, the rooms above the bakery would be empty once Meg had married Frankie and moved out.

Meg's thoughts turned to her sister. There wasn't an hour in the day when she didn't think about her and she was getting more and more concerned about her whereabouts. Not hearing from her for so long was worrying and unlike Sarah, even though she had a mind of her own and had never confided in Meg that deeply.

The sight of Daisy waving at her through the bakery window brought her out of her reverie. She opened the bakery door and said hello to her friend and her babe-in-arms.

'Lord, I'm glad I caught you,' Daisy said with relief. 'Did Janet tell you that I've already been in? I thought she finished at 1?' As her baby son placed his small hand outside his blanket and started to bawl and shriek, Daisy joggled him to keep him quiet. 'I swear he knows when I'm having it hard, he's never shut up this morning.'

'He knows that you are worried and stressed. Give him here to me and come on through to the bakery. I'll turn my closed notice for a while. The main rush has gone – it will be just those going home from finishing work at the mills that will call in on their way back home in another hour or so.' Meg came from behind the counter and turned her shop sign over then took the bundle from Daisy.

'I swear I could throw him in the cut some days,' Daisy said, a note of panic in her voice. 'My life's worth bugger all since he came on the scene. Tom wants nowt to do with me, I can't work. My mother daren't have him because my father says I've made my bed and I must lie on it, so all I do is try to keep alive and keep the roof over our heads with the bit of mending that I can do when he is asleep.' She swept a tear away from her eyes and looked at her three-month-old son who instantly stopped crying once he knew he was secure in Meg's arms. 'See – he knows that I don't love him,' Daisy sobbed, as she followed Meg into the back room.

'He knows you are upset,' Meg replied. 'Babies sense things. Now, come on, I'll make you a brew and a sandwich. You know I'll help whenever I can. You can grab a loaf from out of the basket before you go and here's a Victoria Sandwich that's past its best as a treat. I was going to have it but I'd rather you were fed.'

Meg looked down at the baby dozing in her arms as Daisy placed the kettle on the open fire and took the chair next to it, where Ted Lund used to sit. 'Here take him now. He's gone to sleep, he likes the warmth and smell of the bakery.' Meg passed the precious bundle back to Daisy so that she could make sure that her best friend was fed for the day.

Everyone had foreseen Daisy's future. Everyone, that is, except Daisy herself who was now feeling sorry for herself, left high and dry after Tom Askew had abandoned her as his fancy woman once she had become pregnant by him. However, Meg realized that there was worse to come yet. Who knew how long Tom would continue paying for the upkeep of a house for Daisy now they were no longer together? She could see Daisy being thrown out upon the streets as her parents had washed their hands of her. Perhaps she should offer the rooms upstairs to Daisy once she was married – but then quickly thought better of it. Much as she loved her friend, she didn't want a baby crying night and day above the bakery or Daisy entertaining strange men at all hours. Incredibly, even now with a baby on her hip, she hadn't learned her lesson and still flirted with any man who gave her time of day. Maybe best not even to let the idea get into her head about moving in at the bakery . . .

With that in mind, Meg decided not to tell Daisy that her and Frankie's wedding day was about to be set. She brewed the tea and placed a ham sandwich in front of her friend.

'You are a good'en, lass,' Daisy said gratefully. 'This will stop my belly from growling.' Daisy ate the sandwich then rocked her baby as she looked into the fire. An old refrain crossed her lips, one Meg had heard many times over the past few months. 'I never thought I'd get caught,' Daisy muttered. 'And then the bastard didn't want owt to do with me. I thought he loved me.'

'Well if it's any consolation, like I've said, I thought Tom Askew would have stood by you, but he was married. No matter what he said, you should have known his wife and family would come first.' Meg sighed. 'You'll be alright. Charlie here will soon grow up and then you'll be able to go back to work, providing that you behave yourself and don't end up with another fella.'

'Another fella?' Daisy laughed bitterly. 'I wish that they'd all burn in hell. None of them are worth owt.'

'Oh, aye, so it wasn't you that I saw leaning on the corner and flirting with the rat-catcher when he came up our street?' Daisy had clearly not realized she'd been seen – Meg saw a flush rise on her face.

'That was different, that was a bit of business,' she said hastily and put her cup down.

'Got rats in your bedroom, eh! All I'm saying is be careful! Folk talk and I'm not having you put yourself in danger,' Meg said trying not to preach to her best friend.

'No, I know, it was just a one-off and Lord, did he stink! I swear I'll never have him back in my bed. Besides, I think I may have got myself a proper new fella but I'm not saying much more, I don't want to jinx it.' Daisy sat back more content with her stomach full and baby Charlie asleep in her arms.

So much for having owt to do with any of them, Meg thought. 'There's no helping you, lass, is there? Just leave the men alone.' Meg looked at her best friend. 'Anyway, you've forgotten, haven't you, what I was going to do today?' Meg grinned as Daisy tried to recall their previous conversation.

'Oh, Lord, I forgot,' Daisy said, honest regret on her face. 'This little bugger makes me forget what day it is let alone what anybody else is up to. Well! Did you do it? Is old Ted Lund's bakery finally yours?' Daisy knew the answer before Meg replied from the look on her face.

'It is. I signed for it this morning. The deeds are now in

my name. This is all mine. Can you believe it?' Meg grinned, proud at what she had achieved in such a short space of time.

'Aye, I can believe it, you always were the sensible one, and I should be more like you. Now I suppose you'll be marrying Frankie and you'll both live happily ever after, while I live with my shame.' Daisy looked down at the sleeping baby. 'When he's like this, I love him, but when he's twisting and crying I'm lost and I feel so low.'

'Oh Daisy, it will get better as he grows, he'll not be a baby forever . . . and you never know, Tom might come back into your life,' Meg said knowing full well that Daisy still loved her fancy man from the mill, no matter what he had done.

'No, he can stop with the fat cow he's married to. If he can't support his son now he need never bother. I'll raise him on my own. As long as you will always be there for me, I'll cope.'

Daisy closed her eyes and felt herself drifting off to sleep knowing that she and Charlie were fed, warm and safe.

'Have forty winks here in the chair while I clean the floor in the shop,' Meg said quietly.

'No, I'll go back and put him down properly. I might be lucky and get an hour to myself.' Daisy lifted her baby gently and carried him through to the shop. 'Thanks for being there for me. You are the only one that understands.'

Meg passed her a loaf of bread and the Victoria Sponge and Daisy balanced food and baby as she stepped out into the street.

'All we women understand that we could all have been

in the same situation as you and it's more luck than good planning that we aren't. However, a lot choose to be hypocrites, so take no notice of their looks and snipes. You know I'll always be here for you Daisy, just like you were when I needed you.'

'Ta, pet, that means a lot to me,' Daisy said and then made her way back down the street with the baby still asleep in her arms.

Meg watched her and knew that she'd be back another day for free bread and an ear to listen to her woes. Daisy had confirmed what she'd heard on the street – she was selling herself to any man that offered her a few pennies and her reputation was only going to get worse. Meg shook her head: she could never do that, she had too much pride.

She hoped that the new man in Daisy's life, whoever he might be, was not just using her. Frankie knew just how far he could go without being told sternly no and they had been engaged all these months. Poor Frankie must be frustrated with her sometimes, but she was in control of her body and her future, not him, and although she knew Frankie would never have left her pregnant, it had happened to many a young woman before. She was her own woman and that was how it was going to be if she had her way.

Chapter 3

Sarah Fairfax lay in her bed and closed her eyes. *Just another few minutes*, she thought as she heard Sam stirring.

'Come on lazy bones, stir your shanks, the tide will be coming back in if you don't get a move on and you'll have missed the day's best pickings,' Sam called. 'Move, and then you can go and see what you can pick up around Covent Garden – just watch out for the peelers.' Sarah felt a sharp dig in her ribs as he poked her into action.

'Leave me be, another ten minutes won't make any difference,' she mumbled and rolled over on the makeshift bed filled with straw. Then she rubbed her eyes as the dawn's early light shone through the filthy windows of the ramshackle room that she shared with Sam Waites, a cockney lad she had met after leaving the employment of Larry Hopkirk, who was as down on his luck as her.

'Them Fulham gang will get any worth out and they'll give you a good hiding if they find you on their patch. You know what they are like, from last time you came head to

head. I'd to show 'em what I was really made of. Now shift!'
Sam said sharply and pulled the one cover that she had on
her off onto the floor.

'For God's sake, Sam, I never get any peace,' Sarah complained but swung her legs out of the bed. She put her feet
into her boots and bent down to lace them tight. She'd not
bothered to undress; it made no difference whether she
kept herself clean and tidy, nobody was bothered about her.
She yelled at Sam to turn around and not watch her as she
relieved herself in the pee pot from under her bed.

'I don't know why I should, I've seen all that you've got
plenty of times. Having a piss is what everybody does. I ain't
bothered if you watch me,' Sam said, although he did turn
round to grab a sailor's kitbag, which he pulled across his
shoulder ready for the day's pickings that the tide had left
behind on the bank of the Thames. 'You go down to the
usual spot around Millers Wharf and I'll do down by the
Tower. Nobody likes that stretch, what with the Thames
peelers and the Customs House just after the bend, but keep
your head down.'

Sam turned back to face the lass he had found freezing and
hungry on the uncaring streets of his home city. He'd taken
a liking to her and offered her shelter and food in payment
for her help.

'I suppose there's nowt to eat?' Sarah asked as she pulled
her drawers up and fastened them.

'You think right. I'll meet you on Southwark Bridge
and then if we've had good pickings we'll get a muffin or

two from Old Bart. He fancies you – he'll give you one for nothing if you give him a quick peck.' Sam grinned at Sarah as he opened the door onto the busy dockland street where they both lived.

'You mind what you are doing,' he reminded her. 'I know it's usually good pickings on that bend of the river but it's not worth aggravating those bluebottles by mudlarking right under their noses.'

Sarah yawned and pulled a shawl around her shoulders as he pulled the door to, leaving her looking around the shoddy place they called home and trying to forget the empty feeling she had in her belly. It might just be four walls with a bed, table and chairs, but it was better than walking the streets like she had found herself doing when she had stupidly walked out of the household of the couple who had treated her no better than a dog.

Music-hall entertainer Larry Hopkirk and his wife had promised Sarah everything to encourage her to leave Leeds and come down to London with them, but it turned out that they had just needed her to be their scullery maid in a household of bullies and snotty cows, all of whom Sarah had learned to hate with a vengeance. Her home, just off George Street behind the South Quays of London's Docklands, might not be of the finest quality, but she answered to nobody, and she had Sam to watch her back in a city that cared not if you lived or died.

Sarah shook her head and brushed away a tear, remembering her sister Meg, who had tried to do her best for her young sister and whom Sarah had just taken for granted. Now she longed to see her face and even hear her chastizing her. She'd even beg forgiveness from Frankie, her intended, who she had hated so much in the past. She knew now that although they had nothing compared to some in Leeds, it was a lot more than she had now in the hovel she called home, with only a pickpocket friend for company.

Sam was a lot harder than Harry, the lad that she used to love who had lived next door to them. Sam carried a knife and he'd not think twice if he was forced to use it. He was also good with his fists and although he had started sleeping alongside Sarah, so far he had not touched her in any way. She knew sooner or later it would all end in tears, but for now, he kept her fed and a roof over her head, of sorts.

She sniffed and wiped her nose on her sleeve. It was no good feeling maudlin: the dawn was creeping its fingers over the never-sleeping city, so it was time for her to go down to the banks of the Thames. There she could look for treasures lost overboard from the many boats and ships that sailed the mighty waters of the busiest river in the world.

Every day Sarah set out in the hope of finding something that would change her life but so far she had just found the odd silver spoon, lost overboard by a careless captain; exotic fruits, dropped by careless dockworkers; and the general nick-nacks that were lost or thrown into the Thames. Later that day she would risk her life pickpocketing with Sam around Covent Garden and the streets leading away from the busy market. That was where the money would be made to feed them both, but also where they risked being caught by the peelers or even worse, attacked by their victim.

Sarah pulled the door behind her as she left. No need to lock it, there was nothing worth stealing, she thought as she walked out into the grey morning, the streets already bustling with Londoners going about their daily business. Flower sellers were calling for custom, as were milkmaids, while carts laden with veg and bread trundled along the streets, the sellers eager to feed the hungry hordes. The stench of the docks, the smell of the sea and the fish caught within grew stronger as Sarah walked past the busy Wapping Basin. There, some ships were fully rigged, alive with sailors scurrying like rats, making ready their vessel for the next voyage, while the steam-hauled boats poured thick smoke into the already murky skies, thick with smog and smoke from the many coal fires of the busy city.

From Wapping Basin she made her way down to the lapping shoreline, ignoring calls from sailors looking for a prostitute to spend their money on. She might have fallen far, but she would never be so low as to sell her body to just anybody. Meg had learned her well when it came to having pride in herself.

She walked along the Thames banks and peered down into the shingle and flotsam that the receding tide had left behind, picking up anything that looked edible or could be sold, no matter what the value. An empty tobacco box took her eye; it was of good teak wood and had the word Havana stamped upon it. Sarah had never heard of Havana, but she guessed it was a place, somewhere warm and a lot more welcoming than the murky Thames on a cold day in January. For a moment, she wondered about the journey that the box had made just to be thrown overboard when its contents had been used.

Fifty years ago nobody would have been down by the Thames – at least nobody that had to be – it had stunk so much, but now as Sarah wandered along its shores it was cleaner, after the architect Joseph Bazalgette had re-planned all the sewers, stopping them from emptying the city's contents into the mighty river. The Thames was beginning to change. Embankments being built further upstream were making it somewhere people could enjoy boating and seeing the magnificent scenery of the busy city. But that morning, as usual, Sarah would stay down by the docks and wharves, where there was more chance of that one find that could change both her and Sam's lives . . . if she was lucky.

She scoured the shingle, pulling at anything that made itself known to her and searching desperately for anything that shone or could be of worth. Feeling her luck changing she found a lost silver spoon half-buried in the mud. She smiled as she saw the hallmark, knowing that Sam would get a good price at the pawnshop and that they would be fed that day.

As she approached Millers Wharf she noticed a brown paper package wrapped around one of the wooden wharf's legs. It had just been caught in one of the struts by the receding tide. She walked quickly towards it, hoping that whatever was in the parcel was going to be of worth, then waded out up to her knees to retrieve it, flinching when the cold water covered her skirts and hoping all the time that whatever was inside would be worth a fortune.

It was all carefully tied up with string and of a decent weight. She returned to the bank, then, cold and wet, started to open the package, her heart beating fast as she tugged at the string with her cold fingers. She tugged and tugged, hoping this might be the answer to her prayers – only to gasp with horror and feel herself sick to the core as the contents of the parcel were revealed.

Inside was the naked body of a baby girl. Her face and body were all blue and bloated from being in the water for a length of time.

Sarah gasped and fell backward onto the shingle. How could anybody parcel a baby up and throw it into the Thames? Had she been alive or dead when they had done it? Was it a desperate mother who had done the dreadful deed or was it one of the despicable runners of the many baby farms? They had a reputation for not caring for the offspring they promised to raise, just taking money from the caring mothers and then disappearing after doing away with the child? It didn't matter. Whoever was to blame for its appearance, it was now Sarah's problem.

She looked at the small corpse then peered around to check if anyone else had seen her with the parcel, wondering whether to throw it back into the Thames. After all, it was dead, and had been for some time by the look of the skin. But she couldn't.

Somebody must have loved the baby. Surely it deserved a better fate than being thrown back into the Thames to be washed out to sea and eaten by the fishes. The poor wee thing deserved a proper burial, she thought, then looked upstream past Saint Katherine's Docks to the dark outline of the Tower of London. Beyond that lay the Customs House.

That was the answer. She would bundle the small body up in a shawl and leave it there. Surely somebody would take pity on the poor soul and give it a Christian burial?

Sarah took off her shawl, feeling the cold winter even more as she laid it down on the shingle. She squinted through half-closed eyes as she transferred the baby into it then checked it was concealed after she'd knotted it. She picked it up, along with her few salvaged possessions, and quickly made her way along the bank of the river to Saint Katherine's Steps. She quickly climbed them and joined the throng of dockers, sailors, and prostitutes who plied their trade at Katherine Docks.

She clung fiercely to her bundle, making sure nobody knocked it out of her hands or suspected what the contents were. She made her way around the dark walls of the mighty Tower, thinking of all the tales that Sam had told her of the kings and queens and ordinary people that had been held and executed there, especially the two poor twins whose lives had been taken by evil King Richard. Whoever had done this to the baby should be put in there, she thought as she saw the Beefeaters standing guard at the Tower entrance. She hoped that they would not even look her way as she made her way past them to the Tower Head stairs that led back down to the river. She could then follow the water to the nearby Customs House. Maybe she could even hand her bundle into an official there and tell him of her find.

'What are you bloody well doing this far up?' came a rough voice in her ear, making her jump and nearly drop the bundle. 'I told you not to go near the Tower, it's not safe to be seen scrounging around here. You said so yourself, and besides, I've finished this bit myself.'

Sam grabbed her arm as she tripped going down the stairs. 'What you got there then? A bag of gold? Can we have a decent meal today?' He scowled at her full shawl and at the bag full of foraged pieces from the shoreline.

'No, Sam, it's a baby, somebody's drowned a baby. I was taking it to the Customs House because I don't know what else to do with it,' Sarah whispered and looked around her hoping that nobody else had heard her.

'Why the hell did you pick that up? You should have left it where you found it! You can't take that anywhere, especially the Customs House. They'll think it's yours and that you have killed it, you stupid bitch,' Sam growled.

'They'll believe me when I say I've found it. It needs a Christian burial, Sam.'

'No, they will look at you and think that you are too young to be burdened with a baby so you decided to drown it. You are so stupid sometimes. Give me it here and I'll sort it,' Sam said angrily snatching the shawl and contents from her.

'You'll take it where it can be found? You'll not throw it

back in the water?' Sarah said as she watched him walk away in the direction of the Customs House with the body.

'I'll do what needs to be done,' Sam told her firmly. 'Now go and wait for me next to old Bart's stall. Here, I'll save your blushes.' Sam walked back to her and shoved some money in her hand. 'I found tuppence ha'penny on the steps that we've just come down. Somebody will be cursing themselves for losing it, but their loss is our gain. Now get yourself gone and think no more of your find.'

Sam turned and went on his way down the shingle. He had no intention of taking the baby to the Peelers or the Customs House. He would throw it back where it had been found, back into the river, like the numerous others that were found discarded and unwanted in the mighty Thames.

Sarah was thankful that she had not to flirt with Bart as she paid for the two hot muffins that he took out of his make-shift oven and stall by the side of Southwark Bridge. She found him disgusting. His teeth were blackened and his hair hung down like rat tails upon his shoulders. But his muffins were the best to be found for many a mile and she couldn't stop herself from eating one as she walked to the centre of Southwark Bridge and waited for Sam to join her.

The city was waking up properly now. Horses and carriages trotted past her, and people of all shapes and sizes were making their way from one side of the river to the other. Winchester Flour Mill on the far side of the river was busy unloading a new cargo – indeed, all the wharves down the river's banking had ships and craft starting to moor by the side of them, unloading their cargos from all over the world.

However, all Sarah could think about was what would become of the baby that she had found. She hoped that Sam had not got in bother with the authorities when he had handed the remains over. She looked down into the murky waters and imagined herself throwing a baby over the bridge edge. She knew she just wouldn't be able to do it, no matter how unwanted the child was. The mother must have been desperate . . .

Sarah sighed and wiped a tear away from her eye, as she thought of her old home back in Leeds. She had been so moody and awkward with her older sister, and now she realized that Meg had only been trying to keep her on the straight and narrow. How she missed Meg, but she must never know how low she had fallen. Her pride stopped her from telling Meg just how bad things were and that she would love to return home. She'd ploughed her own furrow in life and now she would have to put up with it. Besides, in the last letter that she had received from her sister, she sounded happier without her, and that meant Meg was free to marry Frankie Pearson, who would be glad that Sarah was out of his way. When she had money to spare she would write and tell her all was well in her life and try hard to hide the truth.

A few minutes later, Sarah saw Sam walking towards her, with no sign of the shawl or the dead baby.

'Did you manage to explain to those that you left it with?

I could have done with my shawl back,' Sarah said starting to realize just how cold she felt.

'I left it for someone to find just outside the Customs House. I just hope nobody saw me doing it. I'll pick you up a new shawl from somewhere. Give us my muffin, gal, I'm fair hungry,' Sam said, hoping that Sarah would believe him.

'Surely, somebody will do the right thing by the poor soul.' Sarah replied. 'Thank heavens you didn't throw it back into the drink. I couldn't have lived with myself. It made me realize just how desperate some women are.'

'Well, never mind. Let's not go to Covent Garden, we'll go and see what we can pick up in Lindsgate Market and it's not as far to walk. It looked busy as I passed after leaving the Customs House. There will be good pickings there and you are always happy wandering around there.' Sam saw Sarah's face lighten up. 'So, what else did you find this morning? I found them coins, a coconut, and this wood dish. Nothing to make us any more money.'

'I've done better than that,' Sarah said. 'I found this.' She pulled the silver spoon out of her bag.

'Lord, we will eat today!' Sam said thankfully. 'Come on, next stop Joshua's then. He'll give us a decent price – he can melt it down if nothing else. That's way better than any dead baby.' Sam started off back over the bridge.

'You did leave that baby where it would be found, didn't you, Sam?' Sarah said in a worried voice.

'Yes, stop fretting, it will be looked after. Come on, gal, there are some pockets to be felt and they are waiting for us.'

Chapter 4

Meg sat in the parlour with Frankie after having their Sunday lunch, prepared by the new cook that Frankie had recently employed and served by Ada.

'Well that was wonderful, she certainly knows how to cook,' Meg said. 'However, I don't know why you have taken a cook on at this moment of time.'

'I thought it was time to employ a cook,' her fiancé explained. 'After all, we will soon be married and by the way you were talking, you didn't sound as if you wanted to run the house and kitchen. Especially if you will insist on still running your own business.' Frankie tried to keep any sound of disappointment at this from his voice but he had wanted Meg to be happy just being his wife and mother to the family that he was hoping to have once married.

'I never said that,' Meg corrected. 'I just don't want to let go of my own bakery. I can run it and be at home. There really was no need for you to employ a cook. Ada and I would have managed the kitchen. After all, Ada has been doing well as the maid of all and when we are married this autumn then her duties will become lighter, not increase.' She took Frankie's hand and patted it. 'I know you only had good intentions but I sometimes worry about the amount of money you spend.'

'That is not for you to worry about, my dear,' Frankie chided gently. 'I shall be the breadwinner, in more ways than one, once we are wed. You and our family will be my responsibility. Of course your bakery can be an interest but I wouldn't want you there everyday. After all, your husband and home should come first. Now stop worrying your pretty head about money and my affairs.'

Meg hesitated for a moment but then decided to say what she had thought for a while but had not been in a position to say. Now that she had a property of her own, she thought it was time to air her views on Frankie's dealings.

'But I do worry about you,' she told him. 'Any wife-to-be would worry about her husband's affairs if she thought them to be a bit reckless.'

Frankie frowned and took his hand away from hers, sitting back with a surprised look on his face. 'Reckless!' he repeated. 'You are talking nonsense! Buying your own business has gone to your head. I'm sorry – you forget yourself, my dear. I own three patisseries and deal with an exclusive clientele. My business is totally to be relied upon. Just because I found myself the other year without a decent cash flow doesn't mean that I am struggling now.'

'I'm sorry, my dear, I didn't mean to pry and offend. I'm

sure that you are making good money with your wonder-ful delights. I should not have said anything.' Meg reached for his hand back and patted it, realizing that Frankie had become very defensive at her questions. 'Now, for a much more pleasant subject. Have you been to see the vicar yet at Saint Mary's? Do we have a date set for our wedding?' She smiled at Frankie and moved closer to him, to calm the tension between them.

'I have. I was going to tell you straight away but the cook announced dinner as soon as you entered the house, so I thought I'd wait with my news until now.' Frankie looked down at his feet and then put his arm around Meg's waist and looked into her eyes as he held her hand and kissed it. 'I did see the vicar at Saint Mary's. He was only too happy to marry us both. He was the same one I spoke to before when we were planning to wed and he also remembered burying your mother. He was overjoyed at our union.'

'Yes, he was a good man. Reverend Longfellow if I am right?' Meg smiled. 'He was very caring, despite our family not being regular churchgoers. I often see him nowadays and he always says hello.'

'Yes, that's the man. Lovely man. In fact, he suggested that we should wed this spring, the season for all young couples who are in love, and even suggested Holy Saturday, the day before Easter Day,' Frankie said and tried to judge Meg's reaction.

'That's a little too early, Frankie, especially when we are in no rush,' Meg said. She looked at Frankie, guessing straight away at what had actually happened. 'You haven't set the date for that, have you? You do recall we mentioned September?'

'It's just that he was so happy for us and he kept saying how a spring wedding would be so blessed – and it was when we originally planned. That the daffodils and primroses would be out in the churchyard and that it was the holiest of months. So, I found myself in a corner and agreed to his proposal of April the 8th. I've waited so long for you to walk down the aisle on my arm, September was nearly another six months more to wait.' Frankie took a deep breath and looked at Meg. 'Please don't be angry, just think of it: the leaves on the trees down the churchyard path will be beautiful and green not brown and dying. They will be as fresh as our love for one another.'

Frankie squeezed her hand tightly and kissed Meg on the cheek, but he knew that she was not happy with his decision.

'Oh, Frankie, it is too early. I've no dress, the cake is to be made . . . and just how many guests will you be expecting at our wedding? There are not many guests on my side of the family. It will be mainly friends, but what about yours?' Meg sighed. 'I wanted to run my bakery for six months before we tied the knot. That will be barely three. I thought you knew that?'

'I did, but don't you think I've waited long enough? Besides, there's nothing to worry about: Hopkin's will make you a beautiful dress, and how about we both partake in the making of our cake? You bake it and I'll ice it. I've been thinking of the design for months. Three tiers, with the most exquisite roses draping down it and delicate lat-ticework.' Frankie smiled. 'It will be alright, I promise. The wedding of the year if I have my way. I can ask all the great and good that are my customers. Let's make it a wonderful day to remember.'

Meg knew that Frankie had been patient for over three years, and wondered if that patience might run out soon. A thought struck her. 'What about Sarah? Will she be there? Last week I wrote to Larry Hopkirk at his home address just to ask if she was still working for him at the theatre or some other address, but so far I have had no reply. I don't want to get married without her, she's the only relation that I've got left.'

'She'll turn up like a bad penny,' Frankie said flatly. 'She's always been selfish, has that one. But think of it – in another few years, we will have a family of our own. That many children will be running around this house, we will need more than Cook and Ada. This house is made for children.' Frankie stood up. 'Forgive me, but please say that you are happy with the date. I've set my heart on it and you will make such a beautiful spring bride.'

'Very well,' Meg said after a few moments' silence. 'But please don't go over the top with plans. A simple wedding, that's all we need. As you say, I can make the cake and you ice it. Luckily, I bought in plenty of dried fruit from Joe. I'll soak it in some sherry and start making preparations to make it. It's only right that we both show off our skills on our wedding cake.' Meg stood up and linked her arm through his. 'I know that you are wanting family as soon as we marry, if God is willing, but I'd like a year or two with us just by ourselves. To build our businesses up and make sure that our family will be secure.'

'That, my dear, is for me to worry about. I keep telling you: finances are a man's domain, you shouldn't worry about such like. I'll find us a most agreeable place to hold our wedding breakfast and I promise I will not be too frivolous. Let me know your guest list and I will see those invitations get printed. And spare no expense when you visit Hopkin's for your dress, put it on my account. It has not been used as much since my mother so ungraciously left us.'

'Will you be asking your mother? It would be rude not to,' Meg asked and saw a cloud come over Frankie's face.

'I suppose I will have to. Lord knows why, she obviously does not care about me. Apart from a card at Christmas and for my birthday, I hear nothing from her. I doubt she will have the nerve to show her face: she still owes me a great deal of money.'

Frankie walked over to the bay window looking onto the busy streets.

'She doesn't like me, but she's still your mother,' Meg reminded him. 'Ask her Frankie, or else you'll only regret it. Blood is thicker than water and she only thought she was doing you good.' Meg came over and put her arms around his waist and her cheek on his shoulder.

'Doing me good? She doesn't know the meaning of the saying,' Frankie replied. 'The only good she was doing was for herself and her many lovers. How embarrassing it is to see your mother flaunting herself at these young men who only see her for my money!' Frankie turned and held Meg tightly. 'I don't want us ever to be like my mother and father. She never took any notice of my father. He had to do everything she said, else woe betide him.'

'We'll be nothing like your mother and father. We will be the happiest married couple in Leeds. As long as we respect one another and have no secrets between us then nothing will ever come between us, I promise.'

Meg kissed him passionately and looked into his eyes. 'I love you, Frankie Pearson, and always will. Our wedding will be one filled with love, whether there are a hundred people or just the two of us, so remember that when you are planning the posh do that I know is going around in that head of yours. I'm a lass from the back streets of Leeds, I don't want anything too posh. I just need a man I can trust and love on my arm for all my life, and one that will share his worries with me.'

'I promise it will be a day to remember, no matter how large or small, and I promise I will share my worries and love you all my life,' Frankie said holding her in his arms and kissing her.

Thank goodness she had agreed to that date, he thought to himself. He had already accepted Lady Bea Benson's generous invitation to hold the breakfast at Langroyd Hall.

Later that evening Meg sat down at the table and wrote yet

again to Larry Hopkirk. If she was to be married in April, she would like Sarah to be her bridesmaid at her side. She wasn't happy that Frankie had set the date so early, but it did mean that she could no longer put it off. After all, she did love him; she was just being selfish and wanting to enjoy her time single and independent.

She knew all too well what marriage meant. She would no longer be responsible for just herself and her business but her husband's well-being, the family home, and the family when it came along. All that made young girls into old women before their time especially if there were money worries in the family – and no matter how Frankie bragged about his money, she had a good idea all was not as rosy as he made out.

She reread the letter to Larry Hopkirk, almost begging him for information about her wayward sister. 'Please let him reply to this one,' she prayed aloud as she sealed the envelope. Without Sarah at her wedding, she had no other relatives attending and that would be unthinkable.

Chapter 5

Meg gathered the ingredients around her that she needed: flour, dried fruits, cherries, spices, demerara sugar, butter and eggs. It was early morning, Janet had not arrived yet and while she was waiting for the first batch of her bread to cook, she thought she might as well make the mix for the first tier of her wedding cake. After all, with Frankie setting the date so soon, there wasn't any time to waste. She needed the cakes to mature and soak in the ample measure of sherry that she would dribble into each of them to make them moist and delicious.

She had already lined the largest cake tin that she had, so she emptied the first lot of ingredients into her largest mixing bowl and started to cream the sugar and butter before adding the other items. She beat the mixture so vigorously that her arm was aching as she took a minute's rest to think about her up-and-coming wedding. It was too rushed for her liking but she could see no reason for delaying now that Frankie had almost put everything in place.

Meg got on with beating the mixture, shaking her head, wishing that Frankie had consulted her more with the wedding plans. She only hoped that he'd discuss his choice of venue for the wedding breakfast with her – somewhere not too grand. Somewhere ordinary. After all, they were a couple with no rich roots and they shouldn't think otherwise at the end of the day. He might own his home but she had guessed a long time ago that he had not been born with a silver spoon in his mouth despite his adopted French accent and his posh ways. His mother was definitely no lady – Meg had realized that on the first of their meetings. Despite that, she loved Frankie and knew that she would be happily married to him; he was mild-mannered and caring, and that was a lot better than some of the men she had encountered. She also knew that now she had the security of her own business she could weather any storm that blew itself their way. With family came financial pressure and she did not want to bring her children up in poverty and hardship as her parents had her and Sarah.

Meg reached into her pocket but before she could retrieve its contents, she heard the doorbell jingle in the bakery.

'It smells like Christmas again!' Janet said as she walked through the shop and hung her coat up behind the bakery door. 'What's in your bowl?' Janet took a sneak peek at it as she put her apron on and checked she looked respectable for the upcoming customers. 'It's too early for hot cross buns.'

'Oh, don't mention those or Simmel cake!' Meg said. 'It seems that I'm going to have a busy Easter. Frankie has gone and booked the church for our wedding for Easter weekend. I think all sense went out of his head when he was talking to the vicar because he too will be busy with work.' Meg spooned the mixture into the cake tin. 'Can you just check the batch of bread in the oven and put the next one in if it's ready?'

'Yes, of course, and I'll put the rock cakes, scones and sponges out onto the shelves. You've been busy this morning,' Janet replied as she opened the oven doors to take the large tray of bread out, placing it down on the table and then patting the bottom of the test loaves to make sure that the bread was cooked through before putting the next batch in. 'I didn't think you wanted to get married until autumn?'

'Don't, Janet,' Meg said. 'I didn't but he's booked the church and he's also agreed to book a place for our wedding breakfast. Wherever it's going to be it will be a bit of a one-sided affair as I have hardly any family to ask, and the neighbours and friends that I would have asked would feel totally out of place anywhere posh, like I know he will probably book, knowing his standards.'

'I think I'd have said something. It's your wedding as well as his, you know?' Janet said hoping that she wasn't talking out of turn.

'I've kept making him wait,' Meg admitted. 'I don't think I'd better say too much. I've also made it perfectly clear that this bakery is always going to be run and owned by me and me alone, which I could tell was a bit of blow to him.' She made a dip in the middle of her mixture so that the cake had room to rise evenly then started to cut some brown paper to wrap around the tin so that the outsides did not cook too quickly. 'Marriage I understand is all about give and take, so I'll make do with whatever he arranges.'

'I'd want more of my own way. Start as you mean to go on, my mam always tells me, and that's what I aim to do.' Janet walked through to the shop and Meg smiled at her self-assured young assistant whom she soon hoped would be running the bakery for her – if she decided to become the perfect wife and mother. But not yet. She wasn't quite yet willing to sell her soul for sake of a wedding ring.

She placed the cake to one side. Reaching for the tray of fruit teacakes that Janet had left behind she followed her assistant into the shop and looked out onto the still-dark streets. 'I hate this time of the year, the days are so short.' The clock on the shop's wall, showed that it was just six-thirty; dawn would be at least another half hour away.

'At least you live over the bakery. I don't enjoy my walk from Victoria Street to here in the morning. I meet with some right ruffians. Although I walk with my dad so far on his way to the bottle factory, it's just the last few streets,' Janet said as she placed the scones and cakes out under the glass counter and picked up the list of requirements that George would soon be calling to collect for sale 'in Dinsdale's emporium' as he jokingly called it.

'Well, I've been thinking about that,' Meg told her. 'I wondered: once I am married would you like to live above the bakery? You wouldn't have to make the walk every day then and it would be doing me a favour having someone living in. That is if you want to?'

Janet turned to Meg with a huge smile on her face. 'Are you ... are you really offering me my own room?' she stuttered delightedly. 'I can't believe it. I share a bed with our Lizzie and she pinches all the blankets every night and she snores! I've wanted to move out of home for months, but haven't the means. It would be like all my Christmases have come at once.'

'Well as long as your family agrees, the rooms will be yours. I won't charge you for them because I'll expect you to put the hours in like I do at present, especially if Frankie and I have children. You'll need to be on hand to get the oven lit and have everything ready in time for George and our early customers. Headingley is not going to be the most convenient place to live but I'm not going to forsake my little bakery,' Meg said.

'Oh, my Mam will only be too glad to get rid of one of us,' Janet laughed. 'She was only saying that she wished that I'd been born a lad and then I'd have been long gone. Either that or I should get myself a fellow.' She grinned broadly. 'I haven't found one that takes my fancy yet ... or one that fancies me, come to that.'

'Oh, I don't know, you've one that is quite smitten by you pulling his horse and cart up now,' Meg told her. 'You'd better get his trays ready, else he'll have something to say.' Meg had seen the grey horse that pulled George and his cart come to a standstill. She watched George put a nose bag around its head filled with oats for it to eat before coming in to flirt with Janet and share the latest gossip.

'Who, George! He's sweeter on you than me,' Janet said quickly, but promptly dusted down her apron and patted her hair before quickly counting the loaves on the wooden trays with Dinsdale's stamped upon them. She then opened the door wide for George to enter.

'Morning, George, you are early, I've only just put your bread out and I've yet to see what else you want,' she said and smiled as he took his cap off and said morning to them both.

'No bother. I'll have a brew if there's one on the go?' George grinned at his favourite two women.

'Of course, there's always a brew for you, George,' Meg replied. 'Do you want to come through to the bakery or do you want Janet to bring it to you in the shop?' Meg knew full well that once of a day George had been sweet upon her but now his attentions had transferred to Janet . . . and she could not be happier for the pair of them.

'Nay, I'll drink it with Janet, while she's getting my order ready. I'll keep her on her toes, and besides you'll be busy, if I know you, Meg.' George leaned against the wall of the bakery as Janet quickly ran into the bakery, returning with a hastily brewed mug of tea which he drank as he watched her every move.

'Right, I'll leave you two alone,' Meg said. 'I have got a wedding cake to put into the oven and I'll need to keep my eye on it for most of the morning.'

'Oh, you are making your wedding cake? Have you set

a date now then?' George asked with interest. He'd be sad to see Meg married; he still held a quiet flame for her even though Janet was now the love of his life.

'Yes, Frankie has set the date of April 8th so I've to get on with things. I never thought of a spring wedding but it seems he has set his heart on that date. So, yes, George, I'll finally become Mrs Pearson after all these years of dithering and delaying.'

'Well, I hope that you'll both be happy . . . and I'm sure you will be because he is such a lucky man,' George said quietly.

Even Janet could see the small look of regret in his eye and told him her good news. 'Meg says that once she's married that I can perhaps live here above the bakery. That will mean that I'll no longer have to obey my mother's and father's rules. That will make such a difference to my life.' She had guessed long since that George wanted to walk out with her but he had never plucked up the courage to knock on her family's door, knowing that her father was a stickler about gentleman callers for his eldest daughter.

'That will be grand, and you'll not need to walk to work every day.' George grinned at both women. He'd be calling more often at the bakery on York Street most definitely, he thought as he sipped his tea.

Meg went back to her baking, listening to Janet and George flirting with one another, Janet giggling like a school girl. She was delighted that at least Janet was happy.

But a worry was growing with each passing day, especially after at long last receiving a reply yesterday in the late

afternoon post from Larry Hopkirk. It had been exception-
ally curt. She had really set about making her wedding cake
to lift her spirits and stop from worrying about her younger
sister. It should be her that was living in the rooms above
the bakery if she would only return home, she thought as
she sat down in the chair next to the open fire and read the
letter again.

3rd February 1898
2 Lonsdale Square
Islington
London

Dear Miss Fairfax,
I am afraid I cannot help with regard to your search for
your sister Sarah. She left our employment as a scullery maid
over nine months ago and gave no forwarding address. It was
my belief that she was hoping to return home to you. I'm
sure knowing Sarah that she will be safe and well somewhere
and that she will eventually get back in touch with you.
With the best of wishes,
Larry Hopkirk

Meg folded the letter back up and put it into her pocket then
wiped a tear away from her eye. A scullery maid! So Sarah
had never been working on the stage, despite her claims.
What other lies had her little sister told her? But more to
the point, where was she now, and was she safe wherever

she was? London was at least five times the size of Leeds and miles away from home. Meg had visions of her walking the streets in rags or worse still, lying dead in some back alley, abused and beaten. 'Oh Sarah,' she sighed as she looked into the burning embers of the fire.

There was definitely no chance that Sarah would be returning for her wedding, she thought as she rose to take the last batch of bread from out of the oven. But that didn't matter; if she knew that she was safe and well, that would be enough. If she would come home she could live in the rooms above the bakery and step into her shoes if she wanted. Janet could work alongside her and even share the rooms with her. There was room for two easily.

George shouting his goodbyes brought Meg out of her reverie.

'Aye, goodbye George, tell Mr Dinsdale I'm asking after him,' she called back. 'I'll be coming to see him shortly. I've some private business I need to discuss with him.' Meg quickly wiped another tear away from her cheek before she went back through into the shop with a false smile on her face.

'I'll tell him to expect you,' George replied, waiting in the doorway, his cart fully loaded. 'He's busy with his other shop that he's just bought. He'll be a millionaire shortly just like your soon-to-be husband.'

'I wish, George,' Meg said. 'I wish them both to be millionaires but I think that is just a wasted wish. Both can work all the hours that God sends but they'll never become that rich.'

'Aye, happen you are right, but they might both surprise you, especially Joe Dinsdale. I'm sure his pockets are sewn up.' George laughed. 'See you in the morning.' He winked at both women and then untied his horse, taking its feed bag and stirring it into motion. Janet watched him head down the cobbled street to meet the coming dawn with his baking for the now awakening workers of Leeds.

Meg stood behind Janet and put a hand on her shoulder. 'He's a good lad, is George,' she said quietly. 'You could do a lot worse. He's steady and reliable and Joe Dinsdale is teaching him how to do his accounts books, so he must trust him.'

'I know, he's a bit younger than me though. Only by six months, mind,' Janet said and blushed as she turned the bakery sign to Open.

'That's nowt to worry about. You get on with courting him. He deserves a nice lass in his life, and if I help with giving you your own place I'll be glad for both of you.' Meg sighed and felt as if she was going to well up with tears again.

'What's wrong, Meg, you seem a bit down this morning?'

'It's nothing. I'm just worried about my sister and this wedding being set so fast has made me start panicking a little.' Meg tried to smile.

'Sarah will be alright. From what you have told me of her, she can look after herself,' Janet tried to reassure her.

'I don't know if she can or not, Janet. I've heard back from her old employer and she no longer works for him. She's not even been helping on the stage as she told me, she's been his scullery maid and she left his employment months ago.' Meg let out a sob. 'Where the hell is she and why did she go in the first place? She is so stubborn and pig-headed. She could be anywhere!'

Seeing the first customer of the day heading towards the door Meg hastily reached into her pocket for her handkerchief and blew her nose. 'Anyway, I shouldn't be troubling you with my worries. As you say, she will be just fine and she will get in touch with me in her own time. It'll be pride that is stopping her from doing so.' Meg breathed in deeply. 'Now, let us get on with the day. I'll mix another of the cakes and you serve the customers. Shout if we get busy and you need a hand.' Meg smiled wanly and took comfort in Janet's hand patting her gently on the back before going into the shop to serve the first customer of the day.

Meg's heart was breaking as she stirred the mixture and wiped away her tears. She should be celebrating the big moment in her life, but the worry over her younger sister was clouding everything. 'Lord, let her be alright,' she whispered as she rested her arm once more after aggressively beating and creaming the mixture. As long as Sarah was alright, Meg could forgive her for anything.

Chapter 6

'What the devil have you done that for, you stupid woman? Why, in your wildest dreams, did you think that I would be in agreement for that horrible upstart of a little man to hold his wedding banquet here? Even his accent is false and I hear that he has not got a penny to his name.'

Lord Richard Benson snorted at his wife as he cracked open his egg at the breakfast table, wishing the egg was Frankie Pearson's head as he smashed it once more just for good measure. 'You do know he tried to join the Gainsborough Club? The audacity of the pompous man. He's a nobody and always will be.'

'Oh, Richard stop being such a snob,' his wife remonstrated. 'He's quite a well-to-do man. Perhaps not born with a silver spoon in his mouth, but you wouldn't know that until you get to know him. Besides, he entertains me and my friends, and you must admit his delicacies are simply scrumptious.'

'Too delicious, by the look of his bills on my desk. I am

loath to pay them ... The thought of him making eyes at you and touching you,' Richard Benson growled. 'The man does not know his place.'

'He does neither,' Beatrice replied. 'You are letting your jealousies run away with you. I hope that you have paid him for the last months as he will have invoiced all the lovely things that he supplied us with for Christmas, and while I might not know the amount, I am sure it will be a small fortune for him.' She gave her husband a hard stare.

'Oh, I'll get around to it sometime. If he will enjoy your company he must pay for it. In fact, why don't you tell him that the use of our home is in part payment for what we owe him? That sounds to me like a very good idea.' Richard Benson guffawed and smiled at the disgusted look on his wife's face.

'I can't do that. I promised him without mention of any money. Besides you don't do that to a friend.' Beatrice raised an eyebrow and looked across at her husband. 'When exactly did you last pay him?'

'Oh, I don't know, a few months back? His bills are of no consequence, the little man. He's like an irritating fly around my head. If you are not talking about him then your friends and their husbands are. So, I let him wait.' Richard Benson wiped his mouth with his serviette and looked across at his wife.

'You will pay him and you will pay him today, Richard,' his wife said firmly. 'You can just go into Leeds and into his shop on the Headrow and pay him what we owe and apologize begrudgingly in person for late payment. Do you hear?

I had no idea that we were in debt to the poor man.' Beatrice scowled and summoned the butler to clear her place and take her coffee into the morning room.

'Well, I'll not be the only one not paying him,' Richard told her. 'A few of my chums at the club leave him to the last, for the same reason that I do. That he gets more attention from their wives than they do. You all must be blind or have lost control of your senses.' He grunted. 'I don't want you to go near him again or his shop ever again.'

'You go in and you pay him, Richard, do you hear? And stop being so stupid, he's a baker, dear. Not one of us ladies is remotely interested in him! He and his fancies are just a novelty while you old dinosaurs are out shooting or playing billiards. Besides, he is about to get married. Although I think he could do much better for himself, even though she is a good baker like himself I hear.'

Beatrice gathered herself together. 'I'm going to the morning room to do my sewing. Make sure that you do go and pay him this morning. Never a debtor nor a lender be, that's what my father used to say to me. And think again if you try to stop me buying from him,' she said, giving Richard a withering glance.

'Aye, well you'll be paying it out of your own funds from now on – and as for your father, he didn't have a penny to his name. I'm not going to ever be like him,' Richard Benson shouted after her and watched his wife leave in a huff. He cursed Frankie Pearson yet again.

*

'Mr Pearson, Lord Benson at the shop's counter, he needs to speak to you urgently,' Norah said as she came into the bakery looking flustered. It was one thing to serve Beatrice Benson but having to speak and serve Lord Benson himself was another matter. His whole demeanour made Norah nervous: when he spoke, she knew he was to be obeyed.

'Oh, Lord what does he want?' Frankie muttered. 'It's usually his wife that I deal with. It must be of some importance if he is actually visiting my shop. Another minute and I'd have been on the way to Headingley. I need to see how the manager is doing there, and I hope that he doesn't detain me too long.'

Frankie sighed and started to wash his dough-covered hands. 'Show him up to the tea room, Norah, sit him in the quiet corner next to the window and give him a cup of tea. I'll be up to see him directly.'

As Norah nodded and went to lead Lord Benson up the stairs, Frankie gathered his thoughts. He hoped that all was alright within the Benson household. He disliked Richard Benson because he was so pompous, but at the same time he was well aware who controlled the purse strings at the hall, so above all Frankie hoped that he had come to settle his considerable bill at long last.

'Is the Frenchie making me wait?' Richard Benson growled at a trembling Norah who was serving him a tea and a complimentary éclair.

'No, sir, definitely not. He will be with you shortly,' Norah said and was glad to hear the footsteps of her employer coming up the stairs. As Frankie arrived, she curtsied then returned to her duties.

'Ah, Lord Benson, so sorry that I've kept you waiting. I'd just finished helping out making some bread in the bakery, my hands were covered with dough.' Frankie passed his now clean hand to be shaken but Lord Benson ignored him and sipped his tea. 'I hope Norah has made you comfortable – a cup of tea and an éclair I see.' Frankie looked at the cake that had so far not been touched.

'Yes, she's seen to my needs, seems a pleasant enough lass,' Benson said after a moment. 'Not keen on your cakes though, Pearson, no matter how much my wife raves about them. Puff of air, that's all they are.'

'I trust Lady Benson is well and that you don't come bearing bad news?' Frankie said, ignoring the comment about his baking. Everyone was entitled to their opinions, even if they were wrong.

'She's well, not that it is any of your business.' Benson grunted. 'I've come because she tells me that it is about time I paid the bill that we owe you. However, I also wanted to state what I think is only right as to the conversation and the promise that my wife has made to you.'

Richard Benson looked sombre and sat back in his chair enjoying the worry on Frankie's face.

'It's good of you to come and settle your account. I appreciate it,' Frankie replied uncertain what else Lord Benson was referring to.

'Aye well, she tells me that she has offered you our home

to hold your wedding breakfast in,' Benson explained. 'She forgets who owns it sometimes and expects me to go along with her ideas.' He leaned forward, staring at Frankie.

'It was very kind of her to do so. I am most grateful. I hope that it's not caused a problem between you?' Frankie saw a slight smile begin to appear on Richard's face. 'It will be a wonderful day and I am most grateful for Lady Beatrice's generous offer.'

'Aye, well it hasn't! But you'll not think it that generous when I tell you what I've to say about the matter.' Richard Benson put his hand into the inside of his jacket pocket, brought out an envelope and passed it over to Frankie. 'In that there's your for September to November. I don't pay some of my wife's smaller bills that fast – after all, it's only fripperies that she usually buys. However, seeing that you are using my home for your wedding, I've no intentions of paying December's bill. It was for a goodly amount, an amount that will just cover the charge of use of my dining hall and the staff that no doubt you will want to wait on . . .' Richard's grin widened as he opened the envelope with the various invoices and cheques within. 'That small charge will mean not a lot to you, a man as well-versed in business as yourself. You'll understand that's only right I do so. My staff, they're not going to be able to do their work for me while they're attending to your needs, so it's only right that I charge you for that time.'

Frankie looked across the table and picked up the envelope. 'Of course, I understand,' he said slowly. 'I thought at the time that it was far too generous of Lady Benson. I quite understand and I will mark your account as being paid up to date.' Lord Benson clearly wanted to prove that he was master of his own home.

'I'm glad that we have agreed,' Lord Benson said, his mood suddenly far more affable. 'Wouldn't want your wedding day spoiling now would, we old boy?' He rose from his chair. 'Your wife-to-be will be looking forward to such a grand affair. Wedding breakfast in a grand hall! Not bad for two bakers from Leeds.' He pulled on his gloves and looked around him at the tearoom. 'After all, it is a lot grander than here.'

'My bride-to-be doesn't yet know we are to hold the reception at the hall. I've kept that as a surprise,' Frankie said

'Then you must keep it that way. I'm sure she is worth every penny spent upon her, and I'm sure that you will both have a wonderful day celebrating. Now, I must be on my way, I have got a luncheon to take with some good friends at my club. Can't keep good friends waiting.' Richard Benson smiled and tipped his hat. 'By the way, I've told Bea that if she shops here in the future she settles her own bills, so I'll not be visiting you again.' There was more than a hint of satisfaction in his voice. The Frenchman might be getting married in his family home but he would not be getting any more of the Benson fortune.

Frankie watched his visitor leave and although he had tried to keep it hidden, hefelt gutted, shook to the core. The bill for December to Langroyd Hall had been huge. If he wasn't going to receive payment for it, he would be struggling to keep afloat. He was at least a hundred pounds down and what was worse, that parting shot meant he had lost the hall's custom for sure. He was certain Bea Benson would not go against her husband's wishes – her husband might as well have simply told her not to shop with Frankie. But he would keep the hall for his wedding breakfast though: if he had paid for it then he was going to use it, although of course Frankie knew of a lot of cheaper places.

Still seated at the table in the tearoom, Frankie closed his eyes and hung his head in his hands. What an underhand trick to play. All because Lord Benson was jealous of his wife's friendship with him, of that he was sure. He'd lost his best customer just at a time when he needed her the most.

Frankie looked at the cheque made out for the autumn months: it would hardly be noticed going out of Richard Benson's bank account but it would just disappear into Frankie's own growing overdraft. He regretted opening his chain of patisseries up so fast. He should have kept his head down and concentrated on his first love, the patisserie on the Headrow. Perhaps Meg was right: keep it small and local but made with love. She seemed to be making money and without half the worry that he had.

He shook his head. Perhaps he should tell Beatrice Benson that he had decided not to hold the wedding breakfast at the Hall – after all, he had not told Meg of his plans. But, no, that would give Richard Benson greater satisfaction if Frankie had to grovel for the money he would then be owed for December – let alone the January bill, which was yet to be delivered – and Meg deserved a special day with nothing spared for her happiness.

Richard Benson sat drinking his glass of port in a sumptuous leather chair surrounded by his cronies in the Gainsborough Club. Most of the men around him were married to his wife's friends and they listened to him as he guffawed about how he'd got out of paying the bill owed to his wife's favourite shop owner.

'I tell you, Wilkins, all our women folk swoon as soon as they see him. Well, I wasn't having it anymore. I've told Beatrice that she must not order anything more off him unless she wants to pay him out of her funds, and I can't see that happening.' Richard swigged his port and looked at one of his closest friends. 'He's the same with all your wives, puts on that smarmy French accent, and leads them all astray. Well, no more at my home. Once he's married, that will be an end to it. No visits by him, nor my wife to his shop. I wish to God she had never agreed to him getting married at our home. However, I cooked his goose this morning when I charged him for not paying his heaviest bill. Whatever he does he loses face.'

'I must admit, my Penelope is always talking about him and his bill does seem extremely large each month,' Robert Wilkins replied and the rest of the group of men nodded their heads in agreement.

'He's leeching on our wives and our bank balances,' Tom

Browning piped up. 'I suggest, gentlemen, that we put a stop to our reckless wives making fools of themselves and stop them from visiting his shops and entertaining him. That will learn the cad. In fact, the other day my Martha said she wished I smelt as good as him, that's how near that she had got to him. I raised an eyebrow then and had words.'

'Aye, he's up to no good,' Benson said. 'Gentlemen, let us all stand together on this matter and put Frankie Pearson in his place. All of us will stop giving him our trade, tell our wives not to go near him, and see how long his fancy shops survive without the likes of us. We will not allow him into our club either, he might think himself something but he's just an upstart.' The group nodded their heads in agreement.

'He's an upstart that's celebrating his marriage under your roof,' Wilkins pointed out.

'Aye but who's going to be there? I bet you my last shilling that on his wedding guest list are all our wives and their spouses. He knows nobody else! Well he can't celebrate so much if he has no one in attendance.' Richard smirked and finished his port.

'You are a hard man, Benson, and Pearson deserves what is coming to him, but what about his poor wife?' Wilkins asked.

'It'll not spoil her day,' Benson said promptly. 'From what I hear she is only from the back streets, she'll not be comfortable at the Hall anyway. It is him, the pompous fool – he thinks that he's something that he isn't. Time for him to learn a lesson.' Richard sniggered at the thought of Frankie

Pearson feeling the pinch if all his friends stopped giving him their business. He'd learn him for being so friendly with his wife and sending ludicrous bills for his French rubbish. 'To our lovely ladies, let's keep them safe from working-class letches.'

Richard raised his glass, looked around him and sniggered as all his cronies cheered.

Chapter 7

Meg stood across the street from her bakery and smiled.

The sign writer had just left, along with the painter, and now the little bakery looked like a completely different shop. All the windows had been repainted and tidied, and the front door was now varnished and gleaming, encouraging people to enter. The sign above the door read Meg's Bakery. Wholesome, Good Baking, just like your Mam makes. That's what she was – Mam to all of the street, she thought as Janet slipped her hand through her arm and hunched up to her.

'You should be so proud of yourself, you've turned your life completely around,' Janet said quietly, noticing a tear welling up in Meg's eyes.

'I know, I never thought in my wildest dreams that the bakery would actually be mine one day. I hoped it would be, but sometimes my dreams were lost amongst all my problems.' Meg sighed and smiled at Janet. 'I'd like this just to be the start. I love the feeling of owning my own business. I daren't tell that to Frankie though. I think he is still secretly expecting me once married to be a faithful wife and mother and to relinquish the bakery to him.'

'The world's changing, Meg .If you want to still run your own business, do. Mr Pearson should be able to afford a maid and a nanny to look after any family that you have surely?' Janet said as they walked back into the warmth of the bakery.

'Oh, I could never leave my own children in somebody else's care. I'd want to bring them up with my love and attention. A nanny or even a father is not the same as having your mother looking after you. I already feel guilty when it comes to our Sarah – perhaps if I had given her more time and shown her more love then she would not now be missing. I should have been more of a mother to her, let alone leaving my own in somebody else's care.' Meg went to stand behind the counter to look at what was left from the day's trading, putting her finger on the calendar showing the day's date, February 8th.

'You are too hard upon yourself,' Janet chided gently. 'From what you have told me of her, Sarah was always set in her ways. She would never have been satisfied unless she went her own way. She'll appear one day, bedecked in jewellery and fine clothes after making her way in the world.' Janet looked up at the clock. 'Do you want a brew? I can stay on for a bit longer. I'll make us both one, another half hour and the mills will be blowing their whistles and then we will have the last rush of the day.'

'No, you go home, Janet, I can handle the late buyers. Besides I bet Daisy lands by. Why she trails out with the baby in the evening air I don't know. It's not good for it, and she'll not be able to get warm in the place she's living with not having enough heating to keep herself warm. Don't you end up the same way as her, let her life be a warning to you!'

'I'll not ever be like Daisy. I keep my legs together. That's where she went wrong and he was a married man, she should have known better,' Janet said with disgust in her voice.

Meg looked at her. The lass was only four years younger than she was but seemed to be a whole more worldly-wise than she'd been at her age. 'Don't be so hard upon her. She loved Tom Askew, she trusted him. He's as bad, if not worse, than her. He's the one who left her holding his baby without any support. He was willing to have his fun but when things went wrong and the baby was on its way he soon decided which side his bread was buttered,' she said. 'Go on, get gone home, and get your beauty sleep tonight. George will be here first thing and he will be counting the seconds before he sees you right now.'

'I don't know what you mean!' Janet said but couldn't help but grin.

'You do, missus, he's staying longer and longer of a morning. Joe Dinsdale will be after him,' Meg said and Janet blushed.

'He'll not be coming for much longer. Mr Dinsdale has got a new lad to replace him and George is to run one of the shops for him,' Janet told her. 'It'll be a big step up for him, he'll be glad for the extra money.'

'He'll need more money if he starts walking out with you,

my lass. He'll be a good catch will George, he's a nice lad. I'll be sorry when he stops coming here for the baking.'

A thought struck her. 'Tomorrow, would you mind if I left you running the bakery around nine-thirty?' she asked. 'I need to visit Hopkin's on Boar Lane to discuss my wedding dress.'

'Oh, how wonderful. I wish it was me at Hopkin's! You are so lucky to be marrying a man like Mr Pearson. I can only dream of shopping there. He will be able to provide you with such a wonderful life.'

'I know I am lucky. He truly loves me and I him. I am blessed and sometimes I just don't realize it,' Meg said and tried to forget the nagging feeling she had when it came to her fiancé's finances.

'Well, I wish you both the very best. You have been so kind to me and I'll never forget it. Especially if I am to live above the bakery as you have promised.'

Meg stood outside Hopkin's. Even though she could afford to shop there occasionally, she never did. It still seemed as if she was being watched and felt out of place in such a grand store. She had the feeling that everyone knew that she was from the backstreets and was out of place looking at the grand things that were displayed for the more affluent classes.

She caught her reflection in a mirror as she climbed the stairs to the specialist bridal department and that made her feel even more uncomfortable. She might look respectable in her pin-tucked high necked white blouse and flowing green skirt but she knew where she came from and that there was no going back upon her heritage.

Putting such thoughts behind her, Meg walked into the department filled with everything a young bride would need for her big day. Even the air seemed perfumed and she held her breath as she looked around at the dresses on mannequins then peeped through to the sewing rooms where she could see seamstresses hard at work making handmade dresses for excited brides-to-be. On one side of the room was a large wooden cabinet filled with gloves, hair pieces and purses, all beautifully decorated with pearls and flowers, shining and looking pristine. On the other side was a row of off-the-peg wedding dresses that she knew would be less costly than the handmade dresses. She made her way to them, making sure that her hands were clean before she started to look through them.

'Can I help Madam?' A young very pretty assistant came and stood by her side and smiled.

'Yes, I was just admiring your dresses. I am to be married in April and have come to seek your advice and to purchase a dress and accessories.'

'These are our off-the-peg dresses,' the assistant pointed out. 'Perhaps Madam might like one that is special to her and made to measure. If so, I will get one of our seamstresses to come and take your measurements and see to your needs.' The assistant urged her to walk with her towards the room where the seamstresses sat.

'Oh, no, that would be too costly for me, a true fitting

would be far too extravagant, and I would not feel happy having to justify such a cost for just one day,' Meg admitted. 'I already feel that if I had the time and the experience that I should be making my own.'

'Oh, I see. Our dresses are quite expensive but they are the most well made in Leeds. Every care is taken in making sure that our brides get exactly what they need for their day.' The assistant smiled. 'You say that your wedding is in April. Is Madam looking for something in white or perhaps a different colour?' The way she said it made Meg blush – of course there was no reason for her not to be in white, although she understood why the assistant had asked – she probably rarely dealt with brides who were getting married in a mere two months' time.

'Oh, white, it's got to be white, I've always set my heart on a white wedding dress as our dear Queen Victoria got married in. Besides, my Frankie will expect me to walk down the aisle in white, I'm quite sure he wouldn't expect any other.'

'Frankie is your intended?' the assistant asked as she reached up to take some of the pre-made examples from off the rail just above both of their heads.

'Yes, Frankie Pearson. He shops here quite frequently. We are to be married on the 8th of April. He wanted a spring wedding, where I would have preferred an autumn wedding, but spring is the time for weddings so I can understand him wishing it so.' Meg felt the colour rise in her cheeks.

'Oh, Mr Pearson, yes, he was here the other day for a

fitting,' the assistant said. 'Charles in Men's Outfitters was talking about his visit. I believe he said that you would be coming to us to choose your attire and to make sure that you charged it to his account. Such a gentleman, you are such a lucky lady.' The assistant placed the dresses on the counter then said carefully, 'Are you sure you will be happy with an off-the-peg dress? Mr Pearson was quite extravagant in his choice, from what Charles was telling me. Our seamstresses could fit you with a beautiful dress that would flow beautifully over an S-shaped corset. You need to impress on your big day – all eyes should be on the bride.'

'I don't intend to wear a corset, I've of no need for one,' Meg said abruptly and walked over to view the dresses that had been taken down from their hangers. She should have known that Frankie would have made sure that he was going to look dapper at his wedding, but she was sure she would also. The dresses might not be fitted and personalized but they did look beautiful. Along with some hand-picked accessories, she would look as beautiful as any bride could, she thought as the assistant held up each dress for her to inspect. It would compensate for the money that Frankie would have frittered away on himself.

She held each dress up to herself and the assistant commented on how dainty and small her waist was, obviously trying to make amends for the mentioning the all-too-fashionable corset that nipped and tightened ladies into an unnatural shape.

Meg felt the quality of each dress, finally deciding on

one that was made in white taffeta, the high neck of which was embellished with lace that also fell down the bodice into frills. 'May I try it on?' she asked and was shown to a fitting room where the assistant helped her place the dress on, making Meg feel embarrassed that another woman was seeing her near-naked.

She stepped out of the fitting room and found a full-length mirror. She drew in a sharp breath, hardly recognizing herself. She looked beautiful and would be even more so when she had placed her long hair into ringlets for the day, she thought. Her waist was highlighted with a satin bow and the long skirt billowed out and rustled as Meg walked about in it. She smiled and looked again into the mirror, noting the sleeves were long, with puffs at the shoulders which tapered down to her forearm. She could not have dreamed of a more beautiful dress, she thought as the assistant fussed over the length of the skirt.

'The skirt is a little too long. We can soon amend that at no more cost to yourself, it's part of our bridal service,' the young woman said. 'Now a pair of long gloves to match: these satin ones with the pearl buttons would be ideal.' She passed Meg a box with a plain pair of gloves inside and smiled as she saw how much Meg looked admiringly at them.

'Oh, yes they are beautiful, they go so well,' Meg agreed. 'But they will be expensive?'

'If you can't spend money upon yourself on your wedding day then when can you?' the assistant asked and placed the gloves on the counter. 'And shoes? These small white kid leather boots would go so well, it would complete your look – unless you were also thinking of a train or a veil?'

A pair of small leather boots were taken from off the stand next to the counter and placed in Meg's hands. She felt how soft and how beautifully made they were but she was all too aware that it was another expense, one she knew Frankie was barely able to afford. 'I don't want a train or veil,' she decided, 'but I do like the boots and also the combs with the flower garlands on, they are more me.' Meg pointed to a stand with hair combs upon it. If she was to buy the boots she had balanced the expense by choosing a comb instead of a veil.

'Try the boots on once you have slipped out of the dress,' the assistant suggested. 'And I agree. A comb of flowers would look perfect in your hair. That one with lilies and orange blossom in would be ideal. You could have a matching bouquet.' Meg considered that for a moment then nodded.

'If you are happy with the dress, I will see that the hem is taken up just by an inch. I've popped a pin in where the seamstress needs to alter it to the correct length. Now, is there anything more that you may need for your big day? Would you like everything sent to your home? I know Charles had been told that whatever you bought while here was to be billed to Mr Pearson, but he, unfortunately, did not give the delivery address.' The assistant began to fill out the bill of sale, after Meg assured her she would not need help changing.

'I'll take what I've purchased home with me today. There's no need to send a delivery boy, and I will be back in to collect my dress if you really do think it needs the hem altering, although I could do that by hand myself,' Meg told her as she went to undress and try the boots on.

'Oh, no we couldn't let you do that, especially as Mr Pearson said that it was going to be a society wedding. Charles had been mightily impressed by which guests he was thinking of inviting and the location of your wedding breakfast. It will give us great satisfaction to think that we have dressed you to the best of our ability on your wedding day.' The assistant chattered away as she wrote a note to the dressmakers then wrapped the gloves up along with the chosen comb.

Meg came out of the dressing room and passed her the boots and dress and made sure that her hair looked tidy as she gazed into the mirror before replying. 'I think he's getting a little carried away calling it a society wedding,' she said.'We may both be in business but we don't mix with the good and great of society.'

'Oh, I understood that Lord and Lady Benson were to attend and the Fairburns, who made their money in India,' the assistant said, not seeing the worried look creeping over Meg's face. 'He also said that your reception was to be held in Langroyd Hall – now how lovely is that for you! Langroyd Hall! I often look across at it and dream of myself walking up those grand steps. I can think of you now in this beautiful dress.'

'He likes to do things right, but I'd still not call it a society wedding. The wedding itself is being held in Saint Mary's so perhaps he's exaggerating a little.' Meg tried to smile but she felt her heart fluttering. Had Frankie really asked all these grand guests without her knowledge and had he not thought that no matter how grand Langroyd Hall was, it was the last place on God's Earth she would want her wedding breakfast? No matter how much business she brought to Frankie's patisserie, Meg despised Beatrice Benson, thinking her shallow and flirtatious.

The joy of the morning's shop soon dissipated as she walked back with her goods, hoping and praying that Frankie had just been bragging about his wedding plans. As it was, she would soon find out as they were both to attend Saint Mary's for the first reading of their banns on Sunday, a wedding that she was beginning to have second thoughts about, no matter how much she loved her Frankie.

Chapter 8

Bells were ringing out all over Leeds, summoning people to attend their local church for the morning service.

Meg grabbed her gloves and shawl and looked at herself in the mirror. She'd not seen Frankie all week and the words of the shop assistant had been on her mind since their conversation. The box of satin gloves, the kid white boots as well as the delicate comb covered with silk flowers were on her dressing table and drawers, a constant reminder. There were questions to be asked of Frankie once they had attended church, she thought as she gave herself one more glance in the mirror then ran down the stairs and unlocked the bakery door to walk out onto the street.

She was late. After sleeping badly and worrying about one thing and another she was in no mood to hear what he would have to say. The more she thought about it, the more she knew it was something that Frankie would do. He liked to think of himself as something more than he was and would excel in boasting about the guests and venue of his wedding.

She just wanted a quiet affair, mainly to guard Frankie against spending money he could ill afford, which it seemed he had already done at Hopkin's. Although she now had her accessories back in her bedroom she felt frivolous and stupid about spending his money too. After all her wedding day was just another day, and in the light of her own bedroom, the boots, gloves and posies had lost their appeal, every time she thought of their cost. The assistant had been very good at her job, Meg reflected. Even if she hadn't managed to sell Meg a handmade dress, she had made the sales up with the fripperies, which really were not needed.

'Morning Meg', 'Morning, Miss Fairfax' – various people greeted her as she hurriedly walked down the cobbled streets wrapped in her shawl, her Sunday best hat upon her head. She rarely attended church, but her mother's words had echoed in her ears as she placed her hat on her head then secured it with a hat pin. 'Women have got to hide their glory when they go to church. Always make sure you wear a hat.'

Hide her glory? Her hair was a mousy brown, nothing special, and why should she wear a hat to stop men looking at her in church? Meg wondered. They should be thinking of higher things than the women in the congregation, she thought as she turned the corner and joined the many people that were heading towards the church service. Some were going willingly, others not so willing, with children being dragged by their parents, checked for clean necks and freshly polished shoes. She was relieved to see Frankie standing at the church gates waiting for her. He stood like a sentry, immaculately dressed in his best suit and a top hat on his head, looking every inch the gentleman he wished to be. He smiled as she approached him.

'I worried that you weren't going to show. The bells have been chiming for a good half hour and the church is fairly full. It's not that big is it when you walk into it, there's much grander in Leeds,' Frankie commented quietly after giving her a kiss in greeting. He took Meg's arm with pride as they walked down the path to the porch with the rest of the congregation.

'It might not be big and posh, but it's my parish church. A lot of good people come and worship here,' Meg said sharply and unhooked her arm from his as they passed over the church's threshold and walked a few steps down the aisle to a pew at the back of the church.

'Are you alright, Meg? You didn't look that happy to see me,' Frankie whispered as he placed his hat by his side. Both bowed their heads in reverence to God and to show how humble they were in his presence as they sat on the pew together.

'I'm alright, just late as you have pointed out,' Meg whispered back and then lifted her head without glancing at him and focused on the vicar who was about to take the service.

Frankie looked at her and reached for her hand and squeezed it as the service began. Something was wrong; he could just sense it.

Midway through the service, after the hymns and prayers but before the sermon, the vicar stood and gave a sign that he was about to make that week's announcements. Both Frankie and Meg watched breathlessly as he went through the couples that hoped to be getting married in his church within the coming months. Right at the end of the list, their two names were mentioned followed by the standard rubric that if anyone had a reason to doubt any of the marriages for them to speak now. No one said anything.

'I know it's silly, but I worried in case someone said something,' Frankie whispered as he smiled at Meg as she stood up to sing the following hymn.

'Now, who would do that? Unless your devoted Lady Benson wanted to keep you for herself,' Meg said with a hint of sarcasm in her voice.

'What are you saying that for? You know that there's nothing in that. You should be happy on our announcement day,' Frankie whispered back and looked at Meg and realized straight away that she knew where he had planned the wedding reception to be and was not happy.

'Now is not the time to talk. Wait until afterwards.' Meg whispered back and concentrated on the service. She'd kept her calm all morning, but now she would have her say she thought as she bowed her head and said the Lord's Prayer.

'What's wrong then? This morning should have been full of joy and love, but you look as if you wish you weren't about to get married,' Frankie said after they had shaken the hand of the vicar on their way out of the church and exchanged pleasantries to the ones that wished them well.

Meg stood outside the church gates that she knew so well and sighed. 'I don't want to talk here. Come back home and I'll discuss what's worrying me. I'll make us both some lunch.' She felt her hat shifting as the breeze picked up, and secured it back in place.

'I thought as a treat we would dine at Whitelock's,' Frankie told her. 'I've booked a table, it's a way of celebration that we are actually after all these years about to wed.' He took her arm. 'How about we discuss your concerns there? I've booked the table in the quiet corner, just for us both to be alone.'

Meg's sigh this time was even longer and louder. 'You see, this is your problem, you do things without telling me,' she said in a frustrated voice. 'If we are to be married and work as a couple, you are going to have to be more open.'

They walked down the street in the direction of the Headrow and then turned down onto Briggate and into the White Swan Yard where Frankie's favourite place to eat was.

Frankie stopped in his tracks and looked at Meg. 'Surely you are not mad at me for ensuring that we have a romantic Sunday dinner that neither of us has to cook? I booked it because I love you.'

'Just like you have booked our wedding breakfast to be held at Langroyd Hall? I suppose it was that awful woman Beatrice Benson that offered you the hall and you couldn't resist her,' Meg said, feeling tears come into her eyes as she thought of the way that she had seen her looking at her beau.

'Oh, someone has told you about that! I was going to tell

you over dinner this afternoon, but it seems my plans have been scuppered,' Frankie said and took her hand as they walked on.

'Yes, Frankie, the assistant at Hopkin's told me about your plan and your guest list. From what she was indicating it's all planned and sorted, I bet, without my say so. Even a shop-girl gets to find out about your wedding before your wife-to-be,' Meg said quietly.

'I didn't mean for it to happen that way. The tailor at Hopkin's must have blabbed, he did seem a curious sort of fellow, wanting to know everything and anything. Before I knew it, I was seemingly having a large wedding with all and sundry there.' Frankie stopped at the door of Whitelock's restaurant and waited for one of the butlers to come and seat them. He reached for Meg's hands and held them tight. 'I'm sorry, my love, I'll tell you all about it, and if there is anything you need to change at all, then it will be done.

'Very well, Frankie, but we need to discuss other things as well as the wedding breakfast. I'm worried about a few things. I love you dearly and I can't wait for our wedding day, but we need to sit down and talk and say exactly how we feel. It's no good setting off into a marriage on the completely wrong footing,' Meg said then smiled her thanks to the waiter who showed them to their seats.

'Now, what are we going to have to eat?' Frankie said dismissing Meg's comments and looking at the menu. 'I think I'll have the turbot.'

Meg just shook her head. Of course, he would have the

turbot – after all, it was the most expensive thing on the menu and her dear Frankie had to keep up his appearances. That's what everything was about with him, no matter what, but she was going to have her say.

'It's things like that, Frankie. I worry that you spend too much. If we are lucky enough to be blessed with a family we can't pretend to be something that we aren't.'

At the waiter's return, Meg ordered the roast beef then sat back in her chair as Frankie requested the fish.

'I love you, Meg, I just want us both to be happy. I can tell Bea Benson that we have decided to no longer hold the reception at the Hall, although she did insist that we used her home for our wedding, free of charge.' Frankie was tempted to say to Meg that events had moved on and that the hall had now been paid for but thought better after the look on her face and tone of voice. 'The turbot is a treat to celebrate our banns, surely, you don't begrudge me that?'

'No, I don't really. I didn't realize that the hall was free of charge! Then that was kind of her. However, I still think that it is a bit grand for our small wedding. I'll be struggling to have five guests there.' Meg pursed her lips. 'I just worry Frankie that you are full of grand ideas that are so above my station in life. I'm not used to spending so freely and it isn't that long since I know you were struggling.'

'Well, you can just stop your worrying. I promise that no matter what it takes, my first objective in life is to always make sure that my family never goes without anything and to make sure my business is always in profit. Now, have you heard from Sarah?' Frankie asked, hoping to change the subject before Meg delved deeper into his finances.

'No, not a word from Sarah. I would so like her to be at our wedding, but most of all I just want to know that she is safe. I worry so much about her.'

'Yes, I can understand your worry. But Larry Hopkirk is a good employer, I would have thought, he'll take care of her, my love.'

'Oh, Frankie, but she hasn't worked for him for some time. I got a letter the other day, from Mr Hopkirk. In fact, she's only ever been his scullery maid. All this talk of being on stage and helping him was a big lie.' Meg began to sob and Frankie passed her a handkerchief and smiled at the other dinners who were looking at the unhappy couple and wondering what the problem was.

'Now, calm yourself, my love, you are letting your thoughts run away with you. Sarah will have found herself another job in service. She'll be writing to you shortly when she gets round to it. After all, she never did like writing from what you have told me in the past.'

'The trouble is I keep remembering about reading about the terrible murders around the Whitechapel area made by this monster that they called Jack the Ripper. It would seem that no woman was safe walking the streets of London,' Meg said softly. 'She could be one of those women that are walking the streets, Lord helps us! She could be one that is lying dead in her own blood and I'd never know.'

'But, that was ten years ago! All has changed, I'm sure, and

Sarah will not be in any danger,' Frankie tried to reassure her. He nodded his agreement to a glass of port that the waiter offered them both. 'Here take a sip and stop worrying, We were supposed to enjoy our dinner together, not argue and worry over things that have not even happened, Now tell me what your dress looks like, and have you thought about a bridesmaid other than Sarah if she has not been in touch?'

Meg sniffed and pulled her handkerchief out of her pocket. 'You are right, I'm making problems when there aren't any, but I can't tell you about the dress. It would be bad luck!' She wiped her dampened eyes with her handkerchief and smiled. 'I suppose all young couples get these doubts before they get married.' Meg gave a wan smile. 'And as for Sarah I guess you are right – she will be fine, she always did land on her feet did that one.'

'That's better. And yes, there will be a lot more couples with more doubts than us. At least we both have homes and an income. No parents aimed with shotguns at the groom as his bride walks down the aisle.' Frankie laughed 'Now tell me, how is your business doing? Any new recipes? What sells best for you at the moment? Will you be doing anything special for Valentine's Day? I'm about to make a spectacular gateau full of cream and meringue, something for my cus- tomers to share with the one they love. We too must make this day special – it will be the last one we spend together as single people.'

Meg sniffed and smiled then looked across at Frankie. She did love him and every man had his faults and she was definitely not flawless. As for Sarah, she would be alright wherever she was. It was true what everyone said: bad news carries fast and if anything had become her, she would have heard. 'I'm not doing anything too special. I'm going to bake some ginger biscuits and ice them with flowers. My customers don't have the money to waste on fancy things and most have turned their backs on romance after being married and struggling for years. It's only the likes of Janet who are deeply in love – even though I think I'm not supposed to know about her and George.'

'And us, my dear, what would you like for us to do that day?' Frankie asked the woman he loved.

'A card will be sufficient, Frankie Pearson, nothing more, don't be wasting your money. We know we both love one another without anything too fancy,' Meg said and returned his smile. 'How's your business? It is always a quiet month in February, the weather is against us and ladies are not shopping for leisure.' She looked up at the waiter and felt her mouth salivating as her lunch was placed in front of her. It was thoughtful of Frankie to have booked a table, it was a real treat.

'Thank you,' Frankie said to the waiter and then looked across at Meg's lunch and wished he had chosen the roast beef. 'My business, well, you know it's doing well. All my bakeries are doing well, but I thought the one in Headingley should happen to be aimed at the ordinary customer. I might play about with some of your recipes, if you don't mind. It will not hit your trade as we are miles apart.' Frankie started to tackle his turbot lunch.

'Oh, that's not what I expected. I thought that you'd always stick to upper-class patisserie. I've always thought you looked down on my recipes,' Meg replied as she relished every mouthful of her dinner.

'Not at all. I just found my baker is more skilled in every-day baking. Headingley is a different area than the centre of Leeds, and my customers there are not as wealthy. It makes sense for me to change my practices. I presume my profits will be higher if I keep my feet on the ground and bake what people really need.'

Frankie kept his eyes focused on his dinner plate. He couldn't look Meg in the eye. In reality, the bakery at Headingley was leaking profits like a sieve and far from playing to his baker's strengths, this would be his one way of saving it. As for the new bakery at Ilkley he already put that one up for sale. He should never have bought it in the first place. He needed money to cover his debts that were rising by the day, although that was the last thing that he wanted Meg to know.

'Any help that you need, just let me know, I'll gladly share my recipes. In fact what if I come and meet your baker? I've never ever been in the one at Headingley, it's about time I visited . . . and the other at Ilkley.'

'Yes of course my love, you must come and visit at Headingley, Ivor is my baker there. Just give me a day or two to suggest alterations to what he bakes. In fact, come for lunch, my cook will make us a Valentine's dinner, hopefully with beef that looks as good as yours,' Frankie said with a slightly jealous look at the little Meg had left on her plate.

'Is your fish not as good as you had hoped? You can't get anything better than a piece of good Yorkshire beef, you should know that.' Meg grinned. Sometimes money and pride meant that Frankie missed out on the best things in life. She was glad that he had asked her for her advice, though; she would share it willingly. Perhaps he was starting to realize that catering for the upper classes was not all that it was cracked up to be. And, alright, she would also be happy to be married at Langroyd Hall, providing that he was not being charged for the use.

'As usual you are proving to be right. I keep looking across and thinking that I should have ordered that instead of this whale,' Frankie admitted. 'When can I expect the wedding cake to ice? Have you made all three tiers?'

'I've just the largest of the three to make and then I'll keep feeding them until the middle of March. Will that give you enough time and do you know how you are going to decorate it?'

'That, my dear, is quite sufficient time, but the decoration is my secret. I hope for it to be quite spectacular. Now, are we having a substitute bridesmaid, just in case Sarah does not appear in time? No matter if you think me shallow, it should be anybody but Daisy now she has fallen by the wayside. Although I'm sure Sarah will have made herself known to us by then, so it is only a precaution.'

'It should be Daisy, but I agree, under the circumstances, I couldn't ask her,' Meg replied. 'I thought perhaps Janet? She's a bonny lass and a good friend even though I'm her boss. I'm going to ask Joe Dinsdale to give me away. He's been good to me these last few years, nearly like a second father. Who are you going to ask to be your best man? Have you anybody in mind?'

'Yes, my old friend Miles Mitchell. He lives in Ilkley, we went to school together. You'll like him.' Frankie took Meg's hand and kissed it. 'We are going to be so happy. We have everything that we could wish for and more. Tell Janet to go and choose a dress from Hopkin's and put it on my account. We need her to look at her best.'

'There's no need for that Frankie, she already has some beautiful clothes. Her mother is a seamstress, even though they are not wealthy and there's a lot of them. It's amazing what she can do with some second-hand rags. Save your money.'

'Very well, but I hope she doesn't let us down.'

'Frankie, I wouldn't care if she turned up in her birthday suit, as long as you are by my side and I've heard from Sarah by then. You shouldn't count so much on looks and wealth – there's more to life than both of those.' It would be too much to expect him to change, she knew.

'I know but I want our day to be so perfect, I want our life to be perfect.'

Frankie smiled, keeping up the pretence for Meg's sake. He wished that his life could be perfect because it was far from being so at the moment.

Chapter 9

Frankie held his breath and felt his heart beating fast under his best jacket. His head felt light and he couldn't focus his mind on the job at hand. It was time to take a hard look at his finances and not shirk from them. Pawning a few pieces of jewellery was not going to get him out of the debt that he was in this time.

He patted his inside pocket checking that the deeds of his home were still in there as he entered the bank chambers and waited to see his bank manager. A feeling of complete failure washed over him as he thought of the day when his father had celebrated the purchase of his first home and told his young son that he would never have the yoke of debt around his neck and that the banks were just thieves in disguise. Now, he was about to mortgage his home, to get him out of the temporary embarrassment of lack of money.

'Ah, Mr Pearson, please join me.'

Edward Hitchins, the manager for the Yorkshire Bank, opened his office door and looked down at the young businessman. The man was in trouble and Hitchins felt slightly sorry for him — he looked as if he could do with a good night's sleep. 'How are you, sir? It is good of you to come and discuss your affairs this morning.'

'Thank you, Mr Hitchins, I am hale if not hearty. Perhaps I will feel a little better once we have talked,' Frankie said, following the manager into the office that he had sat in all too often of late. He breathed in the smell of expensive cigars and went to sit in the large leather chair that was offered to him, feeling like a school child just about to be scolded by the headmaster.

'Well, I'm sure we will be able to reach an agreement,' Hitchins said, looking at the papers in front of him. 'I must begin by saying that you have been a little reckless with your finances. However, all is not lost seeing that you have very wisely decided to sell the bakery at Ilkley and I believe that you are to offer the deeds of your family home for collateral this morning.' Hitchins lifted his jacket tails and sat back into his high back studded chair. Young Pearson was another one who had tried to run before he could walk. 'You know, your father was a good man, he was very careful with his money. I talked many a time to him in the past and asked him to invest in other properties to expand but he was happy with just the one. Perhaps you should have followed his example.'

'I know, I've been a fool, it has taken me this long to realize,' Frankie admitted. 'My fiancée keeps lecturing me. She has her feet truly on the ground and doesn't ever let me forget my faults.' He tried not to think about what Meg would say if she knew that he was about to mortgage their family home.

'Well, let us hope that she is the tonic and guiding hand that you need,' Hitchins said jovially. 'There's nothing wrong with wanting to expand your business but it has to be able to make a good profit and be worth taking risks for.' His tone changed. 'Sadly, looking through your accounts and books, you are putting your home at risk if we complete a deal. Now, have you made me the list we discussed of outgoings and income, and any outstanding bills that remain unpaid? We need to start off with a clean slate and keep you within a limit so that we are not confronting this mess again in a short while.'

Hitchins took the list of debtors and the deeds from Frankie and unfolded them all, taking his time to absorb the information, during which Frankie felt increasingly uncomfortable. 'By the looks of this first bill on the top of your pile, it doesn't look as if you have learned much from our other meetings. This bill from Hopkin's is inexcusable, sir. Do you realize the seriousness of this matter? You are putting your future happiness in jeopardy with your recklessness.' The bank manager leaned heavily on his desk and stared at Frankie.

'I know. It has suddenly dawned on me that I cannot be as reckless in the future,' Frankie apologized. 'The bakery at Ilkley is about to be sold and I am looking at cutting back on costs at both of my patisseries. The Hopkin's bill is for my wedding attire, else I would not have been shopping there.'

Frankie drew a breath and leaned back. 'Believe me, I know how serious this is now. It grieves me to have to let the bank get hold of my home, especially in the light of my wedding.' Frankie put his head in his hands and sighed.

Hitchins looked at him fiercely for a moment. 'Well, perhaps it has taken this for you to come to your senses. I know your property well, I was the one who first financed it, so I know that it is worth considerably more than we will be willing to lend to you. We will only lend you sufficient money to clear your debts and to give you some collateral in the bank.

'I need to look at these books and bills that you have laid in front of me and then I'll write and inform you how much we value your home at, but I must make it clear that this is the very last time we will be able to help.'

Edward Hitchins stayed silent for a moment, allowing his words to sink in. He looked stern once more as he sat back in his chair. 'I'll be honest, Mr Pearson, it will take you all your efforts to keep yourself solvent. Perhaps now is not the right time to be thinking about getting married, unless she is wealthy.'

'Meg is not wealthy but she is very savvy with her money,' Frankie told him. 'She has built her business from nothing and she lectures me about my spending and grand ideas. In fact, she never stops.' Frankie smiled slightly. 'She will keep me on the straight and narrow once we are wed, I just know it.'

'I'm glad to hear it.' Hitchins' attitude softened very

slightly. 'Now, let me see what I can do for you, and, of course, if and when the bakery at Ilkley sells then you will have halved your debt and will have helped yourself with the interest payments. I'll be in touch shortly and in the meantime spend only what you need and look hard at both of your remaining businesses.' The bank manager rose from his chair and stretched his hand out to be shaken. 'I wish you well, Mr Pearson. Just keep your feet on the floor. You have a good business at heart, you just need to curtail your spending.'

'Thank you, sir, I hope to hear from you shortly. Of course, I will do whatever it requires for my embarrassment of a bank balance to be resurrected. In fact, I am about to travel to Ilkley now to meet an interested buyer, so that should soon be resolved.'

'That is good to hear, one less worry for you on your wedding day. Good day, sir.'

Frankie put his top hat on as he left the office where he had felt so intimidated. He hated having to squirm in front of a bank manager, the arrogant old man, but at least he had secured funding to carry on for the next few months. Now to head to Ilkley to secure the sale of the bakery there and meet his old friend Miles Mitchell to ask him to be his best man.

'Hello my old friend! When I got your letter saying you were to visit me, I thought things are either bad or he's getting married.' Miles Mitchell shook Frankie's hand and slapped him on the back as he alighted down the coach steps.

'You know me too well, my dear friend,' Frankie laughed.

'However, I've also some business to do here in Ilkley, I'm to meet a purchaser for my patisserie later . . . but you are right, I am to be wed to my Meg.'

'Patisserie! The trouble with you, you were too long abroad in that filthy French country, it's a *bakery*, lad. You and your fancy words.' Miles grinned and shook his head 'So, you have finally got her to marry you? She's kept you waiting long enough.'

'Aye, we are to be married on the 8th of April. I have finally persuaded her to put my ring on her finger,' Frankie said walking briskly by his friend's side.

'Then let's celebrate! A swift noggin and a good feed in the King's Arms should set you right for the day, my friend. You look as if you are in need of a good meal. A baker that is getting thinner by the day, now that is not a good sign,' Miles said as he opened the door to the King's Arms, the warmth and the smell of beer hitting them both as they made their way to a quiet table in the corner of the large wooden-floored inn.

'I'm not the only thing that's going thin, my bank balance is as well,' Frankie admitted. 'I've just come away from a lecture by my bank manager and that is why I have to make sure that I sell my bakery, as you will have me call it. To be honest, I'm in a pitiful state and there am I about to marry the woman I love and assure her that I can promise her any-thing she ever wishes.' He wondered if Miles could really understand. His best friend had always been industrious and worked his way up from being a solicitor's clerk to joining the rolls as a solicitor himself.

Miles caught the eye of a serving maid and ordered two gills of Ilkley's finest and two plates of best stew before looking at Frankie. He realized that things must be bad, else Frankie would not be so open in his admissions. 'You sound a bit down. Can your mother not help you? What happened to your inheritance? Surely you should have come into that be now? It is so long since I've seen you, I've lost track,' Miles said with concern.

'Oh, the story is a long one, but my mother thought my inheritance was better in her care. She called me too reckless to have such a sum in my bank. However, I'd spent a lot of my money by then, thinking that I could repay anyone that I owed, buying my patisserie on the Headrow in Leeds and starting to build another up in Headingley. She left me penniless and almost bankrupt then.' Frankie sighed and drank deeply from his beer. 'If it hadn't been falling by luck in with Lady Beatrice Benson's group of friends, I would have lost everything. They have been such good customers and buoyed my business up, making me invest in the bakery here at Ilkley. However, I've had to admit that I've overstretched myself yet again. I'm nothing but a fool.'

'I'm sorry to hear all this. You always did have a passion for the best things in life. As a child, you always were dressed ten times better than any of us and you would seem to want for nothing. Perhaps you could blame your mother for that too – she was always admired by most men for her fashionable looks and she seemed well-to-do.'

'Aye, at my father's expense. He was always bent over his

desk accounting for every penny. I should have learned from him, but I didn't. Like I say, I've been an absolute fool.'

Frankie sat back and smiled at the servant girl who brought two plates filled with beef stew. She placed them in front of each man then curtsied as she left them to eat their dinners.

'If you get this bakery sold in Ilkley, surely that will help clear your debts?' Miles asked as he seasoned his plate.

'It'll go some way to it, that is if it does sell. I'll see none of the money and that is going to be hard to explain to Meg, as she knows nothing of the problems. Although I think she suspects that I am not wealthy, especially when she helped me out the first time by introducing me to the pawn shops, thinking that she was helping. Unfortunately, my debts have grown and you can't pawn property, only to the bank.' Frankie ate the first mouthful of his dinner and enjoyed the taste of the rich gravy.

'Well, I'm sorry to hear of your plight. It goes without saying that dinner is on me, and if I can lend you a small amount of money, I will see what I can do,' Miles offered although he hoped that Frankie would not take him up on it.

'I would never borrow from a friend like you, I would not want to jeopardize our close friendship,' Frankie said hastily. 'I may not see you for months but I know that you are always there for me, and believe me, that counts for a lot in this world.' He smiled ruefully. 'I will accept dinner from you, however and am most grateful. Now, the burning question, will you be my best man at my wedding on the 8th of April at St Mary's in Leeds? You must come and see my Meg and see that I'm lucky in love if not in wealth.'

'It goes without saying, my good man, it will be an honour to see a cad such as yourself walk down the aisle with a woman that can tame you by your side. Tell me the time and I will be there,' Miles said and was glad that the mood had lightened.

'It is at eleven in the morning and the wedding breakfast is at Langroyd Hall,' Frankie told him as he soaked up the gravy of the stew with the bread that had been provided.

'Bloody hell, man, that will have cost?' Miles blurted.

'Well, it wasn't supposed to. Bea offered it to me for nothing but then her bloody husband got involved, so yes, it now has cost a fortune. But I'm not backing down, now it has been settled and actually paid for.'

'"Bea", is it? Very informal for her ladyship. Something going on there, you old rogue?' Miles sniggered.

'No, I'd never be unfaithful to Meg. Which brings me to ask, are you living with your wife or lover nowadays – or perhaps with both if I know you?' Frankie asked.

Miles patted his mouth with his napkin.

'Do you think that I have a death wish?' he laughed. 'Both of them I keep far enough apart. One woman demanding of me at once is enough – and besides, it gives me time to play the field a little as well. I was just thinking what a bonny serving maid we had seeing to our needs. I might see if there is a service I could give her after you depart.' Miles grinned across at Frankie.

'We don't change, do we? You like your women and I like my money . . . or should I say I like spending it?' Frankie said. Miles ignored him, watching the young serving girl. Frankie decided to leave his friend to pay court to the bonny faced lass. He had an appointment that would make or break his life and hoped above hope that the potential buyer for the bakery would have the means to settle on a price that would keep old Hitchins happy at the bank. He now had more than himself to worry about.

Frankie did not want to become a copy of his mother. She had always thought only of herself and her position in society, and sitting in the bank chambers had reminded him how unhappy his father had been. He'd worked every hour to keep solvent. Frankie was not going to follow in his mother's shoes or let Meg carry the burden he had given them. It was time he faced his demons, admit to himself that he was not that posh and come back to earth with a bump.

A week later Frankie sat in front of Edward Hitchins in the Yorkshire Bank office once more. He had received the bank manager's valuation of his family home and the offer of a mortgage on the property – even if the valuation was less than Frankie considered it was really worth.

'Well, Mr Pearson, it seems that the sale of your bakery is going through nicely and I see that you have signed and agreed to our terms,' Hitchins said. 'Your account will soon be back in the black if you keep your head down and don't let anything else go wrong or spend rashly.'

Edward Hitchins leaned forward in the same threatening manner he had at their previous appointment. 'I hope that this will be our last meeting under these circumstances. My bank is not here to bail you out of any stupidity and it will not be doing so in the future. You are running out of collateral, so bear that in mind when you next see a dandy coat in Hopkin's.'

'I will indeed, sir. I aim to improve my financial status and am about to make changes,' Frankie said quietly.

'Then see that you do, sir. See that you do. Because we will not be here for you next time, and your new wife and family will be out upon the streets.' The bank manager growled. 'Now, good day, sir. I have other clients to spend my time upon, ones with money!'

Chapter 10

'Is that the last of your wedding cakes out of the oven?' Janet asked as she looked at the large square cake that filled the bakery with the smell of baking fruit.

'It is, thank the Lord, and it hasn't sunk in the middle. That's my part of the cake done and dusted, now it's up to Frankie to ice it.' Meg stepped back and regarded the bottom tier of her wedding cake and was glad that the bake had gone to plan.

'I bet it will look magnificent once it is erected. I wish I was able to see it once it is complete.' Janet sighed. 'It is going to be a society wedding, I just know it. The newspapers are bound to want to report it, Mr Pearson's shops and your own are that well known.'

'Frankie's might be but I don't think mine is. I just serve our local community. Frankie's is a little posher. Anyway, miss, you are going to be at our wedding. I told Frankie that I'd like you to be my bridesmaid. It's only right that you are, as you are my right-hand woman in the bakery and I value your friendship. Are you willing?' Meg smiled at the look of glee on Janet's face.

The smile turned to worry in an instant. 'Oh, I'd love to, but what am I going to wear? It'll be such a posh do, breakfast at Langroyd Hall. Lord, I'm well out of my depth there.'

'Frankie did offer you a dress from Hopkin's if you want? But I've seen you in some lovely dresses. How about that pale blue one with the long white lace sleeves, you look ever so beautiful in that?' Meg suggested.

'Oh! No, I couldn't go to Hopkin's, lasses like me don't go into that posh place,' Janet said, to Meg's slight relief. 'They'd look down their noses at me and I wouldn't feel comfortable. Besides, my mam can make anything just as good as anything they can. She's a wonder with a needle, in fact, she's got some lilac coloured cotton that I have had my eye on for a week or two. That will make a perfect bridesmaid dress. Tell Mr Pearson it's very kind of him to offer, but no, I'll sort myself out.' Janet regretted her words as soon as she had said them; she shouldn't have turned an opportunity to shop at Hopkin's.

'As long as you are sure? That colour would be perfect. As you know I'm in white but if you are dressed in lilac we will match the row of lilac trees that will be flowering on both sides of the church walkway. A true spring wedding.'

Janet gave a little giggle. 'Oh, I can't believe that I am to be your bridesmaid. I thought that either Sarah or Daisy would be helping you down the aisle, not me.'

'Well, I still haven't heard from Sarah and at one time I

would have loved Daisy to be my bridesmaid but you know how it is and Frankie has never liked her.'

'I hear that she's been seen walking out with one of the workers from the glass factory down Abrahams Yard,' Janet gossiped. 'I hope she's behaving herself with him, else there will be another baby on the way.' Janet blushed as she saw Meg scowling at her, and realized that she might have overstepped the mark.

'She's never told me who her new man is. I wondered why she left the baby with me the other night,' Meg mused. 'Let's hope that he's a good man and that his attentions are honourable, as you say. As for Sarah, I pray every day just for a few lines from her, or better still that she turns up on my doorstep, no matter what state she is in.'

'She will one day, I'm sure.' Janet saw Meg's eyes fill with tears and tried to get back onto a more pleasant subject. 'Are you asking Joe Dinsdale and his wife?'

'Yes, I'm going to visit him after we close this evening, I want to ask him to give me away. My father died some time ago and he's the closest thing I have. He's supported me through thick and thin so I owe him a great deal.' Meg wiped her eyes and smiled. 'And don't worry when it comes to George, he's invited too. After all, you two might be the next couple to get wed the way he has been looking at you lately.'

'Nay, I don't think so, although, I do like him, ' Janet said, although her embarrassed smile made Meg suspect she had hit close to the truth about her feelings towards the grocer's lad, soon to be manager.

The shop bell interrupted their conversation. 'Oh, that's a customer,' Meg said. 'I'll go. Janet, can you wash those patty tins and make another batch of shortcrust pastry? I think we will make some maids of honour for tomorrow, they will make a change from coconut tarts and besides, I seem to have run out of coconut. It's with making coconut pyramids yesterday and I forgot to tell George we needed some more.'

Meg secured her hairpins and welcomed a break from the heat of the ovens as she walked into the shop.

She smiled at the tall well-dressed woman that stood in front of her, secretly admiring her hat with the pheasant feathers displayed in it. 'Good afternoon, may I help you?'

'Yes, I'm absolutely famished,' the woman said. 'Standing outside yelling to the world has given me such an appetite and I was just passing and happened to notice that you had some scrumptious-looking scones in the window.' The woman smiled and asked, 'I don't suppose you could butter me one as well if that's not too much trouble. I'm going to have to wait for a drink of tea until I get home and that's quite a walk yet.' She shuffled a sheath full of leaflets and sighed as she leaned back against the wall exhausted and Meg suddenly remembered that she had seen the woman along the Headrow a few weeks back – their eyes had met for a brief moment.

Meg reached for a scone and smiled at her customer. 'Of course, we could butter you the scone. You look weary. Would you like to sit through in the bakery and enjoy it with a cup of tea? That is, if you don't mind the smell of baking all around you.'

'That would be most appreciated, I've been on my feet since eight o'clock this morning and I must admit I chose the wrong boots to wear this morning,' the woman replied. 'Who am I to preach about women being the stronger sex when I myself can't even be sensible in the choice of my own footwear.' She sighed and then lifted her head. 'My name is Alice Dent – it is only right that I introduce myself to you especially as you are offering me your hospitality.'

'I'm Meg, Meg Fairfax, this is my bakery. Please come this way and I'll ask Janet to make you a cup of tea. I think I have seen you once before standing with some other women along the Headrow, in fact, I think you were making yourselves known to one and all,' Meg said quietly as she led her visitor to the main bakery and urged her to sit in the chair next to the open fire.

'That would be me and my little band of followers. There are not many of us but our numbers are growing. Women are beginning to want to be men's equals, and so they should be,' Alice said forthrightly, making Janet glance at the woman who was talking so strongly and was being allowed to sit next to the fire.

'Janet, this is Miss Alice Dent, she requires some warmth and a drink of tea,' Meg said. 'Could you make a new brew and we will have a break ourselves.'

Janet wiped her hands after mixing the shortcrust pastry.

'Please don't let me stop you from your honest toil,' Alice said hastily. 'It's good to see two women working together, especially when it is a woman that owns the business.

109

Women should be more independent, that's what I keep telling my ladies.' She smiled at both women and looked at the interest on Meg's face. 'I'm sorry, I'm used to saying what I think. My parents always brought me up as an equal to my brother, so some would say that I don't know my place in the world. Especially the mill owners of Leeds at the moment who are frightened because I helped to set up a union for the tailoresses that they exploit. Unfortunately, when we called the women out on strike, it was not a success. You probably heard, as it did cause a bit of a scandal at the time. Women saying and doing what they think, it should never be allowed, you know.' Alice smiled.

Janet passed her a cup filled with warm tea and Meg put a freshly buttered scone on a plate next to their guest, then Janet went back to making the maids of honour, not wanting to be part of such inflammatory talk.

'So, Miss Dent, you are fighting on behalf of the women that are, as you say, put upon by some ruthless mill owners, but surely there is not a lot you can do?' Meg asked. 'Women need the work to keep their families fed. I remember the strike and they had no option but to return to their jobs.'

'That they do,' Alice agreed, 'but they should alsobe respected and have the same opportunities as any man. We are oppressed, Miss Fairfax, and it is time we fought back. They will soon stand to our attention if women demand more money and refuse to work for less than their fellow man. Although, as you say, the women's hands are tied because there is nothing worse than seeing your child go hungry.' She bit into her scone and ate as if it was the first thing she had eaten for weeks.

'I believe that we women are as good as any man as you say, Miss Dent,' Meg agreed, 'but I don't know how we are going to change things. In fact, I think women are cleverer than men, from what dealing I have had in life.' Janet couldn't help but take a deep intake of breath in surprise at Meg's announcement.

'Then you must join us! Come to one of our meetings at my friend's home at Adel Grange: do you know the house? We have meetings of like-minded women once a week and aim to mend the world through our strength of standing together,' Alice said as she stood up and brushed the crumbs from her skirt.

'Yes I do know the Grange, it's a grand house. I will think about your kind invitation. What night do you meet?' Meg asked and looked at her guest who had quickly drunk her tea and eaten her scone without any airs and graces.

'Tuesday evening at seven and please bring any other women that you think have the same views as us. Our strength lies in our numbers.' Alice looked across at Janet. 'Can we not tempt you?'

'No, I'm busy looking after my siblings of an evening,' Janet said and hoped that Meg would not contradict her.

'Righto! Well, I look forward to seeing you, Miss Fairfax. I'm sure you will find our meetings of interest, we intelligent women must stand our ground. Now, I'll be on my way, thank you once again.'

Alice walked to the door followed by Meg. 'Thank you for calling and I will attend one of your meetings – probably this next Tuesday. I'd be interested in what you say.'

Meg stood at the doorway and watched the radical woman walk out onto the street without a backwards glance.

'You are not really thinking of going to one of her meetings, are you?' Janet asked, coming and standing next to her.

'Yes, I am. You know I've always thought us women are far more intelligent than most men and that we should have more say in our lives,' Meg said, seeing the worry on her friend's face.

'Won't Mr Pearson have something to say about that? He'll think women like Alice Dent are dangerous. All the mill owners must hate her and her friends,' Janet said quietly.

'All the more reason to go and see what she preaches. Besides, Frankie need never know. He often keeps secrets from me, so this time this can be one I keep from him,' Meg said sharply. 'Now, are those maids of honours ready for the oven? That will be one job less for the morning if you get on with them now.'

Never had Meg met a woman like Alice Dent and she was interested in what she had to say. It was time in her eyes that women stood their ground and not become a man's chattels when married. She would go, whether Frankie would permit it or not. She picked up a leaflet that had fallen to the floor. It was headed LEEDS WOMEN'S SUFFRAGE SOCIETY. Meg glanced at it briefly before putting it into her pocket;

she'd read it later after she had closed the bakery and visited Joe Dinsdale.

'Aye, lass it would be an honour to walk you down the aisle. It's just a pity your mother and father aren't still in this world to see what a grand woman you've grown into.' Joe Dinsdale smiled as he looked across at his wife.

'Aye, I remember your mother, worked hard every day of her life to bring you two lasses upright. Where's your Sarah at nowadays? She went to London, didn't she?' Betty Dinsdale asked Meg.

'She did, she's still there as far as I know, but she's not one for keeping in touch,' Meg replied hoping that Betty would not pry any deeper. She knew that Joe's wife liked a good gossip and she and her friends liked to chew over other people's problems.

'I don't know what your mother would have thought of her going down there. She's terrible young to be left to her own devices. I'd be worrying myself to death,' Betty said and shook her head.

'She'll be right, will that 'en. Stop making Meg worry,' Joe chided. 'She always did have her head screwed on, did Sarah. Agnes brought them up to be independent, perhaps a little too independent, for women.'

'Yes, she had to, else we would not have survived. I'm thankful that she did, it makes you strong,' Meg replied and looked at Betty. To her, she was the perfect Victorian wife, after marrying a man with money and becoming

113

a perfect housewife and mother to his children – but nothing else.

'Aye, these young women, all's changed since my day.' Betty sighed and looked at her husband. 'We'll have to get ourselves dolled up for this wedding Joe, especially if the reception is at Langroyd Hall.' Betty looked closer at the gilt-edged invite that Meg had given them before asking Joe to walk her down the aisle.

'Bloody hell, that'll have cost your Frankie a bit! Does he think himself royalty?' Joe said, forgetting himself for a minute. He didn't reckon much to Frankie Pearson, but as long as Meg was happy with him, it was nothing to do with him.

'He got the use of the hall free,' Meg explained. 'Lady Benson offered him it. She's a good customer of his. Of course, we are seeing to all the food ourselves, so it's just the hall and her serving staff that she is giving free.' Meg felt herself blushing, knowing what Joe would be thinking if not saying.

'She must be a good customer and she must think some- thing of him if she's doing that for your both. I bet her husband had something to say about it, he's as tight as a duck's arse and an arrogant bugger. No wonder she amuses herself a lot,' Joe said and then got gently nudged by Betty, reminding him to be careful what he said.

'It's kind of her, Joe, it is nice to know that folk still have a bit of kindness in them,' Betty said. 'We'll all have a grand day. Now, is there anything that you are in need of for a wedding present? It's no good giving you something that you already have and both of you have homes from what I've heard Joe say.'

'That's really kind of you, but we don't expect anything from anyone, we have all that we need,' Meg said and felt awkward.

'A nice piece of china or silver?' Betty queried.

'We'll get her a piece of silver, Mother, something nice and tasteful, something that's worth summat,' Joe said and stood up and reached for his pipe from off the fireplace.

'Please. You've already done so much for me, I expect nothing,' Meg said as she also got to her feet.

'Nay, a bit of silver never goes amiss. You can always pawn it if times get hard ... not that you'll ever need to, I hope lass.' Joe puffed on his pipe and watched Meg put her shawl around her shoulders in readiness to go. 'We both wish you the best and, like I say, it will be an honour to walk you down the aisle.'

'Thank you, I'm grateful.' Meg said, before Joe saw her out.

Once she had gone, Betty scowled at her husband. 'What did you say that about pawning silver for? She'll never need to have to do that, surely.'

'I don't know so much, my lass. Word is that her fancy Frankie doesn't have any real money. He's sold his bakery at Ilkley before even opening it. Now, that doesn't make sense. And he's a ladies' man! Getting married at Langroyd Hall? Well we all know what that's about. Everyone knows that Lady Benson is no lady. Meg'll not have an easy life when she marries that man. I only hope that he doesn't ruin her bakery because she loves that little shop and it makes her good money.'

'Still, Joe, there was no need to say that, it will have started her thinking,' Betty said.

'Well, I hope it has. There's still time to walk away from it. She's kept him waiting long enough so she must have been uncertain about him herself.' Joe shook his head. 'No, the lass if you ask me would be better without him, and that's a fact.

Chapter 11

'Thank you,' Meg said and looked up at Frankie's maid, Ada, as she placed the gravy boat on the Sunday dinner table and curtsied.

'It won't be long before we sit each dinner time together,' Frankie said as he helped himself to the spring cabbage then passed it Meg's way. 'The day can't come soon enough for me. To have you living with me instead of being so far apart and having to make sure there's a carriage for you to be picked up each time you visit.'

'Yes, it will be a saving for both our pockets. Cabs are so expensive nowadays,' Meg replied as she took hold of the tureen, helping herself to the vegetables.

'I didn't mean because of the expense, my dear, I meant that I worry about you travelling in the carriage on your own. Although you are right, they really don't know what to charge sometimes and half of the poor animals that pull them look near dead.'

'The mouths of the cabby children are to be fed first,

although he depends on his living through the horse, but times are hard for the working classes. It's time things changed.' Meg saw a look of surprise on Frankie's face as she said what she thought.

'Have we been taking an interest in politics, my dear? I've never heard you speak like this before,' Frankie exclaimed and gave a small laugh. 'Such things are better left in the hands of men, don't you think?' He cut into his slice of roast beef then noticed Meg's face was flushed.

'Not in politics,' she said carefully. 'But I do worry about me fellow man, especially the women of our society and more so, the women who do not have a say in their everyday life. If it hadn't have been for Joe Dinsdale, I would have perhaps been walking the streets. I will always be grateful for his trust in me. Not every woman has the same chances. Who knows what our Sarah is doing.' Meg paused then took a mouthful of her dinner.

'But, that is politics, my dear. You see, you are best leaving such worries to me. A pretty head like yours should not be full of worry,' Frankie said and noticed Meg go quiet as she ate her dinner. He decided not to educate her, rather than spoil a perfectly good meal. Instead, he took the opportunity to raise a different subject.

The time had come to tell Meg that he had sold his patisserie in Ilkley. She had to know sometime, he thought, and the time seemed right seeing that she was discussing the fate of fellow workers. 'I think I'd better tell you that I've been keeping quiet about a deal I've been doing for the patisserie at Ilkley.' Frankie hesitated then said, 'I felt that the place on the High Street was not ideal and Roger Henderson, a fellow baker, offered me a good price for it. So good that it was hard to ignore.'

'But you had put so much time and money into it,' Meg said. 'I thought once it had opened it would thrive, like Headingley and your one on the Headrow. I never even got to see it!'

Frankie wiped his mouth with his serviette. 'The offer really was too good, my love. I did the deal when I went over to meet Miles. He's agreed to be my best man, by the way. Roger Henderson is a fine man too, in fact, he has already paid me and the money is safe and secure in the bank. I made a handsome profit.'

He sat back in his chair as Ada cleared the empty plates away.

'Well, I suppose the money will have boosted your bank balance,' Meg acknowledged. 'We are both responsible for spending a little rashly of late, with our wedding on the horizon.' She placed her knife and fork together and passed her plate to Ada.

'Yes, I count myself lucky to have sold the property so easily. However, it would have made no difference if I had sold it or kept it on, I was going to make money either way. I didn't have to sell it!' Frankie said gruffly and wondered if Meg had guessed his plight.

'Oh, I must have misunderstood,' Meg said thoughtfully. 'When you asked me to come and show your bakery here at

Headingley some of my recipes, I thought that your pastries were not selling, so your profits were not thriving. Didn't you feel you would be better cutting your losses with selling the bakery at Ilkley?'

Frankie looked flustered. 'No, not at all my love. The people in Headingley have perhaps more down-to-earth needs and I'd like to corner the market. Now that you have mentioned it, when do you think you could grace us with your presence at the patisserie? I hope it can be this week and my baker can start to see if your everyday fare will sell just as well,' Frankie said. He realized his fiancée was very astute in her business knowledge and he knew she kept a close eye on her purse strings.

'It depends on what time of day that you need me. I'd prefer one evening so that I can still work at my bakery and not lose any time there,' Meg said and watched Frankie think about it. She had never guessed a few months ago that he would lower himself to wanting her recipes and ideas. This was a real climb down from his high ideals.

'Mmm ... Yes, I can always ask Ivor to put in a few extra hours one evening or you could just pass him on the recipes. I'm sure I will have made most of them in the past when I was just starting out,' Frankie replied unable to hide an air of superiority. He hated having to admit that Meg's baking was more popular than his. 'Or, if you have Tuesday or Wednesday evening free that would sit comfortably with me.'

'I can come Wednesday but not Tuesday, I have got an

appointment elsewhere,' Meg said and smiled as a plate of cheese and biscuits was placed on the table, after Ada had asked if she would like to partake in a sherry trifle and she replied with a shake of the head.

'We will make it a week on Wednesday then, I'll make sure I'm present as well. What are you about on Tuesday? Not looking after that poor unwanted baby for Daisy, I hope.'

'No, although I expect to be looking after the poor little mite one evening this week, as I understand Daisy to be courting, a man from the glass bottle factory, although she has not told me as of yet.'

Meg thought for a moment then decided that she would tell him the truth. After all, despite what she said to Janet about keeping it quiet from Frankie, she did believe that they should not keep secrets from each other. She buttered a cracker and took a slice of cheese from the platter that they were both sharing. 'I'm going to attend a meeting out in Adel, at Adel Grange, I was invited to attend by a Miss Alice Dent. I found her views most interesting.'

Frankie placed his knife down and looked directly at her. 'Adel? How do you know somebody who lives there? It's very upper class, my dear. Are you sure you have the right address?'

'Yes, I'm very sure. Alice came into the bakery. I made her welcome with tea and a scone and she invited me to one of her meetings.'

'Meetings, now ... is this connected to the woman who is causing so much upset, telling women they have the same rights as men and talking of women's suffrage? What on earth do you want to mix with the likes of her for?' Frankie scowled as he remembered more about the trouble she had caused with women striking in their place of work and now calling women to arms. 'I hear her shouting with her so-called followers outside the patisserie on the Headrow. She's trouble, is that one, she should know her place.'

'I found her quite amicable and I do believe she talks a lot of sense,' Meg said firmly. 'It is time women were treated with more respect, I'm glad that she is making a stand for women. We are never given the credit we deserve. I've seen how women are treated by some of their bosses. They are used nothing better than dogs sometimes and why are we any different from a man?'

Frankie's face suffused with anger. 'I forbid you to go, Meg, it is not the sort of company that I want my wife to keep. I don't know what has got into of you of late.'

'I'm not your wife yet, Frankie,' Meg snapped back. 'I will be going. She interests me with her talk.' She sighed. 'Surely you don't want a simpering wife with no mind of her own.'

'I want you to have a mind of your own, which you always have had, of course I do. However I don't want you mixing with her – or her friends. From what I have heard about them, they are radical in their ideas. Not the sort of people to mix with, especially for a gentleman in business,' Frankie added and breathed in deeply.

'And what about a woman in business?' Meg asked. 'I think she is just the sort of woman that I need to know. As she says, there is strength in women in numbers, and that is what we need to support one another.'

Meg couldn't quite believe that she had dared to speak to Frankie so forthrightly. A few months ago she would never have spoken her mind in such a way but she had grown in confidence and she knew now that she was just as good at business if not better than her husband-to-be. No matter what he had claimed about selling his bakery at Ilkley, she knew that he would have probably only have done it of necessity. She also knew that she now had the better head for business out of the two of them. Once married, she hoped to prove it if he let her.

'I suppose I can't stop you from seeing the dreadful woman but I think you will regret it,' Frankie said after a few moments' heated silence. 'I do hope that you are not going to be so headstrong once we are married, Meg. A strong wife is to be admired but a pig-headed one is not. We need to set an example for our children.'

Frankie stood and reached for a cigar from a silver tin on the sideboard before pouring himself a glass of port.

'I fully agree a stable home is a happy home,' Meg replied. 'We both will have a lot to learn in bringing up children and being open with one another. I do love you, Frankie, but I will always want a say in the running of my business if not yours and it is with that in mind I will still be attending Miss Dent's meeting on Tuesday. I think she and her followers will have some valid ideas for women in business as well as in general.' Meg smiled. 'Now, let's not argue over such a petty matter. You say you went to see Miles and he's agreed to be your best man?'

'Yes, he's only too pleased to be there for me on our big day. It was good to catch up with him. You will like him once you have met him, he's a real gent.'

'Then everything is in place. Janet is to be my bridesmaid, Joe Dinsdale is only too happy to give me away and you have your best man. The wedding date is set and the Hall is booked. Let us hope that the sun shines upon us and that I have heard from Sarah by then. '

Frankie reached for her hand. 'It is just a fancy that takes you to see Alice Dent, isn't it, Meg? She is not the sort of woman to be seen with.'

'I know that you are worried about my going, Frankie, but please, I need to see what she's all about. The world is changing and I don't want to be left behind and reliant entirely on my husband for support and money.'

'But that's what I am there for, my dear. Like all my generations before me,' Frankie said. He wasn't going to let his wife take charge of his world. He'd seen the consequences of that with his father, and he had been a more astute man than Frankie ever would be.

'Well, that doesn't seem that fair to me,' Meg argued. 'It should be a joint affair and both of us as strong as one another. Besides, I sometimes think that you struggle with your affairs. I haven't forgotten the time when you were having to ask my help in pawning some goods and I never want us to be in that situation again.'

A flash of anger crossed Frankie's face. 'I do wish you would forget about that. I've moved on from those early years. My bank knows that I'm a competent businessman and that they would support me now. Not that I need them,' Frankie quickly added and hoped that he hadn't given the game away.

'The bank . . . You don't owe at the bank, do you? It will be like a ton weight around your neck if you do. I've always kept clear of them but I know that they love adding interest to anything borrowed.' Meg scowled and hoped that Frankie was telling her the truth.

'No, I don't rely on them, but it is reassuring to know that should I need to borrow then they would be willing. Now, this is not about my finances, this is about you attending a meeting at that woman's house. If you feel you must go, then go. However, I do hope that you don't get involved in her movement. You do know her friend Isabella Ford supports the Fabian Society, don't you? I believe the whole Ford family does. I always think there is something deeply suspicious about socialists, with their talk of reconstructing society with high morals through political means. Do they think that the rest of us have no morals?' Frankie said crossly.

'I'm sure they don't think that. However, don't worry, I'm only going out of interest. They are not about to convert me into a staunch socialist on my first meeting. But I do believe she is trying to do good for the working classes.'

As they went to prepare for an afternoon walk, Meg wondered why Frankie had mentioned the bank when his finances were talked about. Was he in debt to them, no matter what he said? His spending was grand but she had no idea how much he made at his patisserie. Unlike her own bakery, he had well-to-do clients who cared not what they spent, and Frankie never let slip details of how he was doing with his business.

She couldn't help but think something was wrong, else he would not have sold the bakery at Ilkley, for which he had once had such grand plans.

Tuesday night soon came around and the more Meg thought about going to see Alice Dent and her friends, the more nervous she got. Both Janet and Frankie had made their views about the woman quite obvious but still, she felt that she should go. Alice dared to say what Meg had thought for a long time.

After catching the horse tram out to the small affluent village of Adel, she walked to the driveway of Adel Grange. She breathed in deeply, straightened her hat and made sure that the coat she had bought second-hand from the rag and bone man that morning was buttoned up and looked respectable. She shook her head and thought herself stupid for letting her stomach churn and to have wasted good money on a second-hand coat that she had gone so long without. Even though Alice Dent had seen her at work at her worst she had felt she should make an effort. To meet someone with money and influence, she should look her best.

'Oh, you are new, I take it you are going to our meeting?'

a young woman said, catching up with Meg and taking her by surprise.

'Yes, yes, I am. I was just summoning up courage, I've never been to such like before or a house so grand,' Meg found herself saying as she had to catch her breath as they walked up the driveway and stood in front of the grand large gothic building that was the home of the Ford family.

'Oh, don't worry about either, the house is not that grand inside and I promise we won't eat you. I'm Isabella, and you must be one of Alice's new recruits. I'm glad that you are joining us. Now, come, we meet in the parlour and share tea and biscuits. We are quite civilized, you know. Quite unlike what some people, especially the men in society, paint us to be.' Isabella smiled and held the front door open as Meg walked up the steps and looked up at the wooden veranda that sheltered visitors from the inclement weather and hoped that she hadn't offended Isabella with her hesitance.

'Thank you. I'm Meg, I run a bakery in the centre of Leeds,' Meg introduced herself as she walked into the hallway and looked around at a house that seemed very grand indeed.

'That makes a change. We usually have plenty of seam-stresses and factory workers at our meetings. It sounds as if you are already making your way in a man's world, which is gratifying to know.' Isabella took her hat off and hung it up on the huge iron coat stand that stood in the hallway and then took her coat off and offered her hand for Meg's. 'I'll take your hat and coat. Our butler is feeling his age so he's not as spritely as he used to be. He's probably sleeping in his chair in the kitchen, so I wouldn't want to waken him.'

Meg slipped out of her coat but kept her hat on her head. It was heavily pinned and she didn't want to disturb her hair.

'Right follow me, this way to the parlour. I can hear Alice pontificating as we speak. She's got such a loud voice on her, all the world has to listen to her when she starts.'

Meg followed Isabella, feeling completely out of place in the large parlour filled with women from all walks of life. But she soon found out that she needn't have done. There were mill lasses still in their clogs and shawls, seamstresses in their uniforms, all seated next to well-to-do women from the upper classes. Not one of them looked at her twice as she sat down in a chair that Isabella indicated as Alice came to a close and looked round at the new arrivals.

'Ah, Isabella, so you are back and I see you have brought Miss Fairfax. It's a pleasure to have you join us er ... Meg? We were just discussing the hours worked by the average woman, and men come to that, and that there should be a limit to what we are expected to work. Do you not think so?'

Meg thought for a second or two then replied, 'You are asking the wrong person, I'm afraid, as my day can start as early as four in the morning and ends when I see fit, with being a baker. However I don't expect Janet my assistant to work the same hours. After all, she has family and a life of her own. So, yes I think some workers are worked too hard and long and a cap on hours worked would be welcome.'

'We at the Fabian Society believe in an eight-hour day,

eight hours of work, eight hours sleep, and eight hours for a home life. Surely that is what every family man or woman should expect. A twelve-hour working day, which is expected of us now, is too long, although it is not long since it was much more than that. We will eventually persuade the government to bring it into play,' Alice said and looked around the room as the women clapped and smiled in agreement.

Meg observed Alice closely. The other women were obviously captivated by her, and she thought about what she'd just proposed. Yes, in an ideal world, eight hours would be long enough to work but it took her at least four to just make the bread, and then she had to sell it. Most of the women in the room either were employed by mill owners or were ladies of leisure, she thought. None of them had to balance their own business books and work long hours to make their business work. It was then she realized that she had risen above her original status as a shop-girl to one of a business owner with a different look on life. No wonder Frankie had not wanted her to attend. She sipped her cup of tea and listened more to what Alice was saying.

'I believe in an eight-hour working day with opportunities for training and employment. Improvements in education and admission to professions that have in the past been closed to us women. All these should be our goals in life, ladies.'

Meg tried not to catch her eye, not wanting to be drawn in again into the conversation. She agreed with a lot of what Alice was saying – particularly that women should be equal in rights to men – but what she was proposing was dangerous in a society run by men. Frankie was right, this was radical talk, but it was radical talk that should have been a way of life for most women for a long time. She sat back and listened to the other women talking, the seamstresses telling everyone of the hours they put in for their employer and the conditions that they worked in and she thought of her sister when she was a burler and mender. Perhaps Sarah had been right to stand her ground against the bullying overseer, however not in such a violent way. The world was not fair and never would be until women were equal with men.

All too quickly, the meeting reached its end and Alice was shaking everyone's hand in the hallway as they left. 'I hope you enjoyed our meeting, Miss Fairfax, and that you will be joining us again?' she asked.

'Yes, indeed I did, I agreed with quite a lot that you said. We should have equal opportunities to men.' Meg pulled her coat on.

'Perhaps you would like to become a member of our Leeds' Women's Suffrage Society along with my friend Isabella and my dear sister-in-law Helen?' Alice suggested. 'We could do with prominent women in our society.'

'I will think about it, but I only have my own small bakery. I'm not prominent at all in society. I'm just like the seamstresses at your meeting, I work all hours to keep my head above water and hopefully make a little profit at the end of the day.' Meg buttoned her coat up.

'Oh, the seamstresses and tailors. I help them as much as I

can with the Provident and Protective League but there is so much work to be done and so much help needed.'

'You are a busy woman indeed, Miss Dent. You are doing so much good for those without the strongest voice,' Meg said and smiled. 'I must go else I'll miss the last tram home.'

'Then here take one of our pamphlets and if you want to join us again please do so. I'm also giving a talk by the Hyde Park Hotel in Leeds on Sunday morning. It would be cheering to see your face amongst the crowd.' Alice handed her copies of the leaflet that she had touted for the past few months asking for a subscription to the Leeds Women's Suffrage Society. Meg recognized it as the one she had been carrying when she visited the bakery.

'Thank you, I will pass them out to who I think may be interested and I will try to come and see you on Sunday morning, I promise.' Meg started to climb down the stone steps hastily. 'Until Sunday, Miss Dent,' she said and then turned hard on her heels to catch her lift home.

Chapter 12

Sarah sat on the edge of her bed and looked at herself in the reflection of the broken mirror that she had found on the shoreline. She was a mess.

Her hair was long and lank and filled with knots, and she sported a black eye that made her wince when she touched it. She blinked and tried to open it properly but to no avail. The skin around it was puffy and had swollen so much so that she could hardly see out of it. She held her head in her hands and felt the tears welling up in her eyes then curled up in the foetal position on the mattress that she called her bed. The bed that had seen her raped and punched until she had screamed for her life as Sam had hit her and had his way with her after hitting the drink and losing money at a dog fight down in Battersea.

She'd never seen him in that state. He had never acted that way before and she hoped he never would again. She'd not stirred as she had heard him coughing and retching in the early morning's light and leave her side without a word, stumbling out into the street without even checking she was alive. It was in that instant that she hated him. She'd have done anything for him before then but now he had taken the one thing that she had always kept sacred, her virginity. How could he? She'd always told him not to and been able to stand her ground but last night with the drink and a temper raging within him, he'd not kept his promise.

Her trust in him was now gone. She could no longer feel safe with him, and she'd seen a whole new side to him that night. His language and his actions made her feel even more worthless, tossed about like a rag doll and her most private of places abused. She had nothing and meant nothing to anyone, she sobbed. How she wished she'd listened to Meg and had stayed at her humble but love-filled home, instead of following an elusive dream that had just turned into a nightmare.

Sarah shook and curled up even tighter as she heard the door open on the hovel that was home. She didn't move as she could feel Sam's presence looming over her and smelt the familiar odour of sweat, tobacco, and stale ale.

'Sarah, Sarah, get up. I'm back.' He reached down and shook her shoulder hard.

'Bugger off, leave me alone,' Sarah snivelled and kept her face turned to the wall.

'I'm sorry. I've brought you some breakfast – look, a muffin from Bart, and I got him to butter it.' Sam pulled on Sarah's shoulder and tried to make her turn towards him.

'I don't care, I'm not hungry,' Sarah sobbed.

'Course ya are, you are always hungry. Come on girl, I've said I'm sorry, I can't do much more than that. I can't take back what I did last night. I wish I could.' Sam sat on the edge of the bed and put his hand on her arm. 'Come on gal, it was the drink and I'd lost what I had in my pocket to those pikeys and their dogs down at Battersea. I should have known better but they kept egging me on and plying me with their bloody booze.' Sam sighed. 'I didn't know what I was doing, honestly, gal.'

Sarah didn't move and even though the smell of the warm muffin made her mouth water she could not look at the one person that she had trusted in the whole of London.

'I'll leave it here then,' Sam said. 'I've a spot of business this morning, I might have been worse for wear last night but we might have the chance of a better life if I move fast on what I heard last night. You'll not be ignoring me then, my gal.' He put the muffin down by her side and got up from the bed. 'I'll be back in another hour or two, hopefully with some good news.' He looked down at the lass he knew he'd done wrong by. 'I'm sorry gal, it'll not happen again. I saw my father do it to my mother too many times and I always vowed I'd never treat my woman like that.'

Still staring at the wall Sarah spoke softly. 'Well, you did and I'll not be taking it again.' She rolled over and looked up at Sam, showing him the damage to her face that he'd done in his drunken temper but hiding the real hurt he'd done by raping her. Her stomach churned as he reached out and touched her.

'I'm sorry. I'll make it up to you. I'll be back with some good news shortly, I promise.' Sam looked downcast and looked genuinely sorry for losing his temper and control in a bout of rage. 'Now eat your muffin and make ready for flitting, cause if all goes to plan, gal, we'll soon have a proper roof over our heads.'

'A home, a proper home, not like this place that we are in now?' Despite her despair over her present predicament, Sarah perked up. The idea of having a proper home made her think of better times ahead.

'That's what I said and you'll not have to go scrounging along the shoreline. I've the chance of something better for us both. I might have lost leave of my senses for a while last night, but not until I'd done a bit of business.' Sam winked. 'Now get that muffin eaten, gal, while I go and see a man about a dog.'

Sam closed the door behind him and left her in the gloom. Had he really found them a new home and a job or was he just saying it to get back on her right side? Whatever employment he had found it would not be legitimate, not with the crowd that he was with last night, she thought as she bit into the muffin and the warm butter ran down her chin. But anything would be better than the state they were now in. Just as long as the beating she had taken did not turn into a regular thing she might as well stay with him. It was either that or sell herself to anybody who looked at her and not many would do that in the state she was in.

Sarah lay in her bed for most of the day, except for a few

minutes spent putting the few belongings that they possessed into her shawl and tying it fast. It was nearly dusk when the latch on the door lifted and Sam walked in.

'Get up gal, we are moving. I've found us a better place and work. Stop feeling sorry for yourself and shift!' Sam grabbed the shawl full of their belongings and then pulled Sarah by the arm. 'Come on, get a move on, we've a home waiting for us and I need to earn our keep tonight. I've work to do while you lie feeling sorry for yourself.' He pushed Sarah out of the door into the filthy street.

'But where are we going? Don't I have a say? I might not want to go,' Sarah said belligerently, pulling away from him.

'You'll go whether you like it or not, gal. Besides anywhere's better than here. Now, get yourself moving. We are off to Spitalfields. There's a house just become vacant and that's to be our home.' Sam laughed as Sarah pulled up her skirts and tried to keep up with him as he strode out across the alleys and streets, carrying their few belongings, heading towards one of the most feared areas in London. 'The folk there were good enough to leave many of their belongings and all. They just upped sticks and decided they didn't like the area anymore.'

'Why's that then? You wouldn't leave everything behind just like that,' Sarah panted, as she ran to keep up with him.

'They were Jewish, decided to be with their own kind and get out of this part of London. Not that they had much choice,' Sam added with a nasty grin as he dodged people walking down the streets.

'What do you mean? Why didn't they have much choice?' Sarah asked.

'Let's say that if you are not part of the company we are about to keep then you are not welcome,' Sam explained as he turned a corner and entered one of the most desolate parts of London known as Whitechapel.

Sarah caught her breath and looked at the dirt-filled streets and the inhabitants that stood outside their doorways. 'You've brought us here? This is no better than where we have just left!' There was a cock fight taking place halfway down the street and on the corner as they turned to enter the street two prostitutes shouted for Sam's attention.

'It's a lot better,' Sam told her. 'You've got a good house and it's got some comforts in it. You'll see, there's a kitchen and two bedrooms ... and more than that, I've got work, we'll not go short. Saying that, you could always join the whores on the corner, you'd make us good money from what I can just remember.'

Sarah stopped in their tracks and stared at Sam. 'Stop it, stop right now. I'd never sell myself, you know that. You took advantage of me last night and you know it.' She stared at him. 'I want to go back Sam, back to where we have come from. Here looks like my idea of hell. It is filthy, and by the looks of the place, it's filled with every cutthroat that ever walked the streets. And isn't this where Jack the Ripper stalked the streets? They never caught him. He could still be about, lurking on these streets.'

'You either come with me or you go on your own and fend

for yourself,' Sam said sternly. 'You'd not last long and then you really would be selling yourself on the streets. Besides I was only joking. I'll not touch you again, I promise. You can make sure of that as all the rooms have locks on them, some fellas that have come on business before we moved in didn't want to be disturbed on the job.'

Sam could see Sarah wavering and pointed up at the street sign. 'Come on, gal, you've got a proper address, that means you can write to your sister and she can write to you. She'll not know how you are living or where the street is. London is London to you northerners, every street is the same, paved with gold, isn't it?' Sam laughed cruelly and pulled on her arm as they walked down the street together with everyone watching them.

'That's what I used to think, but now I know it is worse than anywhere I ever went in Leeds,' Sarah told him. 'I'll not stay, Sam, if you touch me again or I hate the place. But now you say I can write to Meg, it is worth seeing how I fare. She'll be thinking me dead seeing I haven't written to her for so long.'

Sarah felt a little happier. The place that they had been living in had no postal address and Sam had never said she could write home before – besides she'd never been able to afford the postage. He must have landed on his feet and got a good job, but just what she dared not think about. Nobody in an area like that was trustworthy and legal she guessed.

Sam pulled a large key out of his pocket and unlocked a scabby painted wooden door halfway down the street then stepped back with his cap in his hand. 'Welcome to our humble abode. It might be small, but it's better than we are used to and it is clean, unlike the street outside.'

Sarah stepped forward and stood in the main room and gasped. 'How did you manage this?' She ran her hand over the back of a pine chair, smiling at the set of four and the scrubbed table, the sideboard that even had some ornaments upon it, and a picture of Queen Victoria on the wall. 'It's posher than my old home at Leeds,' she said excitedly and then walked into the kitchen and scullery before running up the stairs to view the bedrooms.

Sam sat back in one of the chairs listening to Sarah walking from room to room and grinned. At least he'd made up for his lack of control the previous night. He'd been pretty sure that once she had seen their new home, that she'd forgive him.

'Bloody hell, we are nearly royalty! I still don't understand why the folks that lived here left half their stuff, though. There's even bedding on the bed! We want for nothing,' Sarah said once she'd finished her inspection.

'I knew you'd like it, gal, that's why I had to act fast. I know it is not the best of areas but neither was round the docks and you got used to that. Besides, as long as I do my job and keep my new bosses sweet then it will always be ours.' Looking at her eye again, Sam went over to her and said, 'I'm sorry, gal, I shouldn't have hit you. It was the drink and the company I'd kept all night. I felt that I had to prove myself to somebody and you were gabbling on and I just had to stop you.'

'As long as you don't do it again and you keep your todger to yourself. I'm not to be used like that, and don't you forget it,' Sarah said with a little of her old fight back.

'Right, but things work both ways and just you remember that. You keep your mouth shut and you say nothing to nobody about the comings and goings in this house. We are not living rent-free for nothing. My hours – my life – belongs to the Bessarabians now and they would soon oust us if we ever said anything wrong about them. Just like the Jewish family that lived here whose life they made hell.' Sam stopped and looked downcast for a minute. 'We are in league with the devil now and are running with him, but he pays well and it's work I can do, so never ask me how I've come by stuff.'

'Oh, Sam, what have you done?' Sarah said, hearing a note of fear in Sam's voice that she'd never known before. 'You'll be alright, won't you? I think I'd perhaps have stopped where we were if whoever you are going to work for is that bad.' Sarah looked so worried that Sam put his arms around her.

'It will be right, I can look after myself,' he said confidently.

Sarah dropped her head. Whoever these Bessarabians were, she wished that Sam had not got caught up with them. They didn't sound like the folk she would want to get involved with. What exactly did they do? She hated to think what had happened to the poor family that had lived in the house and had left everything, fleeing their family home in a hurry by the looks of it.

*

For the first time in weeks, Sarah felt clean. Her belly was full, the swelling around her eye had now subsided and there was just a yellowy patch of skin around her eye as the bruising came out. Sam came and went at all hours of the day and night and she knew better than to ask what he was about as he brought many a package and parcel into the home and told her not to be nosy and look at it.

She and Sam were now living on the edge of society and she soon realized that even the peelers didn't dare walk round their area unless they were in pairs. Sam's business took him to Dorset Street, where pedlars never entered in fear of being raped or gutted within five minutes of entering. It was such a den of iniquity and Sarah tried to avoid going with him if she could. If the whores didn't heckle you, there would be a cock fight or dog fight being held somewhere down the street or bets being taken on the next bare-knuckle boxing match to be held in somebody's backyard.

It was the worst street in London. Virtually all of it was owned by a Jack McCarthy and William Crossingham who turned a blind eye to the running of the street, especially when it came to the gang of Eastern Europeans, the Bessarabians – or as they were better known, 'the stop at nothing gang' – that Sam now worked for. He never said what exactly he did but Sarah knew it was to do with a protection racket that the gang ran, threatening hard-working folk for a payment to keep themselves and their properties safe, especially picking on the Jewish community as they were the latest race to be shown little pity in the city.

Sarah picked up her newly bought shawl and placed it around her shoulders then went to the table and picked up the letter that she had just written to her sister back in Leeds. Sam was right: Meg would have no idea what sort of area she now lived in, so at long last, she had taken a chance of writing to her and assuring her that she was well. She could tell her sister what she thought she wanted to hear and not the truth. That would never do.

'Hey up, my cock, where you off to, then?' her next door neighbour, Scabby Mary, yelled as Sarah locked the door behind her and walked out into the street.

'Going to post a letter to my sister in Leeds, I haven't written to her in years,' Sarah said not wanting to speak too long with the prostitute that wandered Dorset Street and lived up to her name, scabs of syphilis covering her face and hands.

'She'd never get a letter off me, cock, can't write my own bloody name let alone anything else. Not going to waste my money on a letter anyway. Your fella must be making money,' Mary said leaning in the shared doorway stopping Sarah from going any further.

'We are managing, now I've got to get on.' Sarah said and tried to push past.

'I hear he can be a real bastard. Handy with his fists from what I've heard. Looks like it by the way that eye of yours has been of late. He wanted you to walk the streets and you weren't having any of it? That's what I heard,' Mary sneered.

'Well you heard wrong. I bumped into something, that's all,' Sarah said looking Mary in the eye.

'We all say that, love. But, aye, you are too snooty to walk the streets, you'd not last long here. Or you'll soon be gone, if what I hear is right and that your fella is to fight one of the Odessian gang men from over by the church way. It'll be bloody carnage whoever wins.'

Mary moved out of Sarah's way, giving her a backward glance before starting to offer herself to passing men, leaving Sarah worried if what she said was right. Who were the Odessian Gang and what had they to do with Sam? There was so much she didn't know about Sam's new life but she had a horrible feeling that if she found out more about what he was up to, she wouldn't like it.

Chapter 13

Meg couldn't believe her eyes when the post boy called into the shop with a letter clearly marked from London in Sarah's handwriting. She had waited so long to hear from her sister and now a letter had come! All she could do was hold it in a trembling hand as she wiped back the tears. Thank God she was alive, that's all she could think as she went into the bakery and sat down in the easy chair next to the fire.

'What's wrong? Are you alright? What are you crying for?' Janet asked, as she reached for a batch of fruit teacakes from the ovens.

'Look, look, I think it is from Sarah, she must be alright!' Meg brushed her tears away and smiled.

'Well, you'll not know until you've opened it and read it, will you now?' Janet lifted the tray of teacakes out and put it on the side to cool. 'I'll make a cup of tea for us both and you read it, I'll get the shop if the bell rings.' Janet smiled, hoping that it was good news.

'I don't know if I dare. Please let her be alright,' Meg said aloud as she tore open the letter and proceeded to read.

29 Dorset Street
Spitalfields
London

1st March 1898

Dear Meg,

I'm hoping that you are still at the bakery and that this letter will find you there.

I'm sorry it has been so long since I wrote, but a great deal has happened in my life since leaving the employment of Larry Hopkirk. I wasn't happy working for him and in the end, only became his maid working in his house.

I was then fortunate enough to meet my beau Sam Waites, a lovely man, you would like him. I know that I am perhaps too young to have a beau, but things are different down here in London. He is letting me live with him in his house on Dorset Street, a grand house, in a good area. I do not need to work, he provides for us both, being an upstanding man in the community, working at the local bank.

I hope that you and Frankie are both well. I presume that you are both married by now and probably have children for all I know. I really should not have left it so long to write to you, but I didn't want to write and tell you how far I had

145

fallen becoming just Larry Hopkirk's maid. My pride was always my downfall.

Sending you all my love and hoping that this letter finds you happy and satisfied in your life.

Your dearest sister, Sarah. xx

'Well, that was short and sweet but at least I know that she is alright and happy,' Meg told Janet when she'd read the letter through a couple of times. 'Although as she says in her letter she is a bit young to be living with a fully grown man, I hope she is taking care of herself.'

Meg felt a great relief come over her. She sat back in her chair feeling happy that at long last she had heard from her young sister. 'At least I can write to her now and tell her about our wedding. Perhaps if her husband is making good money, they could afford to attend. She could even perhaps be my bridesmaid after all.'

Janet was glad to see the relief on Meg's face. 'Where is she living at then in London and who is she living with?' she asked.

'She's living with a Sam Waites, a banker, in Spitalfields. It sounds as if he is very well-to-do. She's not having to work anyway. Trust our Sarah to land on her feet. I don't know how she does it, she goes from crisis to crisis but always ends off better than she was.' Meg smiled and looked into the fire, feeling content.

'You said Spitalfields, didn't you?' Janet asked carefully.

'Yes, Dorset Street, Spitalfields. Do you know the area? It must be grand if her beau is a banker?' Meg said.

Janet thought better than to tell Meg what she was thinking. She'd heard about the area called Spitalfields and Whitechapel. They had been Jack the Ripper's stalking grounds, she was sure. She had heard her parents discussing and reading graphic details of the murders in the newspaper at the time. If Sarah was living in Spitalfields, she was most definitely not involved with a well-to-do banker. But Janet was not going to be the one to tell Meg and spoil her dream.

Meg strode out from the bakery. It was Wednesday and, as promised, she was on her way to the patisserie that Frankie ran in Headingley. It was not quite as posh as the one he had originally opened on the Headrow, but it was still upper class in Meg's view. She had come armed with pages of recipes but did wonder why she needed to. Surely if Ivor the baker could make the fancy stuff that he had been creating for Frankie, then he could make her basic recipes. However, she was beginning to enjoy the walk down into Headingley. Being away from her own bakery was like a breath of fresh air and she was glad that she had decided to save both her and Frankie money and not caught a hackney cab.

As she walked through the relatively quiet streets, Meg saw the signs of spring beginning to show. The buds on the trees were just appearing and the birds were busy singing courting songs. Her heart was lighter now she had heard from Sarah. At least she was safe and by the sounds of it, she was doing well. It was time to look forward to her own wedding.

She made her way to the outskirts of Leeds and the

patisserie that Frankie owned but did not bake within himself. The one that he had risked everything to buy and was obviously struggling to afford even though he would not admit it.

Reaching the broad high street she noticed that the patisserie's lights were lit, so they were waiting for her. She hoped that Frankie would be there as well as Ivor. She had only met the baker the once but she had found him arrogant and she couldn't help but think that he would not be willing to follow her instructions or be happy at her intervention into his world.

Looking in at the window of the patisserie, she saw it wasn't as beautifully set out as the one on the Headrow, but it had nearly all the same bakes, cakes and desserts, according to the delicate labels placed for each bake in the now empty window. She walked into the spotless shop, but no bell tinkled above the door like in her own bakery, so she entered unnoticed and unheard.

Raised voices were coming from within the bakery itself.

'You insult my baking and skills and expect me to come here and listen to an unqualified woman telling me what to do when I should nearly be to my bed,' came Ivor's distinctive tones. 'Whatever she tries to tell me to bake, I will refuse to do it. I am a French patisserie chef. You know this. I did not train to make scones and crumpets, like some common back street baker.' Ivor raised his voice. 'I trained with the best in London, I will not bake such mundane pastries.'

'You will bake what I pay you to bake, whether you like

it or not,' Frankie retorted sharply. 'And be careful what you say about my fiancée. Her baking is excellent and has a marvellous reputation in her own area.'

'Pay me?' Ivor expostulated. 'I nearly have to beg you for my pay every week! I thought when I came all the way from London that I'd be working for the best. Instead, I'm working in an impoverished mill town as an impoverished baker and now, I'm being insulted by being told what to bake.' Meg heard a bowl smash in the bakery as it was thrown with force onto the floor. 'I quit! I've had enough of the hours, the impossible orders, and the lack of pay. Keep your wife as the baker or perhaps do it yourself instead of playing the dandy . . . a dandy with no money.'

Meg held her breath and stepped to one side as Ivor, still in his baker's uniform, burst through the bakery door, snarled wordlessly at her as he passed her then swung open the patisserie door and walked out onto the street, slamming the door behind him. She watched him stomp off down the street and then turned to find Frankie standing there.

'Meg, how much of that did you hear, my love?' Frankie asked.

'Enough. I don't think he was very happy, was he? Perhaps I should go and you call him back?' Meg suggested.

'No, let him be on his way. If that's what he thinks then I'm better without him. Perhaps it is him and his attitude that is not working in this bakery. If so I'm better off without him.' Frankie rubbed his brow, which was creased with worry. He shook his head. 'I don't know what I've done to deserve all this. I just try to give the people what they want, but whatever I do, someone does not like it.'

'Oh, Frankie, don't take on so. You'll manage, we'll manage. If it's any consolation, I didn't like him, I thought him arrogant,' Meg said and kissed Frankie on the cheek. 'I was dreading showing him what I make at my bakery. I guessed he would only have scoffed at the simplicity of it. And, yes, I did hear what he thought of me and him complaining about his pay. Seems to me he'd complain about anything,' Meg added softly.

'I haven't had any orders from Bea Benson this last week and I'm worried about that, along with various other things on my mind,' Frankie confessed. 'Now, I've no baker for here, I might as well close up completely.'

'Things are never as bad as they seem,' Meg encouraged. 'Now, there's no need to worry about a baker for here, not when there is both me and you and I've got Janet who is proving to be just as good at baking as I was at her age. Now, what are you going to do? Why not put a notice up and say that due to circumstances that you will be closed all day tomorrow? Then we will sort something out between us.'

Frankie took a moment to compose himself. 'I'm sorry, I should be the one taking control of the situation,' he said. 'Could I suggest that Janet could help out as much as possible at your bakery and you could come and bake for me here at Headingley? Perhaps that would work? I don't want to leave my patisserie on the Headrow – nobody else could fill my place and my delicacies still sell well in there.

After all, that is what I was in a roundabout way suggesting but I honestly thought Ivor would not be so against the new changes.'

Meg knew she had to raise the other important issue. 'It sounded as if he was worried about his pay,' she pointed out. 'Frankie, I don't want to ask you this, but are you struggling? I only ask because otherwise why should he mention the lack of wage?'

'As I said, Bea Benson has not been placing an order of late, which has made a difference.' Frankie hesitated. 'Plus her friends have all paid their outstanding bills but for some reason, they are not coming into either of the shops. I'm at a loss to know what I've done to any of them.' He gave a dramatic sigh. 'It seems I have fallen out of favour with the great and the good.'

'Then it is all the more reason for me to come and be your baker here in this bakery, and bring my recipes with me,' Meg told him. 'Now, show me the bakery and let me see that you have everything in there that I will be needing. Has Ivor left you with anything already made?'

Meg took the lead and walked into the back of the build-ing, which was furnished with the best quality shelves, tables, and a gas oven, but when she went into the store room, she was shocked by what she found . . . 'Oh, Frankie, the shelves are nearly empty – no wonder Ivor was not happy.'

'I didn't realise. He never told me we were so low on stock here. He didn't tell me a lot of things,' Frankie said and shook his head again.

'Never mind, I'll get Joe Dinsdale to send you some stock if he can tomorrow and I will ask Janet to take over at my bakery for a week or two until we get yours back up and running. I don't want to have to travel the full length of Leeds early every morning, though. I'll let Janet stay in my room. That will help her and could I possibly stay in the guest bedroom at your house for a short while – although it will not be long now until we are living there as a married couple! Perhaps Ivor leaving had to be. Maybe this has come around to show us both that we should pull together rather than compete with one another ... which is what I sometimes think we do.' Meg hugged Frankie as he looked so down in the mouth.

'I'm sorry, I'm just useless with money,' he finally admitted. 'I've been trying so hard to get my accounts back in order, but now my main customers have deserted me, I don't know what to do. The money that I have banked the last week or two will only last so long and the bank will be after my blood if I don't start making money soon.'

'Oh, Frankie so now you have got involved with borrowing from the bank? They will never leave you alone if you owe them a lot.'

Meg sat down on a chair feeling deflated. On her walk to see Frankie and his bakery she had felt so happy; now her world was crumbling in front of her eyes. If she married Frankie and he was indebted to the bank that would put her bakery at risk.

'If you want to walk away now, I wouldn't blame you,'

Frankie said self-pityingly. 'I'm not the best catch in the world.'

'But you sold the bakery at Ilkley! Surely if you paid the money in for that sale it would clear any debts you owed?' Meg asked.

Frankie just shook his head. 'It kept them happy for a while. I'm in trouble, aren't I? Unless I can start making good profits on both my business all will be lost. If I were you, I'd walk away now.'

'Oh, Frankie, how have you got into so much trouble in such a short time?' Meg felt her heart beating fast and her head dizzy with shock. 'Look, I'm not about to walk away. I'm used to being without money and you know I wasn't marrying you for your brass anyway. Tomorrow, we will stock this bakery. I'll move into your guest room, and in the evening we will sit down and take a serious look at your accounts. I've learned a lot since buying my own business and I know how to cut corners and save money. You are just going to have to cut your cloth to your needs. No more shopping at Hopkin's and getting hackney cabs for me. We will walk like we always used to have to do, and I'm sure here will make money once new confectionery is introduced into the bakery.'

Frankie was silent for a moment, unable to quite believe his luck that the woman he loved so much would be willing to do so much for him. 'I'm sorry, I'm really sorry. I've been struggling for weeks now and I've watched you going from strength to strength,' he said finally. 'That's why I thought if

I had your recipes and cakes in my shop it might make my fortunes turn around. I really have made myself look at the situation that I'm in. All I want to do is give you and our family a stable home. I'm a disappointment to my mother and I must be a disappointment to you now. All my fancy catering skills have come to nothing. I should have kept my feet on the ground and been just plain old Frankie Pearson from Leeds instead of making myself out to be something I'm not.'

'And you can stop feeling sorry for yourself,' Meg said sharply. 'This is the time for action, not to wallow in self-pity. Together we will pull you out of the pit you have got yourself into. We will put our heads together and turn our lives around. Because it is *our* lives. I am not going anywhere, Frankie Pearson.'

Back home in her room above the bakery, Meg sat on her bed and looked across at the wedding dress hanging on a coat hanger behind the door. If she had had any idea it was simply adding to Frankie's debts she would have rather walked down the aisle in her nightgown. The fripperies that she loved so much just made her stomach turn when she thought how much they had cost.

Meg wiped a tear away, and for all her fine words to Frankie earlier, she honestly did start to question her marriage to her one-time rich French baker. However, she had told him the truth. It had never been about the money, it was for love she was marrying him and that had not changed, nor would it ever change. She'd honour the wedding vows that she had already effectively made in her head – for richer, for poorer; in sickness or in health – because she loved him.

And now he needed her help more than he had ever done. Tomorrow she would take some things out of her own store, ask George to deliver some goods from Dinsdale's, and go and live at Headingley until nearer the wedding. There was only six weeks to go, and hopefully in that time, they would both have a good idea if the bakery at Headingley was worth keeping on. Frankie would just have to sell it to clear his debts if not and bury his pride. Hopefully, that would raise enough money to get him out of debt.

The following morning, Janet had a hundred and one questions for her employer. 'I don't understand why you have to go and run the bakery at Headingley. Can't Mr Pearson employ somebody else?' Janet said as Meg loaded up two baskets with ingredients needed at the bakery. 'Does he not have everything like this already?'

'I told you, Ivor the baker walked out on him last night and he's let the stores run down so badly that he needs stock urgently. I've asked Joe Dinsdale to drop some things off as well so that I can make enough stuff while I'm there these next few weeks.' Meg piled what she wanted ready for the lift that she had agreed with Joe down into Headingley.

'A few weeks? I thought you said initially that it might be a few days!' Janet cried.

'It might get to weeks, I don't know, but like I said you can live here, rather than trail from your home everyday.

George will welcome that, I bet he's never away, now . . . but no hanky-panky in my bed thank you. Think of it as a trial for when I do get married, because we had planned that you would run it for me, once I was wed.'

'Aye, but not on my own, I could do with a shop lass to serve customers,' Janet said.

'I did it on my own for a long time. You'll manage and if you don't, then I'll get you some help.' Meg gave her a reassuring smile. 'Don't worry if you can't manage, I'll sort something out. It's just that Frankie needs my help, he's in a bit of a spot.'

Janet shook her head. Part of her was excited about her new position and having her own living space but at the same time she wasn't sure she was ready to run the bakery on York Street. It was a huge responsibility.

'You'll do it, don't worry! I'll do the accounts and place the orders in. All you have to do is bake and serve and I know you can do both because I hope that I have taught you well. Now, George is here, I'll let you tell him your news as I run upstairs and get a change of clothes and my night attire.' Meg ran up the stairs and left Janet looking perplexed.

'What's up my lass, tha looks fair vexed,' George said as he came into the shop in his new tweed suit looking more like the shop manager than the shop lad.

'She's letting me run the bakery, just like that. Not a mention of it last night and yet this morning she's off to live at Headingley,' Janet moaned.

'Aye, well she'd have been doing that in a few weeks

anyway and Joe says she's going to be back most days.' George winked and smiled. 'You've got the rooms above and all I hear, all to yourself to do what you want in them.' He grabbed her by the waist and quickly kissed her, releasing her quickly as he heard the floorboards on the landing creaking before Meg made her way down the stairs. 'I was just saying, Meg, that she shouldn't worry, she'll be able to run here in your absence and she will always have me to help her out.'

'There will perhaps be a little too much helping out of an evening? George, don't you get carried away!' Meg teased as she passed him the first basket of goods for the back of his cart and smiled as he put the rest on for her. 'Don't worry Janet, I'm not abandoning you, I'll come back at least three times a week to make sure that you are alright. Now, you've got a key, haven't you? You know how to light the ovens and you can remember what goes on first of a morning? I wrote a list first thing this morning of who usually comes in and what they usually want, but you already know that anyway.' Meg caught her breath and looked at Janet. 'I've faith in you, Janet. Look after my bakery and my rooms. It was going to come to this eventually anyway even if it is a bit rushed and a surprise this morning.' The situation reminded her of when Ted Lund had gone off to Ireland leaving her in charge – but the big difference was, Meg trusted Janet. She walked forward and hugged her assistant. 'I know here is in good hands and I'll be back shortly.'

'I'll manage. I have had a good teacher, so now you go and help your man out.'

Janet watched Meg get into the horse and cart next to George and waved them off down the street. She breathed in deeply and, feeling a mix of anxiety and pride, she walked back into the bakery, the bakery that she was now running in Meg's absence.

Meg had worked most of the day, seeing to the bakery in Headingley. She had filled the shelves, got used to working the gas oven that a few years ago she was scared to touch – good preparation for when hers was finally installed – and was now ready for taking charge at the bakery that had been neglected so badly. She sat on the settee looking out onto the gas lit street for Frankie's return and felt her heart beat a little faster as she saw him pass the window and enter. He put his hat and stick down on the hallstand and then smiled as Meg came through into the hallway and greeted him.

'I've dreamt of this moment when you will be standing there waiting for me to come home from a hard day's work,' Frankie said quietly and moved forward to kiss her.

'And I too, waiting for your return and making sure that you have had a good day. We should relish this evening, as in future evenings, we will both be returning home from a hard day's work and will probably be too tired to enjoy one another's company.' Meg stood on the tip of her toes and kissed him gently on the cheek.

'We should, my dear.' Frankie said and put his arm around her waist. 'Perhaps an early evening after dinner?' he whispered into her ear.

'That's just what I was thinking my love, time for talking business from tomorrow onwards. Tonight just let us enjoy one another's company.' Meg smiled and took him by the hand. 'Your cook has made a light dinner and I've told her and your maid that once we've eaten to enjoy their evening as we won't be wanting their services. I thought on our first night together we need our privacy.'

'You think of everything my Meg, that's why I love you. I will not be beaten by my mistakes with you by my side, 'Frankie said gently as they both looked at one another. Their worries of work and money put to one side for one evening, where they were going to enjoy the love between them.

Chapter 14

Meg lay in Frankie's arms. It was not yet light but both were awake. They had to leave the comfort of one another to go about their business of the day.

'I sometimes wonder why I chose to be a baker – a four o'clock start every morning is not the best,' Frankie called from his dressing room as he pulled his nightshirt over his head and started to dress. 'I usually go without any breakfast until I get to work. What would you like to do? I can always ask Ada to get up that little bit earlier along with the cook if you want us to eat together before work. Although with neither of them living in, it would be an unearthly time of the day they would have to be up to see to our needs.'

'Oh, no, I wouldn't dream of having them serve on us at that time. In fact Frankie, I've been meaning to say there really is no need for you to have a cook when I become your wife. I will be able to see to our needs. I don't really see why you have both a maid and a cook even now. Ada did everything for you, it was surely just keeping up with your friends at the time.'

Meg made her way to the bathroom, carrying the small paraffin-fed oil lamp that she had lit from her bedside table.

'You'd have me scrubbing my own kitchen floor if you thought it would save me money, but perhaps you are right,' Frankie said as he followed her into the bathroom and wrapped his arms around her waist as she looked at herself in the mirror. 'I love you, Meg Fairfax.'

'And I love you, Frankie, but we must get a move on, that bread will not bake itself and you have to get to the centre of Leeds yet. I'm lucky I've just a few streets to walk so there is not such a rush.' She turned around and returned his kisses and looked into his eyes. She loved him so much she thought as they kissed tenderly, breaking apart only when they could hear a knock on the front door.

'Who's that at this time?' Meg said worried that she was as of yet only partly dressed.

'That will be my cabbie with his horse and carriage,' Frankie explained. 'He knows to give me five minutes to go and join him. We have an arrangement: he picks me up at this unearthly time and I give him what is leftover in the bakery of an evening that I can't sell in the shop. So, don't tell me to get rid of him. He costs me nothing. But I will have words with the cook, she is not that good anyway.' Frankie kissed Meg's neck and grinned. 'I'll enjoy your cooking and having you at home.' He hurried into the bedroom to finish getting dressed and ready for his day.

'I might be doing the cooking but I'll still not be involved in the bakeries, so don't you start thinking that I'll be happy running the house and home and nothing more,' Meg said firmly as she brushed her hair and then looked at herself one last time. She joined Frankie downstairs, both of them grabbing their coats from the hall stand. They stepped out into the silent street, all around sleeping except for the patient cabbie and his horse.

'I know, my love, I'm marrying a modern woman and I'll have to get used to it. Now, have a good day. Rosie the shop girl will be with you at six and she will do anything you want her to do. She knows that you are in charge.' Frankie kissed her quickly and then mounted into the carriage. 'Until this evening.'

Meg smiled as the carriage made its way over the cobbled street. She had lain in Frankie's arms all night and while they canoodled, they had talked and dreamt of their future together. It would be a perfect future if everything went to plan and she could take Frankie's extravagant ways in hand.

At least he was now listening, but later that day, they were to look at his accounts together, after delaying doing so the previous evening. The truth would then be out and then Meg would truly know what she was up against with her pauper prince. But she had enough to worry about for now: today she would get to know the workings of the new bakery.

Meg soon got to grips with the gas oven. The flame leapt and came into life, and she remembered how she had first been frightened of the idea of burning gas and the dangers that her mother had warned her of. Soon the bakery was as warm and as welcoming as her own and she set about making her usual recipes for the customers that she hoped would visit the shop that day. There would be no fancy crème de la crèmes, vanilla slices or crème slippers, just good simple baking that filled the stomach, that was affordable but as good. It would be a completely different bakery, she thought as she placed the baked loaves of bread out onto the shelves and turned the shop's sign over to Open. She made her way back into the bakery to take her courting cake out of the oven and replace it with coconut tarts. She placed the warm tray down when she heard the door go and went out to see a young blonde-haired lass taking her shawl off revealing the white frilly apron that she had on underneath.

'Rosie?' Meg asked.

'Yes, Miss, you must be Miss Fairfax. Mr Pearson told me to expect you here when he closed the bakery yesterday, just for the day.' Rosie bobbed a curtsey to her new employer and smiled, looking unsure at what next to say or do.

'Yes, I'm sorry that you missed a day's pay, we will try to make it up to you. Unfortunately, there have had to be a few changes made in the bakery and I'm afraid Ivor was not in agreement, so he decided to leave at short notice.' Meg sighed. 'However, I will be here in his place for the foreseeable future. I don't know if Mr Pearson told you but we are to be married shortly, so you would have been seeing me quite a bit anyway.'

'He did tell me, Miss, and I must congratulate you. Mr Pearson is such a lovely man and it's Ivor's loss that he decided to leave his employment,' Rosie replied.

'Thank you, Rosie. We've not worked together before but you will find me fair and hopefully easy to work for. However I will expect a decent day's work from you, particularly now that our choice of baking has changed. This patisserie is now a bakery. A bakery selling good wholesome bakes, which I hope people will buy. I've re-labelled everything in the window so if you could get used to the new things that we sell and look at the prices that I have written down for you on the piece of paper next to the counter, I'd be grateful.' Meg looked at Rosie and thought how beautiful she was, her hair blonde and cared for, with pink cheeks that matched her name. 'Where do you live, Rosie?' she asked.

'Out at Kirkstone,' Rosie told her. 'My family has a farm there. Just a few acres, enough to keep us fed. Although houses keep being built nearer and nearer our land, so I don't know how much longer we will be there.'

'Yes, Leeds is growing fast. It's becoming a sprawling city and all the little villages are becoming part of it. I'm sorry if your family has to eventually give up their farm; hopefully, it won't happen,' Meg commented as Rosie looked at the list of the new baking. 'Have you had your breakfast? I'm just about to have a cup of tea and some jam and bread. Would you like me to bring something through to you?'

'Oh, no, I had porridge this morning, thank you,' Rosie said. 'My mam always makes us all porridge. She says it lines us up for the day, fills the belly until we come home.'

'Sounds like your mam's a good 'en. I lost my mam a few years ago and I still miss her. She's your best friend is your mam, if you only realize it when you still have her.' There was a wistful smile on Meg's face as she remembered all the good things about her mother.

'Aye, I know, she does right by all four of us, and she can bake,' Rosie said. 'In fact looking at this list, she makes most of this herself. I'm sure it'll sell a lot better than that posh stuff that Ivor used to make and besides, it was nowhere near as good as Mr Pearson's. Ivor just didn't take care of how it looked and he swore all the time. If you don't mind me saying, Miss Fairfax, I'm glad he's gone.'

'I don't mind at all, Rosie. In fact I only met him the once before he left and I took an instant dislike to him, so I can understand why you didn't like him. Now, there's some courting cake waiting to be put out along with scones, fairy cakes, fly pasty and some coconut tarts once they are out of the oven, if you want to come and get them before the customers start coming in.' She looked up at the clock. 'I expected to be busy by now,' she commented. 'It's usually busy at my bakery by now, with mill workers.'

'Give it another hour, Miss and then it will be. Headingley is a little more leisurely than the centre of Leeds. We have mill owners and office workers and shop owners down here. Everything moves a little slower.' Rosie looked around her. 'Your bread looks lovely. I could just eat some of my mother's lemon curd on that for my dinner.'

'Lemon curd?' Meg repeated. 'What's that?'

'It's a spread made with eggs cooked with butter and fresh lemons. My mam makes it when the hens are laying well.

She puts it in jars and then we can have it whenever we want. Have you never had it?' Rosie looked surprised.

'No, I haven't. Do you think I could buy a jar from your mam? I'd like to try it.' Meg asked.

'She'll not expect anything for it, she'll give you a jar, and I'll bring it with me in the morning. I'll not have my porridge, we can share it over breakfast together if you like?'

'That would be very kind of her and that is just what we will do. Now, with the mention of curds, I think I'll make some Yorkshire curd tarts – I bet they would sell here in the shop – and then I'll go and make some biscuits. I don't know what Ivor's been doing, but he's not bothered filling the shelves with baking that people might be tempted with.'

'No, if he didn't have to do it, Ivor wouldn't do it. Come to think of it, he didn't do a lot unless he knew Mr Pearson was coming to visit. He's best gone,' Rosie said and followed Meg into the bakery to fill the shop shelves with the new baking. Hopefully, new customers would come through the doors lured by the sight and smell of freshly baked goods.

'Well, let's see how well we do without him today, shall we?' Meg said and opened the oven to get her coconut tarts. 'We could do with some custom if we are going to get rid of this lot.'

'Oh, they'll come, there's not another baker around here for a street or two and when word gets out that it's not as daft with its cakes, there will be even more customers,' Rosie told her confidently. 'There was only the snobby few that came in for the posher stuff.'

The young girl carried the baking through and left Meg smiling. She was going to like Rosie, she could tell. She was down to earth and said what she thought, and that was the best way to be.

As the morning went by, Meg's smile widened as she looked out at the faces peering through the bakery window. Shoppers were noticing the window display had changed and were tempted in to try the new delights that Meg and Rosie had on offer. Rosie had been right: she'd understood more than Ivor or Frankie about the shoppers of Headingley.

Also selling well was Meg's new recipe – curd tarts, pastry shells filled with milk curds, sugar and currants mixed together with egg and a sprinkle of nutmeg. It was a traditional recipe that her mother had taught her and her grandmother before her and she had nearly forgotten about it until Rosie had mentioned the word curd.

By the end of the day's trading, Meg had a warm feeling of satisfaction as she closed the bakery and walked down the street to where she now called home. Future days would not be so hard now she knew Rosie was capable of running the shop – and she had filled the shelves with jars of biscuits and baking that kept quite well for a day or two. But what was troubling her now was the fact that after supper that night she was to sit down with Frankie and look at his accounts in depth. It would be the first time he had come clean about the amount of debt he was in. Meg was worried how much she would find out he owed.

She walked into the hallway and was met by Ada with a

smile and curtsy. 'Good evening, Miss Fairfax, how has your day been?' Ada asked as she took Meg's coat from her and watched her make her way to the main room of the house.

'A very long one, Ada, but now I think I know how everything works and what the people want,' Meg replied. 'And we benefit from having a good worker in young Rosie Andrews, she's a Godsend.'

She was surprised to see Frankie sitting in his favourite chair waiting for her. 'You are home early?' Meg said and returned his kiss as he stood up and greeted her.

'Yes, well, I've thought of nothing else but going through my accounts with you, it has weighed heavy on my mind all day,' Frankie admitted. 'I can fool myself but I know I can't fool you.' He looked shame-faced. 'But if you are too tired tonight, we can make it another night. I'm afraid of losing you, my love, when you find out just how much debt that I am in.'

'Frankie, stop it, we will look at them tonight as we agreed,' Meg said firmly. 'It is not money that I love you for. I've come from nothing and I don't expect anything from anybody. Now, stop worrying, we will have our supper and enjoy it, and then we will sit down together and work things out.' Meg smiled and sat down beside him. 'You'll be glad to know that we have been making you a tidy sum today. We have been run off our feet and so many people have commented on the change of baking. The people of Headingley are definitely more impressed with straightforward recipes. You've also got a good worker in young Rosie. In fact, I think it was a good day's work when Ivor walked out on you. He's been dragging your bakery down from what I've heard from her.'

'I knew you'd like Rosie, she's a bit like your Sarah but not as brash,' Frankie said.

'Oh, mentioning our Sarah, with everything else going on with the bakery, I've completely forgotten to tell you! She's written to me. She's well and sounds content living with a man called Sam Waites, although she's not married to him. I should hope not, she's far too young, so I hope that he's honourable.'

'You hypocrite, Meg Fairfax, you are living here with me, as of yet unmarried.' Frankie grinned. 'However, I'm glad that she has made contact, I know you were worrying.'

'Yes, but I am older and we are betrothed, that is the difference. I'm going to reply and send her a wedding invitation now I know her address ... not that I think she will bother to attend.'

'No, I don't suppose she will, nor will my mother. I sent her invitation the other day. She will not want to travel from her precious Paris, just to see her son marry.'

Ada walked into the room.

'Supper is ready, Sir,' Ada said politely and then withdrew.

'Have you had a word with your cook yet?' Meg asked.

'No, I haven't had the chance. Besides if you are going to be busy at the bakery, perhaps we should keep her on. I'm not looking forward to giving her her marching orders, she's a bit short-tempered at the best of times.'

'Frankie, stop taking the easy way out. We don't need her and you know we don't,' Meg said sharply. 'She'll find somewhere else to go if you give her a glowing reference, especially when people realize she's cooked for you.'

'I will miss her suety puddings, though!' Frankie said and took Meg's arm as they walked through to the dining room.

'Mine will be just as good, I wonder if Rosie's lemon curd would taste good within a suety pastry?' she said out loud.

'Lemon curd?' repeated Frankie. 'Sounds terrible. Surely lemons and milk just curdle? Whatever has Rosie been telling you?' Frankie placed his napkin on his knee and looked down into his bowl of French Onion soup, which Mrs Baxter, the cook made so beautifully. He would miss that if he was to sack her.

'I'll let you know more about it in the morning,' Meg told him. 'It sounded so good that she is bringing a jar in for us to share tomorrow. She knows her food, I can tell. Now, let us enjoy our supper.'

Meg nearly could have wept after a few minutes' perusal of Frankie's accounts, during which her fiancé sat uncomfortably silent.

'Oh, Frankie you owe on every property bar the one on the Headrow. How could you let them get their hands on your family home? I thought you had more sense than that.'

'I needed the money after buying the property that I bought in Ilkley,' he replied. 'It's only a little that I owe them on this place. I paid most of what I owed them with the profit I made on the sale.' He tried to be reassuring. 'I will be able to pay them back in time, I think!' 'It will take a mountain of fancy cake sales to pay the bank back what you owe them,' Meg said sternly. 'Then there are your actual accounting books. They are in a terrible state! Do you not write everything that goes in and out religiously each evening? It's the only way you can keep an eye on what's what.' She checked some figures again, and a relieved smile crossed her face. 'At least I see all your posh clients are up to date with their bills. That's one blessing.'

'Yes, but they have stopped ordering with me,' Frankie reminded her. 'I seem to be out of favour with Bea Benson and her followers. Even she has not been into the patisserie for a while. I only hope that she is still happy with us holding our wedding at the hall.'

'That is the least of your, or should I say our, worries. No wonder you were concerned at the shop . It's not making any money – you have been making even less than I do at my bakery. Plus Ivor's wage was ridiculous for what he's been doing. Rosie should be paid more than he ever got.'

'Now, I have to put my foot down at that,' Frankie said frostily. 'Rosie is a shop girl, and besides, women will never be worth the wage of a man, they aren't the main earners in a family.'

'Frankie Pearson, if I didn't love you so much, I'd really fall out with you,' Meg said bluntly. 'How can you say that? I used to have to work to support me, my mother, and Sarah, or had you forgotten? You really do need to get a grip not just of your finances but also your outlook on life. You are no longer the spoilt rich boy that can play at working. You need to be a hard-headed businessman, especially if we have children. They don't live on thin air, you know.'

His bank accounts were worse than ever Meg had imagined. He hardly owned anything and nine months out of ten, his outgoings were more than his income. No wonder he had asked her to come to the rescue of the Headingley bakery. It was not making any profit at all, barely covering its costs. Hopefully, when word got about that it had changed, it would soon be profitable – and with Ivor's wages removed from the calculation – but that would not solve all of the problems and the bank charges and interest that were accu-mulating each and every day.

Frankie's money problems were now her money problems and she had always been so careful with every penny she spent. Now she owed nobody anything. Never in a million years did she think that she would have ever spoken to Frankie like she just had, but somebody had to tackle the problem head-on and she was not about to let her good name be dragged through the mud if his circumstances got any worse.

Frankie looked at the dark clouds on his fiancée's face and assumed the worst. 'I knew it would end like this once I told you everything. I suppose you want to leave me to face my own fate?' He ran his fingers through his hair. 'I've kept my own worries to myself on purpose, I couldn't bear to lose you. I will . . . We will turn my affairs around, given a chance.'

'Oh, Frankie, I'd never leave you and our wedding can't come fast enough,' she reassured him. 'But it is going to be an uphill struggle to get you, or should I say us both, solvent. However, this makes one thing very clear. I hope you don't expect me to sign my bakery over to you. There's not a penny owing on it, and that, after all my struggles, is how I'd like it to remain.'

'Of course, my love, I've made enough mess of my life without bringing you down to my level. As long as you still love me, I will do anything to keep you by my side. Money comes and goes, but to find true love and for it to be as faithful as yours, then that is worth a priceless ransom,' Frankie said quietly with his head bowed.

'Then we will face the world with our heads held high, and with determination, we will make our world right, no matter what is thrown at us. But you must stop spending recklessly.' She sat back from the table.

'Now, let's talk of something else. There is little more we can do about your finances tonight. I would like you on Sunday to come with me to the Hyde Park Hotel. Alice Dent will be there and I need you to hear what she has to say. It's time you realized that women are just as strong as men and don't always have to use their sexuality to get what they want. Unlike your Bea Beaumont.'

Frankie scowled. 'I know I've to stop spending but do I really have to listen to that woman? And please stop painting Bea Beaumont in such a bad light.'

'Yes, you do,' Meg said sharply, 'especially after the

comment on Rosie's pay. She works as hard if not harder than any man, so why should she not be treated as an equal? And if you want me to shoulder some of your burdens then I want to be treated as an equal. You will go and listen to what she says, Frankie, just to please me as I will be supporting you as much as you will be supporting me. Marriage is a partnership and I know we will have a good one if we both give and take.'

Chapter 15

'Lord, that is good,' Meg exclaimed as she smacked her lips after eating Rosie's lemon curd on a slice of still-warm newly baked bread.

'Aye, I know, we often have it along with jam made from my Uncle Fred's rhubarb. We've always some sort of preserves in our house.' Rosie grinned. 'I'll bring you a jar of that an' all tomorrow. In fact, if you want any rhubarb just let me know, he's nearly at the end of harvesting the forced stuff that he grows inside his sheds, but in another week or two he will have more than he knows what to do with in his fields.'

'Do you think your mother could give me her recipe for the lemon curd?' Meg asked. 'And I'll pay you for a jar of rhubarb jam. I can't expect stuff for nothing . . . What do you mean when you say the rhubarb is forced? I've never heard of that before.'

'You do not need to pay me for the jam. When I say the rhubarb is forced I mean it is forced to grow,' Rosie explained as they got the products ready for the shop. 'My uncle grows the rhubarb in sheds. It is kept warm by coal fires feeding water pipes in the sheds and the plants are covered in either the night soil from Leeds or Wakefield or shoddy from the woollen mills and grown in the dark. He can grow rhubarb then for Christmas and into spring until the stuff can grow naturally outside. He's been doing it for a while now, competing with the London growers. In fact, growers up here send it to Covent Garden and Spitalfields market nearly every day by train.'

'Oh, I've seen it on the market but I've never tried it. I'll have to see that I do now,' Meg said. 'I think my sister might live somewhere near Spitalfields Market, although I have only just heard from her after her not being in touch for a few years.'

'It's a bit of a rough area, I believe, but I'm sure your sister will be in the better end. As for the rhubarb, I'll bring you a stick or two. My mam forces it into growing under an old dolly tub in the garden at our back door. We've had it for a week or two, she can spare some – I'll be fed up of stewed rhubarb and custard and rhubarb sponge in another week or two, even though it is supposed to be good for you.'

Rosie heard the shop door open and went through to do her job. Meg went about her work but couldn't help but think of what Rosie had said about Spitalfields being a rough area of London. If there was a market there, it would be unlikely for genteel houses to be in the same area. Was Sarah lying to her again – and if so, why?

Realizing there was little she could do about that there

and then, Meg's mind went back to the taste of the lemon curd and their conversation about rhubarb. If she could get the recipe for lemon curd from Rosie's mother she could perhaps make some and sell it in the bakery. It would also be lovely as a filling in a sponge cake and in a suety roly-poly mixed in with sultanas. In fact, she could use it in all sorts once she made it. As for rhubarb, she could make jam and also sell that too.

'Pearson's Perfect Preserves,' she whispered to herself. Now that had a ring to it and it would be another way of making income, an income she knew they badly needed after the previous evening's disclosures.

The following morning, true to her word, Rosie brought a jar of rhubarb jam for Meg to taste, along with a few sticks of rhubarb.

'That is tart,' Meg said as she bit into the rhubarb.

'Dip it in sugar,' Rosie suggested. 'Sugar makes all the difference, although these forced sticks are a lot sweeter than the sticks growing outside. That can get really woody if it isn't picked as soon as it is ready.'

'Oh, that's lovely now,' Meg said once she had done as suggested. 'I can see how this will work in a sponge pudding or a plate pasty, like an apple. Do you think your uncle would sell me some?' She reached for a spoon to try the jam.

'Aye, he'll sell you some, he's out at Woodlesford but he usually comes to see my mam on a Sunday,' Rosie said. 'I'll ask him.' She watched as Meg took a taste. 'It's got a bit of heat in it, hasn't it? My mam adds a little ginger, just to spice it up a bit.'

'It has but it's darn good. Do you know how to make both this jam and curd? Perhaps it's something that we could sell in the bakery?' Meg wondered aloud.

'You mean you'd make my mam's jam here? Lord, I don't know what she'd say to that! But yes, I've watched and helped make it all my life – but you'd need a lot of sugar and jam jars if you were to sell it.' For a moment, Rosie was aghast. She had only given the jam and rhubarb to Meg to sweeten her up and now she was talking about pinching her mother's recipes!

'I can see to that,' Meg said, understanding instinctively what was going through Rosie's mind. 'I could also see to giving you a bit more pay if you were to make the jam because you'd be deserving of it. We could call it . . . Rosie's Home Made Preserve.' Meg saw the immediate change of expression on Rosie's face and the glint in her eye as she thought it over.

'You would and you could!' Rosie laughed. 'I don't know what my mam will say, but I can't see it'll hurt her in anyway. We only use the recipe within the family and if there's more money for me and Uncle Fred if he sells you the rhubarb then we all benefit. I'll say, yes – in fact, I can write down the recipe for both here and now because I've seen my mam make it so often.' Rosie grabbed a pencil and paper from the sideboard. 'You are right it will sell well in the shop – and to have my name on it, now that would be something.'

'It is just an idea at the moment, but both taste so good,

I just know they would sell,' Meg replied as Rosie scribbled the recipe down. 'Let's put the lemon curd that is left over in the jar into the middle of one of those Victoria Sandwich cakes that we have made, and if you bring another few jars in tomorrow we can make lemon curd tarts. They would be lovely.'

Meg's brain was working overtime as she thought more and more of what she could do with the preserve and hoped that Rosie's mother would be okay about Rosie giving her the recipe. The more she thought about it, the more knew she was onto a winner.

'Lord, I'm run off my feet!' Janet complained. 'It's alright Meg leaving me to run the bakery myself but I just can't do it. Even though she's letting me stay in the rooms above, the hours are a lot longer than I'm used to and there is so much responsibility.' She was chatting with Daisy, who for once had actually paid for what she wanted from out of the bakery and looked clean and tidy as she pacified her baby in her arms.

'She never told me she was leaving,' Daisy replied. 'It must have been in a rush, she usually tells me everything.' It seemed odd that Janet knew more about her closest friend than she did. 'Do you want me to help out? I don't mind for an hour or two. I owe Meg a lot anyway – she's kept me fed and always been there for me when other folk turned their backs on me.'

'I don't know,' Janet mused, 'but I could do with another

pair of hands. I've some cakes to ice and I can't get on with them because the shop bell keeps ringing. But you've got the baby, you can't serve with him in your arms!'

'He's dead to the world and will be now for another hour,' Daisy said confidently. 'How about I take him up into Meg's bed and I just help behind the counter for an hour? My little fella is a lot more content now his stomach is full, and that's thanks to my new man.' Daisy smiled and kissed her little boy's head.

'Oh, you've got a new man in your life?' Janet said, not giving away any prior knowledge.

'Yes, Jimmy McEvoy,' Daisy beamed. 'He's one of the managers at the glass factory. He's a good man, not married this time. I'll not make that mistake again. I'm going to be moving in with him at the end of the month and he's promised to marry me. I've been lucky in finding him.'

'I thought you looked better than you have of late. I'm really glad for you, Daisy. Now, it would be a good help if you could give me an hour. It would just let me catch up. I can pay you with a loaf of bread and a bun or two if that's alright?'

Daisy made for the stairway to put Charlie down in Meg's bed. 'That will be grand,' she said, 'but there's no need. I'd planned to tell Meg my news this morning but she's not here. She must have despaired of me of late. But all has turned out well. My dad has had a change of heart, so my mother says I'm welcome back now and she loves my lil lad now she's nursed him on her knee for an hour or two. I'll just pop him down and then I'll put on the pinny from behind the door and serve on for you until he wakens.'

Janet heard the floorboards creak above her head. She hoped that she had done right, but she was desperate and Meg was not there to be asked. In fact, if the morning went well and Daisy was game for it she would ask her to come for an hour each day at her busiest time, just to help her out. It would work out better than burning the cakes or keeping a customer waiting, she thought as Daisy came back down, smiled, put the pinny on, and looked at the price list for the baking kept behind the counter.

'Don't worry, I'm good at sums and I've watched Meg many a time,' Daisy reassured her. 'I know how she wants her customers to be treated.' She smiled as a customer came through the door. 'Go on, I'll be fine,' she said as she turned to the customer.

Janet went into the bakery's kitchen and hoped that she had done right, but it seemed to make sense to her. Daisy was costing nothing that morning and if it worked out well she would mention her help to Meg. Perhaps now Daisy's fortunes had changed Meg might offer her a permanent job with her, seeing that Meg was now living in Headingley and up to now had not shown her face since leaving earlier in the week.

It was late Friday morning. Rosie's mum had given her blessing to Meg using the recipe Rosie had provided (after making sure it was all exactly right). Meg had decided that she would visit her own bakery that afternoon to see how

Janet was coping and then pop in to Joe Dinsdale's to see if he could secure a good supply of lemons for her, else it would be pointless making the curd at that time of year.

Rosie assured her that once the morning rush had gone, she could manage on her own, so with the baking all done, Meg buttoned up her coat and walked the mile and a half to her bakery on York Street. A good brisk walk she enjoyed as a rule, but she was feeling tired. She was juggling so many things at the moment – even her wedding seemed to be taking back place to everything else that was going on in her life. Running two bakeries and keeping an eye on Frankie's comings and goings had to take priority over her happiness at the moment. Frankie had collected their wedding cake from her bakery and had told her that he had already started to prepare it but refused her permission to see it until the day, saying that he wanted to see her face on the day when it was presented to her at Langroyd Hall.

Meg said hello to one of her regular customers as they came out of her bakery on York Street and opened the door expecting to see Janet behind the counter. Instead, there was Daisy, her face happy but looking quite flushed as she realized that she had been caught helping out in her bakery.

'Meg, we didn't expect you!' Daisy exclaimed and looked towards the bakery doorway hoping that Janet would walk through and explain.

'No, obviously not!' Meg said then smiled. 'I take it you are helping Janet out by the looks of that pinny.'

'I am. I hope that you'll forgive us. It gives me someone

away from motherhood for an hour or two. My mother has agreed to look after Charlie just for a few hours and it's helped Janet out why you have been helping Frankie. I've not taken any pay, it is just a favour – Janet would not do anything like that without your say so.'

'Your mother's got young Charlie? Now that is a turn up for the books. But you shouldn't be working here for nothing. I'd better do something about it now you are here.' Meg shouted through to the bakery. 'Janet, come here, let us get this straight.'

Janet came through and looked as flustered as Daisy had been. 'I'm sorry, I couldn't cope on my own, and when Daisy came along and offered I didn't think that you'd mind with it being Daisy and you both being friends,' she said, the words spilling out of her. She stood sheepishly in front of Meg. 'It's only been for an hour or two just till I get the baking finished and have tidied up for the next day.'

'Well, now, what am I to do?' Meg looked around with her hands on her hips and noted all was looking tidy and the shelves were full. 'Daisy, are you enjoying working with Janet? You look a different person, I must say.'

'I am, I want for nowt now Jimmy McEvoy has come into my life,' Daisy explained. 'I came to tell you, but then I found out you were at Headingley. My Jimmy has promised to provide for both me and Charlie, no matter what. However, I'd still like to be able to stand on my own two feet, just in case he turns out to be another bastard. I'm not falling for that again.' Daisy paused. 'Please don't be cross at Janet. I was doing it as a favour to both you and her. Repayment for you both being good to me when I was down on my uppers. Everyone needs help at sometime and you have always been there for me, no matter what.'

'This Jimmy McEvoy, he works in the glass factory, doesn't he? He's been the one you've been walking out with when I've been looking after Charlie.'

'Aye, he is, sorry I should have told you sooner, but I thought you'd think the worst of me.' Daisy started to take off her pinny, thinking that her time helping out at the bakery had come to an end.

'What are you doing? Don't take your pinny off! If Janet says she needs you, then you must stay, and if it helps you out now you have mended things with your mother, then I'll be glad to keep you working here.' Meg smiled. 'I know it's hard work and that I have asked a bit too much of Janet. It is different when you own the business, you put in the hours because it is yours, but this last day or two I have realized just how much I have worked and am still working.'

'Oh, that's a relief. I thought that you would play merry hell with me,' Janet said and smiled at Daisy. 'There you see, you've tidied yourself up, got a job, and got yourself a fresh fella. A few weeks ago you looked as if you'd given up on life.'

'Why don't you say it as it is, Janet?' Daisy laughed. 'You never do hold anything back.'

'It's best to say it as it is, you know where you stand with folk then,' Janet replied and looked at Meg. 'Have you come to look at the books and look at what we want to order? I've all waiting for you as I knew you'd be visiting shortly, but I thought that it would be late afternoon when you came.' Janet was clearly still uncomfortable that she had been found with Daisy helping her.

'Yes, I'll come and look at everything but first I want to be clear. I'm glad Daisy is here, especially seeing now she's courting Jimmy. Actually, Daisy, I was going to walk down there but perhaps you could ask for me if he's a manager? I need to know the price of jam jars, in bulk. Would you mind asking him and I'll pick up the price on Monday? That is, if you will be here and if Janet thinks you will be needed?' Meg watched the two women exchange a look. 'We'll have to talk about your payment of course, and hours, Janet, now I know Daisy is here and working.'

'I'll be here, if I'm wanted and aye, I'll ask him,' Daisy said. 'It's all he talks about, the orders and how much glass they've blown and sold. He's steady is Jimmy, not a fly-by-night.' Daisy looked quizzically at Meg. 'What are you wanting so many jam jars for?'

Janet added, 'We are not expected to be making jam as well as baking, are we?'

'No, you'll not be making jam, I'll be making it at Headingley,' Meg told them. 'Frankie has gas ovens and hobs, and I can control the temperature better over there. Although I might ask you to sell some, if I can make a profit once I've priced it all up.'

'Lord above, you never stop thinking about how to make

185

money,' Daisy laughed. 'You've come a long way from the lass with no money on that back street. I'm glad for you. I always knew you had it in you, you were always a determined devil.'

'And I'm glad that you have found a good man. I bet Janet hasn't told you, but you do know she's walking out with George from Dinsdale's?' Meg winked at Janet as she shook her head at Meg giving her secrets away. 'It seems we all have a good man in our lives.'

'Aye, well let us hope that they are all they promise to be, along with your Sarah's man,' Janet said. 'I was a bit worried when you read out Spitalfields as her address but I didn't want to say anything.'

'You've heard from Sarah and she's living in Spitalfields with a man?' Daisy asked Meg.

'Yes, I have, she assures me she's alright. I've written to her but not got a reply yet. I'm beginning to wonder if life is as good as she's letting on, from what I've heard of Spitalfields. I know there's a big fruit and vegetable market there, so I don't think it is as posh as she says.'

'Isn't that where Jack the Ripper stalked his victims or somewhere near?' Daisy said unthinkingly.

'It is – but just for once, I kept my big mouth shut,' Janet told her. 'Sarah will be alright, Meg, I'm sure she will. It sounds like a posh house that she's living in and at least you have got her address now.'

Meg felt her stomach churn with worry. 'Oh Lord, I should have known that she was living in a rough area.

She'll tell me anything, will that lass. What have I done to deserve a sister like Sarah? I only hope that she replies and keeps in touch.

'Now, let us have a look at how we are doing and then I'll make my way back down into Headingley. That needs a lot more looking after than here. Frankie's baker there had really let things slip, but we'll get it back up and going. The baking is already proving to be popular and Rosie there is a good worker. You'd both like her, she's a farmer's daughter, with good ideas.'

'I bet that is where the idea for jam came from? We should have warned her not to give you any ideas!' Daisy exclaimed.

'Not just any jam, jam made with lemons and perhaps rhubarb, ' Meg told them as she sat down at the bakery's table and started looking through the accounts.

'Both will be that tart, it will never sell,' Janet said.

'We'll see. I think it will, but then again I might be wrong!'

Meg looked at the immaculately kept books and one weight left her. She need not worry about her bakery on York Street. It was in good hands she thought as she looked at the list of goods needing to be ordered from Dinsdale's. Janet might be a little outspoken, but she was as honest as the day was long.

Chapter 16

That Sunday morning, both Frankie and Meg were tired and wanted to make the most of a lie in bed. But that would not be the right thing to do, Meg knew, as she prepared to return to her room.

'When are you going to stop this charade of leaving me early in the morning before Ada catches you in bed with me?' Frankie asked. 'She won't care – she knows we are to wed.' He pulled on Meg's arm urging her not to go back into her unslept bed before Ada came up from the kitchen to see to her needs.

'I don't want her to think I've no morals,' Meg said primly. 'It is bad enough that we are living under the same roof and yet we are not married. I'm no better than Daisy really.'

'You'll live to regret taking that one on, I bet my last shilling on that.' Frankie leaned his head back on his arms and looked at the woman he loved.

'No, I won't. She's changed. The manager from the glass factory sounds to be a decent man and he's already proposed to her.' Meg hesitated. 'Frankie, I'd really like to have her as my second bridesmaid. I'm going to ask her next time that I see her. After all, she is one of my dearest friends.'

She was surprised at his response.

'On your own head be it. You know what I think,' he said, nowhere near as negatively inclined to the idea as she had expected. 'However, let's make a compromise: you have Daisy as your bridesmaid and I'll keep Mrs Baxter on. You looked so tired yesterday evening and you must admit that it is good to come home to a decent meal ready and waiting for you.'

Meg matched his wry smile. 'We are not doing so well at cutting back on expenses, are we?' she said with a half-laugh. 'You want to keep Cook on and I've just taken on Daisy as a shop girl and my bridesmaid. But we have a deal ... Oh, Lord, I can hear Ada coming in downstairs! I'll see you at the breakfast table.'

Meg ran back to her unmade bed and waited for Ada to appear to pull back her curtains for the day.

A little later, at the breakfast table Meg reminded Frankie that he'd promised to come and listen to Alice Dent that morning.

'Yes, for my sins. I still don't know why I should tag along with you. It's no place to be seen for a decent businessman. All she speaks of is putting our expenses up and our outgoings more. No wonder the mill owners hate her – as well as all men, now she seems to be making herself known for the suffragette movement that's just turning women's heads.'

Frankie pulled the bone out of his kipper to the side of his plate.

'I'll stand by her when it comes to mill girl wages,' Meg told him. 'Perhaps not so much on her forward views of women's suffrage. But I do think when it comes to mill girls, if they were men that were employed, the mill owners would be paying them more. And as I told you, I noticed Rosie's wage was a lot lower than it should be. If she is to help me with my new venture and it becomes a success then I'd like her to be paid better.'

Frankie looked up from his breakfast. 'What new venture is this? What are you planning now? I thought that we were cutting back not expanding?' he said loudly.

'Rosie gave me an idea. Her mother makes the best lemon curd and rhubarb jam, she gave me the recipe for both last week. I'm going to make it and sell it in both bakeries. Don't worry – I'll pay for the initial expense from the profits at York Street just until I can see if it sells or not.' She looked down at her scrambled eggs and hoped that Frankie was not going to protest over her new idea.

'But you are forgetting we are a patisserie and bakery, not a jam factory. What do we want with selling preserves?' Frankie asked and wiped his mouth with his napkin.

'Yes, but the lemon curd is nothing like I've ever tasted before, and it adapts well for baking. I made some lemon tarts with a bit that was leftover on Friday morning and by the time I had come back from my bakery they had all sold,' she said. 'I'm not wrong, Frankie, people would buy it and it keeps well once jarred. It would fill that shelf by the door and just bring a little bit more money in if you had it in your bakery at Headingley.'

'This is all money spent – and there were you telling me what I could and could not spend. I'm not happy with spending money on jam. It is not what we do,' Frankie replied gruffly.

'Just let me try and if it doesn't work within the first month then I will not mention it again. In fact, if it is not showing a profit by the time we get married, then I will never mention it again.' Meg regretted her words as soon as she had said them. Would she make a profit? It was a gamble and if she was seen to be spending money recklessly then she would never be able to stop Frankie from spending his on just what he wanted.

'A month, then,' Frankie agreed, 'and we are not stopping long listening to Alice Dent. She can afford to put fancy idea's into people's heads. She will have never been poor in her life if her family home is anything to go by. Don't forget, I'm still the man of the house,' he added and then quietly finished his breakfast.

Meg said nothing but wondered if she had pushed Frankie too far. Was she indeed foolish taking on jam-making when they were trying to save every penny? Frankie, this time, might be right, she thought as she felt the tension in the room between them. She had lectured so much about spending money, and now she was doing just that.

Alice Dent stood on a soapbox outside the Hyde Park Hotel. Unlike Speakers' Corner in London's Hyde Park, this wasn't a place well-known for demonstrations, but the new housing in the area was filling up with the sorts of people that Alice knew could be swayed by her ideas. She was dressed in a warm long tweed skirt with a jacket to match, under which she had a white high collared blouse and a hat upon her head showing off various coloured feathers upon it.

'Well she's certainly well dressed and she's got a voice on her,' Frankie said as Meg and he listened to her usual speech upon the needs of women and the failings of the working places run by men. 'I don't believe in all of what she says. Some things cannot be done without changes in Parliament. She needs to go and make changes there first. She's a firebrand, Meg, I'd still prefer you to keep her at arm's length.' Frankie linked his arm through Meg's as the women in the crowd cheered and some men booed and shouted insults at her.

'Who'll look after the bairns? Married women belong at home,' a man's voice shouted.

'Get home, you toffee-nosed bitch.' A ruddy-faced angry man shouted and swore as he pushed his way forward to knock her off her box.

'Help her, Frankie, that man's going to attack her!' Meg shouted at her fiancé as the man grabbed at Alice's skirts.

Frankie pushed through the crowd and stood in front of the red-faced man who raised his fist to Alice then thought better of it as Frankie, dressed like a gentleman, raised his cane, and hit him over the knuckles hard. 'Don't you dare, my good man. You might not believe in the words that she says but that is not the way to prove it.'

'She's a troublemaker. Look at all these women listening to her, when they should be at home with their men making them their dinners. Women should be at home,' the man said and stood back wondering whether to take on the gent that had come to her rescue.

'Where I'm sure your good woman is! Now go home and leave those that believe in her to listen. Like you, I don't like some things she is saying but it is a free country and everyone deserves an opinion.'

The man swore under his breath.

'She's giving women fanciful ideas. It'll cause bother yet.' The bruiser of a man spat on the floor and decided to retreat from the crowd. Alice looked down at the conflict then continued with her speech.

Frankie walked back to Meg's side.

'Thank you, she could have been hurt.' Meg put her arm through his and squeezed it tightly. 'Are you alright?'

'Yes, I am, but she does know how to inflame views, especially in men. Once she has finished we will return home, my dear. I think that she is best left to her views.'

'But she is right, isn't she, Frankie. Women are not equal. We should have the same pay, be able to vote for our government and be able to study like a man,' Meg said and looked across at Alice as she bowed to the applause coming from mostly young women who wanted change in their life.

'She could be, but you do not need to get mixed up in all this,' Frankie told her. 'You have your own business, you have my respect – and besides, why would you want to be able to say who runs the country? Politics is definitely a man's thing. They couldn't have fancy skirts and women gossiping and giggling with perfume on bustling along the corridors of power! Now, let us go home and enjoy Sunday dinner made by the cook whose job I have saved. You see, women do work, in the jobs that they are good at. Why would they want anything else?'

Meg gave a deep sigh. 'Oh, Frankie, you really don't see, do you?'

Her speech now finished, Alice made her way through the crowd to them both. She looked Frankie up and down and smiled at Meg.

'I wanted to thank you Mr . . .'

'Pearson, Miss Dent. Meg's fiancé. You have her to thank for me being here and for saving you,' Frankie said and held his hand to be shaken.

'Ahh, Meg, of course, you came to my house and were kind enough to give me sustenance the day that I was walking home after rallying in Leeds. It's good to see you still taking interest in our beliefs and bringing your good man with you.' Alice smiled and looked at Meg. 'We might manage to win you over and for you to join our growing numbers. Now, I could do with you joining me next week at Armley. We have a rally and everybody there will count.'

Meg looked up at Alice and smiled. 'I'll be with you in spirit if not in deed, Miss Dent. However, rallies are not what I anticipated taking part in and I have a business to run.

While your cause is good and true I need to keep a good name both for my own business and that of my husband's. I cannot afford to be perhaps arrested for my beliefs, no matter how strong.'

'Oh, I understand, perhaps another time. Now, I can see that you are walking out with your handsome beau and I must support my fellow woman and protester who is about to have her say. Perhaps you will call by another day to one of our meetings?' Alice asked.

'Perhaps, but we are about to marry in another month so my diary is quite full.' Meg smiled then took Frankie's arm. 'Good day, Alice, I hope that you are successful with your lobbying.' She then walked away with Frankie arm in arm.

Meg's attitude was quite different than Frankie had expected and once they were out of earshot, he wondered out loud why she had suddenly gone cold about the idea of joining Alice Dent on her quest for women's rights.

'You seemed to be very curt with her,' he said as they made their way back home.

'I didn't mean to be but the more I thought about what she said, the more I thought she sounded like a bit of a bossy soul. And after all, I've got this far in the world under my own steam. Women will always succeed if they set their heads upon it and don't let themselves be dragged down in society. Alice is a little too radical for me and she was born with a silver spoon in her mouth. She can afford to play with her life, but I'm afraid I cannot. Even Daisy is seeing that now her head is not full of stuff and nonsense. Women will be as strong as any man in the future, of that I'm sure.' Meg was sure she would prove women could do anything their own way if left to it.

'Well, I'm just glad that you have seen sense. Besides if you are to be making jam and the like you'll not have time to play politics,' Frankie scoffed.

'You'll see my jam – or should I say, Rosie's jam – will help turn your finances around. So you can scoff all you like, Frankie Pearson. And next Sunday we will take a cab and go and look at these rhubarb fields and sheds. I've never seen rhubarb grown in a shed before.'

'Will you ever stop bossing me around?' Frankie muttered.

'No, not until the day I die, so if you want to change your mind about marrying me, now is the time to say,' Meg joked as she stopped to look in a cobbler's window at a pair of shoes that had caught her eye.

Frankie put his arm around her and held her close. 'That I'll never do. I enjoy being bossed by such a beautiful woman. Now, you know we can't afford those, so don't even look at them.' He held her close as he kissed her in broad daylight with fellow walkers shaking their heads in disgrace at such an outward sign of emotion.

'Then we are the perfect couple. I listen to you and you listen to me, and if we keep doing that we will be old and grey with grandchildren around our feet before we know it,' Meg whispered.

'I hope so, my Meg, I really do hope so.'

*

At the end of the following week Meg and Rosie surveyed the bakery's kitchen.

'I wish I'd kept my mouth shut now,' Rosie commented, 'looking at all this lot – and this is just the beginning if you are to go and see my uncle this weekend.' She took the crate of waxed lemons to be washed at the sink before she grated and squeezed them all in preparation for making lemon curd.

Meg arranged the rows of warming jam jars that a lad from the glassworks had delivered on a shelf above the cooker and then went to get the basket of eggs, the sugar and the butter to be placed in the two large jam pans on the stovetop.

'I'm going to times your mother's recipe by twenty,' she told Rosie. 'That should make enough jars of curd to make a decent display in the shop, and, providing it sells, give us enough for a fortnight. We'll do the same for the rhubarb jam, as and when I buy it and make it.'

Meg cracked egg after egg and whisked them all together. She then melted the sugar and butter, stirring all the time, before adding the lemons that Rosie had grated and squeezed then added the eggs, still continuing to stir constantly as Rosie had told her to do until the lemon mixture turned into a thick custard.

The room filled with the smell of lemon and butter. The two women looked at one another and exchanged slightly tired smiles: the first batch of curd was a success.

'Mam strains it now,' Rosie said, 'just to get rid of the stringy egg bits that sometimes gets left behind and any large pieces of rind.' She passed Meg a sieve and watched as the first jar was filled with the delicious thick yellow liquid. She smiled as Meg licked a dribble of the mixture that had run down the side of the jar off her finger

'Ooh! That's so good, if that doesn't sell, then there's something wrong with the people of Headingley and Leeds. I could eat the pot full.' Meg grinned. 'I have got a lot to thank your mother for.'

'She's not the only one to make it, so it was no skin off her nose that she gave you the recipe. I hope ordinary folk will buy it, especially with all the eggs that it uses.' Rosie looked at all the jars that Meg was filling and putting to one side to cool.

'It will. Have faith. Once it has gone cold, we'll seal the top with a circle of grease-proof paper over it and tie a lace doily on the top with string. Now, I thought that we would call it *Rosie's Delicious Lemon Curd*. We would not be making it if not for you and we agreed to your name being on the pot. Do you think you could write the labels out for all the jars and stick them on for me?' Meg smiled and looked at Rosie's beaming face.

'You are going to call it after me? Really? I thought that was perhaps a sweetener?'

'Yes, and if it starts to sell well, I'll get the labels printed, else your hand will ache too much to help me with baking. It's only right that you get the glory – after all, it was your idea really.' Meg kept pouring the mixture and then with all the jars filled, stood back and looked at the afternoon's work. 'Jars of gold, that's what they look like and what they are hopefully. Now, let's order some more sugar from Joe Dinsdale – we will need it if we are to make Rhubarb jam and some ginger. We'll call that after your mother, *Mary's Rhubarb Preserve*. Let's make all our jams with women's names on them. If customers see jam with their names on they are more likely to buy it. Plus in the future, we will put *Made in Leeds at Pearson's Bakeries*. Then everyone gets to benefit.'

'Everyone except you, Meg,' Rosie said quietly.

'No, because I'm soon to be Mrs Pearson even though I aim to keep my Christian name over my bakery's door. The preserves are a joint effort by everyone, so it is right to market them as such. Now, on Sunday, Mr Pearson and I will visit your uncle Fred out at Woodlesford and look at his rhubarb production. I hope he doesn't mind us paying him a visit on a Sunday but it is the only time we have off from work. I still hear my mother's voice saying keep the good Lord's Day free from sin and business as no good will come of it. So, I hope that your uncle is not as strict.'

'It won't matter what day of the week it is to Uncle Fred if there's money to be made,' Rosie laughed. 'He will strike a deal be it a Sunday or even Christmas Day. He's no scruples. You've got to stand in one of his sheds dead silent and just listen. You'll be amazed.'

'Why, what is there to hear?'

'You'll see,' Rosie replied and then smiled as she put on her shawl. 'I'll see you in the morning, now that the curd is made. Don't forget, if we are making rhubarb jam a bit of ginger added to it spices it up.'

'Already ordered with George from Dinsdale's, so there's no if about it.' Meg smiled. 'See you in the morning.' Saturday was half-day closing so after a short day, Rosie could enjoy the weekend. Meg knew how precious time with family was as she watched her assistant close the door and wander her way home.

That Sunday morning, Meg and Frankie were on their way to visit the open fields of Woodlesford to visit Fred Whitwell's rhubarb fields. It was a beautiful spring day, the sun was shining and it was a relief to be sitting back in a horse and cab and breathing the fresh air of the countryside instead of the smoke-filled air of the city.

'This is the second Sunday that you have asked me to accompany you. We both should be in our respective churches listening to our banns being read. Instead, the woman that you are, we are doing business. Last week was a waste of time. I hope this one isn't,' Frankie said as Meg looked out of the window of the carriage, appreciating the different view from the built-up back-to-backs of Leeds.

'It is a ride out into the county if nothing else, but I can assure you that your Sunday will not be wasted and I'm sure the vicar will still marry us whether we attend banns or not,' Meg said firmly. 'I know that I will come away with a deal for rhubarb from Mr Whitwell and that the jam made from his amazing plants will sell just as well as the lemon curd. Rosie put labels on all the jars of curd yesterday morning and before she went home at dinner time she had already sold six. I know that it is going to make money, else I wouldn't be wasting time and money on it today.'

'That's all very well and good but I was going to ice the first of our wedding cakes today. I've postponed because of this jaunt. You do realize that our wedding day is getting nearer and nearer and only I seem to be worried about it!' Frankie noted.

'I know, but what is there to worry about?' Meg asked. The wedding had been on her mind, but she'd realized that nearly everything was in order. 'I have my dress, the cake is made and as you say you be will icing it shortly, the church is booked, you have seen to the reception at the hall and we already have a home that we are happy in together. Plus, the invitations are to be posted next week, the few that we are sending, so all in my eyes is in hand.' Meg smiled and reached for his hand. 'I do love you, you know, but I'm also practical-minded, if I can make some money between now and our marriage I will and I'm sure you are the same.'

'Speaking of invitations, I forgot to mention that my mother has not yet replied to hers as yet. I'm hoping that she appears because I can't bear a grudge against her all my life. It's her who has to live with herself after swindling me out of my father's inheritance,' Frankie said, leaning back in the carriage.

'I too hope that she attends, she can't accuse me of being after your money anymore and I hope that she sees a change in me. I'm not quite as demure as I used to be. Now that the invitations are printed I'll send one to Sarah as well, but

I can't see her being present at our wedding. I'm glad that I am to ask Daisy the next time I see her if she would be my second bridesmaid. She looks so different now that she has the support of her family back and her new man looking after her.' Meg knew that Frankie was not that happy with the latter decision but Daisy was a staunch good friend and she wanted her present on her big day.

'You are too soft. She will go back to her old ways, I'd bet my top hat upon it. I thought we were cutting back on expenses,' Frankie said and shook his head still amazed that Daisy was working behind the counter at the York Street bakery.

'It's my cost at the moment, Frankie, so don't worry, she'll not cost you a penny as I know she still has the dress that you originally bought her the day we went shopping a couple of years ago. That will be perfect for our wedding day,' Meg said sharply. 'Now, it looks like we are here at the farm. Look at all these long sheds – this must be where the rhubarb is grown and the surrounding fields I know are usually full of it come summer. People have started to call the area between the cities of Leeds, Wakefield, and Bradford the rhubarb triangle, according to Rosie. It's exported all over the country. Isn't that wonderful another product from Yorkshire that we can be proud of?'

'You can only be proud of it if you like it and I really don't. It is vile,' Frankie said as he stepped down out of the carriage into a less than clean farmyard holding his hand out for Meg to take. He quickly urged her to hold her skirts up as he looked down at his usually immaculately clean boots.

'Well, I like it and I aim to make the most fabulous jam with it and sell it on our shelves,' Meg told him and then turned to greet a short man who was making his way out of the red-tiled farmhouse and holding his hand out to shake. She turned to Frankie. 'Come on, smile, this man is going to help us make our fortune,' she said quietly as she stepped forward and shook Fred Whitwell's hand. She kept her eye on the cow pats in the yard, while Frankie not so discreetly covered his nose with a handkerchief.

'Morning,' the man replied. 'Now you must be Miss Fairfax and Mr Pearson. Rosie told me that you were coming to discuss my rhubarb. Apologies, sir, it's a bit rank. I've just let the cows out across the yard and my delivery of night soil from Leeds has just been carted here and left in a pile over there.' Fred nodded to a nearby wall heaped high with waste from the city's outside toilets and held out his hand. Frankie took it hesitantly after seeing that it too was not that clean and wondered how Meg could withstand the smell around her.

'It's none the worse for that, Mr Whitwell, it will make things grow,' Meg said politely. 'You are doing the city a service and feeding us at the same time with your wonderful rhubarb.'

'Aye, well if you want to follow me. I'll show you the forcing sheds.' Fred set out across the yard with Frankie and Meg following. 'As you can see, the fields all around are just beginning to show growth that will be ready in another week or two as soon as the weather warms. The fields will be full of local women picking it for me to be sent on its way. There's nowt finer than our rhubarb.'

Frankie was shaking his head, wondering how on earth the rhubarb could be grown in the sheds that they were about to walk into.

'Now, it's warm in here and it is completely dark,' Fred warned them. 'You'll need one of these to see your way.' He took three candles from out of a candle box on the side of the long wooden hut's entrance and opened the door to a long dark room that smelt musty and pungent but was really warm. They followed him into the hut whose floors were covered in a mulch of shoddy waste from the mills, manure and soil.

Once he lit the candles, Fred and Meg were amazed to see pink and cream growth with furling light green leaves on the top. 'My strips of gold,' Fred said with pride in his breath. 'Folk can't get enough of it.' He could see the puzzlement on their faces and explained. 'The rhubarb thinks it's spring and grows faster in the dark. You can even hear it growing if you stand silent for a while.'

'Amazing,' Meg said and looked around her. 'That's what Rosie must have meant when she said to listen. I'd wondered what she meant.'

All three stood silent and listened for the sound of the rhubarb growing. As they concentrated, they could hear the very faint noise of a leaf unfurling.

'Aye our Rosie, she likes coming here. You'll have found out that she's a grand lass and a quick learner.'

Fred smiled slightly at the posh gent in front of him who had no nose for the smell of a farm. 'Now, how much rhubarb will you be interested in? Rosie says you are thinking of making jam with it, so you'll need a good pound or two for that.'

He led them back out of the shed, and Frankie was relieved as they stepped back out into the daylight. The shed was too warm and smelly for him and even the farmyard smelt better as he put his handkerchief back into his pocket. He still couldn't quite believe that Meg was about to do business but she was going ahead and ordering some of the plants from the farmer.

'I think, shall we say, twenty pounds now and then once I know if the jam sells I'll order more when I need it?' she suggested. 'Rosie gave me the price list that you sent with her and the price is acceptable. Do you want payment before delivery or will you send me a bill?'

'Nay, I'll send a bill when I've supplied you,' Fred told her. 'Rosie says you are good to her so that is good enough for me and she's told me where you are at in Headingley. I hope the jam sells well for you, and if it doesn't, you can always put it in pies. There's nothing better than a rhubarb pie with custard. My old lass often makes one.'

'That sounds good. I'll try that as well. You'll enjoy that, won't you, Frankie,' Meg said with a hint of wickedness in her eye.

'I will indeed, my dear, but now I think we must return home,' Frankie replied and walked quickly to the awaiting carriage.

'Thank you, Mr Whitwell, I'll look forward to doing business with you. Today has been most interesting,' Meg said as she shook Fred's hand tightly.

'It comes from Siberia you know, does rhubarb. It likes growing here because the climate is wet and cold just like over there. The Chinese knew about it hundreds of years ago but we here have only just got a liking for it. It's fascinating stuff!' Fred told her. 'I don't think your fella cares much for it though.'

'He will when it is selling in one form or another on our shelves, don't you worry,' Meg said and smiled. 'Thank you again. I know we'll work well together because you are as fanatical about rhubarb as much as I am about baking. It will be a pleasure working with you.'

'Aye, I look forward to it.' Fred closed the door of the carriage behind Meg as she sat down in her seat. 'Good day to you both, thank you for your business.'

'Good day to you, Mr Whitwell, it's been a pleasure meeting you,' Frankie replied with his handkerchief still to his nose.

'Aye, you and all. Now you'd better leave these country smells behind and go back to the grime and smoke of Leeds. I can tell you've not liked our country ways. Horses for courses, lad, and my rhubarb will make that lass of yours a good bob or two – so don't you worry on that score.'

Chapter 17

Sarah sat in the carved oak chair left behind by the Jewish family who had been persecuted to within an inch of their lives by the gangs on Dorset Street and looked at Sam as he ate his breakfast of fried bread in dripping with a hard fried egg on top. It would have been a luxury a few weeks back, but now Sam was making good money and insisted on a good breakfast before he disappeared for the day doing who knew what. Only Sam knew what he did throughout the day, but many a time he came back with a bruised cheekbone or burst lip. Sarah had learned better than to ask what he was going to be doing – she knew she wouldn't like it, so she never pestered him for information – but this morning was different.

'Bit of business at the Elephant and Castle today, gal, might be back late. Don't wait up for me, it could get near midnight before I'm home.' Sam wiped his chin on his sleeve and swigged back his tea. 'You keep the door locked and all today, open it to nobody, do you hear? Not even Scabby Mary.'

'What are you up to, Sam? Why don't you tell me what you are about? You come and go at all times of the day and night and Scabby Mary seems to think that you are to be in a fight with a gang, the Odessians or something like that,' Sarah said and watched his face cloud over.

'She should learn to keep her mouth closed just like she should have learned to keep her legs shut. It's nowt to do with her anyway,' Sam said angrily. 'Look gal, we live here because I work and help out the Bessarabians. Nothing I do is legit, but you've to do it if you want to keep body and soul together in these parts.' Sam breathed in and ran his fingers through his hair. 'I've got a fight tonight, gal, and if I lose, we lose everything. It is against one of the best fighters from the Odessians. It's a fight for who keeps this patch of the world and the rest of these streets that are on their wanted lists.'

'Who are the Odessians? And why are you involved in the fight? I wish we had never come here. It's full of crooks and gangs that think they run London.' Sarah suddenly realized Sam was frightened for his life in the fight that he was to take part in. Her man stood there, breathing heavily for a minute or so before he finally turned to her, his face hard.

'Look, it is what you've guessed. I help the Bessarabians run a protection racket,' he said. 'The Odessians are another lot of foreigners from Eastern Europe who will not think twice of killing anybody that stands in their way of taking over these streets. I happened to be in the way of one of their gang when I was ensuring that they weren't coming onto Bessarabian streets. It all got a bit out of hand and before I knew it, the leaders of both gangs had fixed me and the fella I had originally come to blows with in a fight to see who should run the protection around here.' Sam gave what he thought was a cocky grin. 'Don't you worry, though gal, I can beat him. He'll be wishing he was back where he had come from by the time I've finished with him.'

'Oh, Sam, we used to worry about the gang from Battersea, but they seem to be nothing compared to these foreign lot that you've got involved with,' Sarah said. 'I do wish we'd never come to this house. What's the use of all this if you could be dead while you are working for these gangs? They are making money out of people who are just trying to go about their lives. They shouldn't have to pay for protection from anybody.' A more immediate concern came over her. 'And who's going to protect you in this fight?' she asked, panicked that she and Sam were out of their depth and they both knew it.

'I'll be right gal, but if something does happen to me, let me show you this.' Sam got up from his chair and went to the chimney breast. He put his arm up the chimney and pulled out a blackened brick followed by a rusty tin. 'In here is some money, payment from the last few weeks that I've managed to put to one side. I trust you girl, that's why I'm telling you this, now don't let me down. There's enough in here to pay for your train fare back home, and that's what you must do if anything happens to me.'

There was a long silence. 'Promise me, Sarah, that if I don't come back tonight you'll take the money in the morning and leave London. You don't want to end up like Scabby Mary in the hands of the Bessarabians. They wouldn't think twice of making you work the streets once I was out of the way.' Sam shoved the tin back in its hiding place and looked at the worry on Sarah's face.

'Don't go, please don't go and fight tonight! I don't want to be on my own and I don't want you hurt,' Sarah wailed, feeling sick to the bottom of her stomach with worry. 'You can't go, you mustn't go!'

'I have to, gal. Don't worry, I'm better than the fella I'm going to fight. He's fat and flabby. I'm too quick for him. I wouldn't have told you what I was up to but just in case he gets lucky, you going back home would be one less worry for me. I might not say it very often but I'm fond of you, gal, I might even ask you to marry me one day when I can offer something better than I have now and you get a bit older.' Sam walked over to her and kissed her as a tear trickled down her cheek.

'Don't go, please don't go!' Sarah pulled on Sam's arm as he put his cap on his head and tied his muffler around his neck.

'I have to gal, it's a matter of honour and if I don't fight for Stephos – my boss and the boss of the Bessarabians – then I might as well throw myself into the Thames and take you with me, because my life and yours would not be worth living.' Sam paused and put on a tired smile. 'I'll be back, don't you worry, and when I do win there will be a good reward from Stephos and the gang. It could be the making of us, gal.'

Sarah watched as Sam doffed his cap and pulled the door behind him. He couldn't be that certain of winning the fight, she thought as she bolted the door and looked over at the chimney breast where the money box was hidden.

They had never gone hungry since Sam had started work for the Bessarabians but it must be at the cost of other people's lives by the amount of money she had seen in the cash box. You didn't get money like that for just being polite.

Sam was a hard man as she had found out on the fateful night when he had raped her. He had been fairly true to his word but on occasion she had bolted her door and hid from his violent tendencies especially after a hard night's work. He'd then go out the house swaying and swearing to find his satisfaction with some of the whores on Dorset Street, who were all too free to tell her that they had slept with her man and she should be thankful to have such a fella to sleep with.

She looked at the uncleared table and wondered what to do. This was perhaps a chance to leave the world of Dorset Street and Sam behind. Should she steal the money in the box and do as Sam said and get a train home? Should she leave or should she stay? Her heart beat grew faster as she pondered her position.

Meg's wedding invitation stood looking at her on the mantelpiece and reminded her of her dislike of Frankie, the man her sister was to marry and the reason why she had decided to seek another life for herself. She hated the French fop. He was ten times worse than Sam with his posh ways, she thought and that made her mind up to stand by her man.

She would just hope that he came out of the fight at least alive if not unscathed. He might be rough and ready but he had looked after her well these last few months. He deserved a bit of support and loyalty, she decided as she put her head down onto her arms and closed her eyes.

Please let him return, she whispered to herself, suddenly realizing it was more than friendship that had started to bloom for both of them.

The day went slowly and Sarah kept herself busy tidying the house and doing jobs that did not really need doing. She never unlocked the door, not even when Scabby Mary knocked on and yelled her name. She didn't feel like eating, her stomach was churning and as night fell, she sat beside the fire with the kettle on the hob and waited in the firelight for Sam's usual knock to let her know he was home. The ticking of the mantle clock seemed to grow louder and louder with every minute. The chiming of the hours made her heart race and her stomach churn as eleven o'clock was chimed and then eleven-thirty and still there was no sign of Sam.

She was just about to give up hope of ever seeing his face again when she heard a shuffle outside the door and the knock she knew so well but lighter.

'Sarah, Sarah, I'm home, let me in, gal, it's alright, I'm back home.' Sam crouched down, exhausted after his battle with his opponent. 'Come on, gal, let me in, I'm on my last legs here.'

Sarah rushed to the door and unbolted it, letting in an exhausted Sam. She gasped at the state he was in and helped him into the kitchen, putting her arm around him as his legs went weak, relieved that he was at long last home and safe.

The smell of sweat and blood hit Sarah's nostrils as she helped him to a chair before running back to close and bar the door on the night. 'Oh, Sam look at you, you are nearly battered to death. There's so much blood on you.'

Sarah reached for the kettle filled with hot water, placed some of it in a bowl then washed Sam's face and hands while he winced in pain. She wiped his wounds gently and felt his pain as the cuts became clean and showed more clearly the damage that had been done.

'It's not all mine. The other fella came off worse. They had to carry him out of the ring, poor bugger, but I've proved my worth to the Bessarabians. I've earned their respect. Our home and us will be safe for a while, my gal.' Sam winced as Meg put iodine onto one of the worse cuts and patted it gently.

'You shouldn't have to fight like this to gain their respect. It's wrong, Sam.' Sarah looked at his battered face, thinking that the black eye that he had given her was nothing compared to the battering his face had taken.

'You don't understand, gal, if we are to do anything in this life, you've got to pick and choose who you run with. We have got a chance to pick ourselves up out of the gutter. If I stand by this gang then I'll make something of both our lives. Come on, you are not having to scrounge about on the shoreline – you are just keeping house, so your lot is better already.' Sam reached for her hand and held it tight. 'Trust me, Sarah, we are on our way up.'

'It doesn't feel like it when I daren't open my door to anyone and mix with our so-called neighbours. We are in the roughest part of London that we could be and there's you beaten to a pulp for some gang that is not even from this country, let alone London.'

'It'll be right, gal. One day you'll live in a big mansion with green fields all around you and we will have earned respect from all around us. I promise you.' Sam yawned from sheer exhaustion. 'I'm away to my bed now. Stephos said I could rest up in the morning after winning him the street from the Odessians. You could join me in my bed tonight if you fancy, gal, I could do with a bit of comfort this night.'

'No, you need your rest, and I can't but remember the last time that you came home from a fight and used me. We are best apart tonight, Sam.' Sarah hoped that would be the last he'd mention it as he let go of her hand and looked at her.

'I'd be gentle, not like last time,' Sam said and hung his head.

'No, you get some sleep and we will see what tomorrow brings.' Sarah kissed Sam lightly on his burst lips. 'There will be plenty of other nights when your wounds are healed. Now, let's get to bed. I'm exhausted after sitting worrying about you and you should get some rest.'

Sarah watched Sam make his way up the stairs to his bed. Maybe he was changing. He wasn't content to wait for what he wanted – he'd take it with force if he needed to and she was beginning to think that was what he would do again to her if she was not careful. She was thankful that tonight he was too exhausted to argue but on future nights she might not be so lucky, she thought as she blew out the oil lamps and made her way with a candle up to her bed. She locked the door behind her and pushed a chair against it to secure it even more. She'd no intention of being raped again by Sam no matter how sweet his talk was when sober and in need of her.

The following morning, Sam was sitting by the fire nursing his wounds and Sarah was washing his blood-splattered shirt in the sink when there came a knock on the door.

Sam looked at Sarah and shook his head for her not to answer it as she gave him a worried glance. He put his finger to his lips and urged her to be quiet.

The knocking on the door got heavier and a loud voice speaking in broken English yelled through the door, 'Sam it is I, Stephos. Open up for me if you are still alive, my friend.'

Hearing his boss's voice, Sam nodded his head for Sarah to go quickly and open the door. She dried her hands on her apron and went to pull back the bolt on the door, feeling her stomach churning in fear of meeting the gangland boss. She wondered why he was calling on them so early in the morning. She stood back as she opened the door wide and the man that the whole of Spitalfields feared walked through her door. He did not give her a second glance as he walked over to Sam.

'You are still alive then, my friend? You fought bravely, the other man was no match for you. He's lucky to get away with his life!' Stephos Stefani slapped Sam on his back and grinned at him, showing his false gold teeth and the bulk of his muscular body.

Sarah looked at the giant of a man, noticing his tanned skin and long dark hair, and realized straight away that no one with any sense would dare cross this man's path if they didn't have to.

'Yes, I'm alive, he wasn't going to get the better of me, and he was no match. He might have been a big man but he wasn't fit.' Sam looked up at Stephos through a half-closed eye. The swelling hurt and he knew he'd damaged one if not more of his ribs. 'I didn't expect you to visit us this morning, I've not even got my jacket on yet.' Sam signalled to Sarah to pass him his jacket to put over his striped twill shirt.

'That doesn't matter. I just wanted to see how bad you are and give you the news that the area you fought for is now our patch,' Stephos said then glanced at Sarah as she hung back from giving Sam his jacket. 'Another match has been fixed for a fortnight, between you and a boxer fresh from Kiev. He's more your match. We are, how you say, running a book on your fight. We will make money for our gang after everybody seeing you fight last night.'

'I'll not be fit in a fortnight, you'll have to make it later,' Sam said even though he knew that he shouldn't argue with Stephos.

'You will be fit, and you will fight. Today you rest, and tomorrow you go and visit the people on our new patch and tell them who is now in charge of their lives,' Stephos said bluntly and without care. 'You've got a good home here, my friend, and a young woman with a bonny face. Don't forget that all can change if you cross me.' Stephos stood back. 'Show them who is boss and train hard for the fight my friend, because this time it will be harder.'

Sarah watched as Stephos made for the door and felt herself shrinking inside as he turned and put his hand around her jaw. 'You'd make me a pretty penny on the streets, little one. Perhaps you should work for me.' He looked into her eyes and saw the fear and anger. 'Remember, my friends, your lives are mine to do what I want to do with once you are on my payroll.' He let Sarah go and walked out of the door, slamming it behind him.

Sarah relaxed fractionally as she ran to Sam's side. 'You can't box again, and I'm not walking the streets for him. Sam, what have you done? He's the devil himself, he thinks he owns our lives.'

'He does, Sarah, he does, and I'll have to box. You just keep out of his way because I'll not be able to save you,' Sam said and put his head down. The previous night's fight had been hard enough but now that money was being bet on him, the fight would be tougher. The Odessians would pick their best man and he would not stand a chance with damaged ribs that would have not healed by the time of the fight. 'We'll be alright, gal, I'll hit his block off his shoulders, and then we will win part of the pot. With that, we'll make a new life for ourselves and leave Stephos and the gangs behind us.'

Sam knew he was lying to his gal. There would be no pot of gold for him and he'd be struggling to win this time.

'We could go home, to Leeds,' Sarah said. 'You'd easily get a job up there, on the cut with Harry if he's still there.'

'Aye, that's what we will do once this fight is settled, but we can't go yet. Stephos's men will be watching our every bloody move. But Leeds sounds just right, that's where we will go, we'll take you back home.'

Chapter 18

It was just under three weeks to Meg's wedding day and she smiled as she looked at a letter of acceptance of her invitation from Betsy, her old next-door neighbour in Sykes Yard.

The letter looked surprisingly well-written for Betsy and she wondered how her new life was panning out now that she was living with a new husband and all her family around her. Although life had been hard when she lived in Sykes Yard, they had also been good days, with everyone caring for one another, and Meg missed the goings-on there and the gossip between houses. Living down at middle-class Headingley, nobody shared their lives and everyone made sure that their business remained behind the closed front doors of their homes. If she didn't have her girls at the bakeries she would have left her previous life and the goings-on in ordinary working-class lives totally behind, she thought as she folded the acceptance and placed it in her pocket.

'Is that an acceptance to our wedding?' Frankie asked. 'I hope that it is because so far, I have heard every excuse going from everyone whom I have invited. I haven't even heard from my mother yet, although that doesn't surprise me. No wonder I thought twice about even inviting her.' Frankie placed his hat on his head and opened the front door onto the still-dark street as they both made their way to their respective bakeries and patisseries.

'It is,' Meg confirmed. 'The post boy delivered it yesterday evening. Betsy and all of her family are coming by the sounds of it. Some of your toffs friends will have their eyes opened with Betsy and her children.' Meg smiled and thought about the mixture of guests that would be gathering at Langroyd Hall. Bea Benson and her snotty husband would be dreading their presence and would be glad to probably see the back of them after the wedding had taken place.

'I've not had Bea in my patisserie for some time, and I'm definitely missing some of her friends' custom,' Frankie told her again and looked worried. 'And most of those have not replied to our invitation. I suppose they will get around to replying sometime. It's the same with paying their bills – it's always the case with the upper classes, they leave everything to the last minute.' Frankie went to his carriage. 'I might go and visit Bea one evening this week just to check if everything is alright. I can't believe that she has not been and visited me of late.'

'Well, I'm glad that she hasn't,' Meg admitted honestly. 'But I know it must be perplexing for you, as she does spend good money with you at the patisserie and we do need some communication over our wedding reception. I'm surprised that she has not been near you of late. Perhaps she's got the message that you are not available now you are about to be married,' she grinned. 'I'll see you this evening if not before as I'm going to York Street with some of my conserves today.'

Meg watched Frankie's carriage trundle down the road. She knew he was worrying about Bea Benson not visiting: Frankie could do with the trade and she knew he was concerned about the reception at the Hall and if all was going to go to plan. Lady B's little bunch of friends were noticeable by their absence also, she thought as she rounded the corner and walked down to the bakery. Perhaps Frankie had somehow fallen out of favour with them – it was the sort of set that once one person fell out with you, they all followed suit, just like lambs.

She turned the key in the bakery's door and lit the gas for the morning's work before donning her apron. Whatever was going on, Frankie would find out, no doubt, when he visited Lady Benson – and that would be his last visit before he was a married man. Meg couldn't quite believe it. Just a few more weeks and she would then be Mrs Frankie Pearson. The timing felt right now: she had her own business, her own ideas, and she had grown in confidence. She'd no longer be in Frankie's shadow but would be his equal, she thought, as she got to work making her first batch of bread for the morning.

'Morning, Meg!' Rosie yelled as she came in, the door slamming heralding her arrival. 'Lord, it's a lovely day out there. The trees are beginning to bud and there are daffodils are opening up in folks' gardens on my walk into Headingley. Only trouble is, I'm here in the bakery. I'd love to back home on the farm this morning.' She put her apron on and smiled at Meg. 'Still, I need the money and you need me. There will be plenty of good days and evenings shortly now spring is here.'

'I hope so. I must admit, I like the warmer months, and at least both Frankie and I will get to see one another more with the lighter nights instead of going to bed quite so early,' Meg said without thinking.

'I should think you'll be seeing a lot more of one another in another month.' Rosie grinned and then blushed as Meg looked sternly at her. 'Sorry, it's just that you'll be married then.'

'Alright, I know what you meant.' Meg started to grin. 'I can't believe it — less than three weeks and I'll be married. I've put our wedding date off so many times and now it is happening.'

'And you'll be the bonniest bride in the district,' Rosie told her and then got about her task of making scones before the first customers of the day arrived.

'I'm going to my bakery on York Street after the morning's rush to take some jars of curd and jam,' Meg said. 'They are selling so well here, they should do the same at my shop, and then I will just have to persuade Frankie to take some for his shop.'

'That will mean another batch or two being made,' Rosie considered. 'My hand ached after writing all those labels for the jam. I don't mind it aching from mixing cakes or stirring jam but writing has never been my strongest point. But, I'm glad that the jam is selling, and my uncle Fred is glad that you are promoting his rhubarb as well.'

'If it really becomes popular we have to make larger batches and definitely get the labels printed. That will save the strain on your hand and eyes. I never expected that we would turn our hand to jams and curds but I was thinking that we could make strawberry and raspberry in the summer months if these two go well.'

'We might as well turn into a jam shop the way you are talking. I'll be happy just baking if you don't mind, I get enough of jam making at home.' Meg could see that Rosie hoped that she would think the better of the whole idea, but the expansion had really caught Meg's fancy.

On the stroke of eleven, Meg walked out to the hackney carriage that she had ordered and filled one of the back seats with jar after jar of jam and curd for her bakery on York Street, leaving Rosie to look after the Headingley bakery. The business was beginning to pick up: people were enjoying the everyday fare and with the added sale of the jams, the business was proving to be popular. The books there were starting to look healthier and even Frankie had to agree that it had been a quick turnaround.

Meg climbed up opposite the jams and as the cab headed to York Street, she watched the people passing by, all of them going about their business, all busy with their lives but all needing food. Baking was the business to be in but along with her new idea of jam making, she thought she could not go wrong in feeding the good people of Leeds.

Her mind turned to all the things that still had to be done in the run-up to her and Frankie's wedding and the things that she had to sort that day. Sometimes she wished that she could just let Frankie take control of all the businesses and become an everyday housewife, kept by her new husband, but she knew that would never keep her satisfied. She loved the feeling of making money and being successful, particularly now she knew she was good at it. She closed her eyes and thought of Sarah. There had been no further word from her sister, even though she had sent her an invitation. How she wished to see the sulky, surly face of her sibling on her wedding day. She would hug and love her, no matter how much she protested, and protest she would, she thought.

She opened her eyes as the carriage stopped at her bakery.

'What have you been up to now?' Janet asked as she saw Meg climb out of the carriage and ask her to help unload the jars of jam that were to sell in the bakery.

'It's the jam and curd that I told you I was making. It is selling well at Headingley, and I thought that since there's some free shelving in that corner of the shop, we could put it for sale there.' Meg pointed to some white shelves that currently housed an advertisement for Dinsdale's Best Flour, which she quickly moved. 'It will catch everybody's eye here and you two could point it out to customers when they come in.'

Daisy was standing behind the counter, still looking well

dressed and presentable. Meg was glad about that, given she had something to ask her before she looked through the books.

'How much are you charging for the jam and curd then?' Janet asked as she put the jars on the shelves.

'It's threepence for a pound pot or five pence for a two-pound of jam, and the lemon curd is threepence ha'penny a jar. Put one jar to the side and then you can both try it on some bread for your dinner and you can let me know what you think,' Meg said. 'Have you been busy? All looks tidy and the shelves filled, although I don't know if that's a good thing or not. Have you got good sales this week?' Full shelves might mean they'd not had good sales.

'Good morning to you and all Meg,' Daisy said and grinned. 'We've not been busy – we have been rushed off our feet. Janet has made second batches of most things and if you look at the bread shelf, we are almost sold out of every loaf.' She moved away from in front of the main bread shelf to show her the empty trays. Meg might be her closest friend, but when it came to her business that was all she thought about sometimes, at the cost of their friendship.

'Oh, that's good, you obviously manage well without me now that there are two of you,' Meg replied. 'Daisy, can I have a word with you upstairs, do you think?' she asked and looked at the worry that came over her best friend's face.

'Alright, but whatever you've got to say you can say it here, as I'm sure Janet won't mind if I don't.' Daisy stepped out from behind the counter and made her way to the stairs.

'No, I'd prefer to tell you on your own, although Janet will get to know soon enough.'

Janet shrugged her shoulders not caring that she had been left out of the conversation and at the same time worried if she had left the bedroom tidy enough for Meg's liking. The other two women climbed the stairs as she served the next customer from behind the counter.

Meg pulled the door to. 'I wanted to ask you something on your own Daisy, sorry,' she said. She hung her head then looked at her trusted friend. 'Will you be my bridesmaid along with Janet? I'm sorry I never got around to asking you earlier but things have been so busy of late! We only sent the invitations out last week. My day would be perfect with you and Janet as my bridesmaids. You're two friends I couldn't see my day out unless you were by my side. You already know that Joe Dinsdale is to give me away and Frankie will be by my side. The only people missing would be our Sarah and you. Please say you will, Daisy, it wouldn't be right if you weren't.' She touched her friend's arm and looked at her pleadingly.

'But Frankie will not want me,' Daisy replied immediately. 'I know he won't, he never has liked me. That's why you haven't asked me before and why I'm surprised I'm being asked now ... And I think you were embarrassed by me when I found out I was expecting. Nobody likes a fallen woman.'

'I was upset for you more than anything,' Meg corrected. 'And don't worry about Frankie. I'm not asking you to make him happy, it is for me. I need my best friend by my side on my big day and I should really have asked you before Janet. I'm sorry for that.' She put her arms around her best friend and whispered, 'Please, I need you.'

'But I've nothing to wear and I can't afford to buy anything new. My Mam would make me something but she's busy enough with our Charlie, I can't ask that of her.'

'You do not need to buy anything or get your mother to make anything. The dress that Frankie bought you a few years back will be ideal. Or, if you wish open up my wardrobe and take your pick. There's one that will match Janet's absolutely spot on, the one that is peach with cream lace and that will fit you like a glove. I just know it will, as we are both about the same size. No one will ever know it's mine, I've hardly worn it. You have kept so slim and slender – no wonder Jimmy McEvoy is offering you his hand.'

Meg walked to her wardrobe and opened the doors.

'Just look at that wedding dress,' Daisy said wistfully. 'How I longed for a dress like that and for Tom Askew to walk down the aisle next to me. Instead, I ruined my life and ended up the talk of this part of the town.' She ran her hand down the length of the dress and sighed at the delicate lace and embroidery.

'But you are turning your life around now and baby Charlie is a blessing, he's such a bonny baby,' Meg told her. 'You have a good man in Jimmy. He must be to take on another man's child. Now, see how bonny you will look in this dress.' Meg held the apricot and cream dress from out of her wardrobe close to Daisy, as her friend admired herself and imagined herself dressed in it.

'It is beautiful, and I could do my hair a little better than it is now . . . and my mam will have Charlie.' Daisy smiled and looked at herself. Her old self was beginning to shine through nowadays as things were starting to look brighter for her and her baby.

'You must bring Jimmy as well,' Meg told her. 'He's more than welcome – after all, he's a business supplier now. I aim to buy more glass jam jars from his works now I know my jam sells. So, you'll be my special bridesmaid. You'll enjoy the reception at posh Langroyd Hall: you can look down your nose at Lady Bea while you sit across from her and sip your tea.' Meg smiled as Daisy put the dress on the unmade bed that Janet had been sleeping in.

'Oh, Lord, I'd forgotten you were holding the reception out there with all the snobs of the district. I'll never fit in!'

'Of course, you will. If I can, so can you . . . but I must admit I wasn't happy when I heard Frankie had booked it to be held there. It is far too posh for a lass from Sykes Yard. But we are as good as any of them. They all still fart and piss as my father used to say.' Meg grinned.

'Meg Fairfax, you never come out with things like that!'

'Aye, I know but I had to make you see that nobody's better than anybody else and I really need you at my wedding.' Meg squeezed her hand. 'Sorry that sometimes I wasn't there as much as I should have been for you. I've been wrapped up in my business. Even poor Frankie has had to wait too long for me to be his.'

'I knew as soon as you got this bakery that you'd make a success of it and you have. I'm proud to be your friend and yes, I'll be your bridesmaid and feel a queen for the day in this dress of yours. You just need your Sarah showing her face and then your day will be complete.'

'I don't think that will happen but you never know. She might surprise me. Let's face it, she's been good at doing that over the years.' Meg looked around her noticing a pocket watch she knew all too well on the bedside table. 'Looks like Janet has made herself at home in my rooms, along with George and all. That'll mean another wedding before so long if they are not careful.'

'I wasn't going to say anything but he was going out as I was coming in. Joe Dinsdale will have his guts for garters for being late to work, even though he is the manager at his main shop now.' Daisy smiled. 'Us women we always give in to easy to our fellas. That is, except you.'

'Oh, I've had my moments, just so far I havebeen lucky but I have a feeling that it may just be about to run out. Let us say it is a good job my wedding is in a few weeks, else I could find myself in a delicate situation.' Meg rubbed her flat stomach and blushed.

'You are not are you?' Daisy said quietly.

Meg shook her head, 'Not yet I don't think, but let's put it this way, I've given over worrying now my wedding is so near.'

'Meg Fairfax, I never thought that of you.'

'No, it's come as a shock to me as well, but now I understand the pleasures that lying together brings.'

'Aye, lass get that ring on your finger fast, don't be on your own like me. Frankie will make a good father and it goes without saying that you will be a good mother.' Daisy wrapped her arms around Meg. 'And if you find yourself with child, I'll be there for you, not that you'll need me. Frankie will be the perfect husband and father. Does he know?'

'Hey, I'm not pregnant yet, at least I hope not. And if I am, I'm not far gone.' Meg looked at her reflection in the mirror and panicked for a moment that she might not fit into her wedding dress. If she was pregnant, would Frankie want to honour their union? 'If I am, I hope that Frankie will still want to marry me.'

'Don't be daft, he's been wanting to marry you for years. He's not been saying that just to get you into bed. A baby will just make it perfect. An heir for the famous bakery chain of Fairfax and Pearson,' Daisy said and gestured grandness with her arms and then both women laughed as they both said 'patisserie' and fell about laughing.

Nothing or nobody could come between their friendship and they both knew it.

It had been a long day as Meg sat on the edge of her bed back home. She'd seen to Frankie's bakery in Headingley, done the books at his own bakery, and managed to persuade George at Dinsdale's shop to sell and stock her curd and jam, just in small quantities at first until it proved to be popular. It was the way forward, she thought as she lay back and put her hands on her stomach. Perhaps if it proved that popular, she could expand into jam making.

She closed her eyes and thought about her life. The time when her father was brought home dead from the pit, the poverty that she grew up in with no bread on the table some days, and Sarah wailing as a baby kept wrapped up in an empty drawer. Her mother dying and Frankie and his money troubles – although compared to her family's problems, these were nothing. Now, she felt as if it was time for her to perhaps become a mother as well as a wife. She had known it would probably be inevitable once she and Frankie had started sleeping together. Although, Frankie had enough worries on his mind and she didn't know if he would welcome children into his life or not. If she was pregnant already she was not too concerned, her wedding day was around the corner and there was no undoing what they had already done. But no matter, she would still remain working in the bakeries, children or no children.

Chapter 19

Frankie sat in silence in the early morning light that filtered into his bakery. It was warm and homely and he felt safe within its walls. He could forget about life when making the perfect éclair or waiting for a luxuriant cake of his own making to appear like a phoenix from out of the oven.

He looked across at the three not-yet iced tiers of his and Meg's wedding cake stacked upon the side in stout tins of their own. He was going to make a start upon icing them that afternoon – just plain royal icing for now. The intricate icing was to follow the week before the wedding. It was then he would excel and show his skills to all the guests and to his beloved Meg.

He couldn't believe that she was, at last, to marry him, even though he had proved his life to be a sham so far and not at all to be what it seemed, now that she truly knew him. She was the stronger person out of the two of them, he thought as he looked around his bakery and considered the way she had made them both work together to start to make a difference in his finances. It was paying off: his overdraft was not as frightening now when he looked at it and given time he would repay the bank what he owed.

How his mother had been wrong to say that Meg had only been after his money. She had been there to help him save his money not spend it, he thought as he decided to start filling the shelves with the newly baked pastries and chocolate confection that he had just made.

His mind wandered to the invitation that he had sent his mother. Would she even bother to reply? She'd made her feelings about the wedding all too plain and the likeliness of her ever showing her face again was very slim. She had stolen his inheritance from him in one fell swoop and had never shown any regret for it. He'd only sent the invitation out of courtesy, he didn't expect her to attend – especially if she was still with Richard the hanger-on that she had been with last time. If she came she came, but there would be no love shown to her if for one moment she criticized Meg or their marriage.

Frankie smiled at Norah as she arrived at the patisserie door just as he unlocked it for his early morning staff to join him.

'You're always the first, Norah, I'd be lost without you,' he said.

'I like to be prompt. Anyway, I enjoy my work sir, it is wonderful working here and serving all the gentry and their wives as well as the people that just walk in from off the street. I never know who I'm going to be serving from one day to the next,' Norah said as she tied her crisply ironed apron strings behind her back.

'Am I right in saying that Lady Benson has not been in for a while? I don't think I have seen her lately or indeed some of her friends?' Frankie asked.

Norah thought about it for a moment. 'She hasn't for a while, sir, and now I think of it, the ladies that she associates with haven't either,' she said finally. 'However, we have been busy with other customers and the girls upstairs in the tea room have been run off their feet, but I'm sure you already know that and I don't have to say.'

She started to make ready the counter for the first customer then turned to Frankie.

'There is one thing, sir. I was asked the other day if you were going to be selling the jam and curd that Miss Fairfax is selling in your other patisserie? By all accounts, it sounds very good, according to two or three customers that have commented upon it,' Norah said carefully, worried about going beyond her place.

'Did they now?' Frankie laughed. 'I will have to ask her to supply us with some here then. I must admit I did partake of the rhubarb and ginger jam on my toast this morning and did find it most tasty, but I didn't tell her so. She knows already that she has a good product on her hands, just like the rest of her baking. She's making my bakery in Headingley a success as well as her own. I should count myself lucky to be marrying her.' Frankie looked at Norah. 'If Lady Benson comes into the shop, could you tell me please. I need to discuss the wedding breakfast that we are to hold at Langroyd Hall on our special day.'

'Yes of course sir, I'll tell you straight away.' Norah bobbed a curtsy and watched Frankie return to his bakery.

He was losing ground in popularity with his customers, she thought. They were asking for his fiancée's baking and perhaps she should have told him that as well as mentioning the jams. But it was really not her place to do so, she thought, as she placed doilies underneath the freshly baked eclairs and waited for her workmates and the first customer of the day.

Lord Richard Benson looked out of his drawing-room window and noticed a solitary figure making his way up the sweeping drive. He knew instantly who the well-dressed man was.

'That bloody Frenchman is making his way here, Bea. Tell the butler to say that we are not available. I cannot stand the sight of him.' Richard snorted. 'I hope that you have told him that it is now out of the question that he has his wedding breakfast here?' He gave a deep, theatrical sigh. 'Why you first agreed to it I just will never know. I even thought when I charged him for the use of the hall he'd think twice and cancel, but he bloody well didn't.'

'What do you mean, you charged him? How much?' his wife retorted sharply. 'I told you, I offered him the hall for nothing. He had supplied us so well with his pastries and fancies and he's a charming man, no matter what you think of him.' She looked daggers at her husband. Exactly as he had planned, after he had put his foot down when it came to her shopping at the patisserie and refused to pay any future bills, she had been unable to partake of any of Frankie Pearson's little treats.

'I didn't pay the Christmas bill. I told him that the cost would cover the hire of the hall. After all, if he thinks himself that high and wealthy, it would be nothing of a loss to him. The bloody impudence of the man.'

'That would really have hurt his bank balance, Richard, we were already late in paying him, due to your stubbornness.' She glared. 'Is it not enough that you have stopped me from shopping at his patisserie? And yes, I know that you have made sure that all your cronies do the same, so you needn't sit there looking so smug. Anyone would think that you were deliberately making the poor man bankrupt and for what? He's just a charming man who is trying to make a living.'

'He's doing more than that! He has all you empty-headed women going faint at the sight of him. You never look at me the way you look at him, the bloody foreigner. I will not have his wedding breakfast held here and besides, I've asked the Bowles family to come and stay over Easter, so we can't accommodate him.'

'He's not foreign, he was born and bred in Leeds, and he just has a slight accent, from living in Paris for some years,' Bea replied. 'And you never told me we were to have guests at Easter. Is that another of your schemes to hurt him?' She saw Frankie about to climb the steps and ring the bell, so turned and glared at her husband. 'If you don't want him to have his wedding breakfast here, then you make good and refund him the money that you so meanly took from him. After all, you will have done what you had set out to do and ruined the best day of his life. Is that not enough for you?'

'I will not, the man is a menace.' Richard glowered at his wife.

'Then I will make him most welcome and will spend the evening in his company,' Bea threatened .'After all, he will be more entertaining company than you.' She knew her husband. Richard's jealousy of any other man sharing his wife's company would be too much for him to bear.

They stared at one another as the butler came in and announced that Mr Frankie Pearson would like to see Lady Benson.

'Tell the bloody man that *I* will see him in the morning room and that Lady Benson is indisposed. I suppose I will have to deal with this.' Richard Benson swore under his breath as he watched his butler disappear and heard the morning room's door open and close.

'You pay him the full amount and a little bit extra for his inconvenience and you also tell him that I will be placing an order for Easter with him shortly, seeing that we have unexpected guests staying and now that we can't host his wedding,' Bea said firmly. Her husband's face turned red and purple with anger.

'You push me too far sometimes, Bea. I'll pay the bloody Frenchman just to have a peaceful life, else I know that you will lead me a dance. But you send a maid with your order, do you hear, you'll not enter into his bloody bakery.'

Richard huffed and puffed as he walked across the parlour and out of the room. Bea was sorry that Frankie was not to have his wedding breakfast at the hall, but at least she had made sure that he had the money to pay for somewhere else to hold it and had got her way with using his patisserie again. Frankie Pearson was soon to be a married man, and he had always shown faithfulness to his true love. She hoped that their wedding day would run smoothly and in a place that they were both happy with.

In the morning room, Frankie greeted Lord Benson as cordially as he could and asked if plans were still in place for the use of the hall for his and Meg's wedding. Lord Benson's face was grim as he replied, 'My good man, there has been a terrible misunderstanding. My wife has just realized that our hall will be full of our own guests this Easter. I'm sorry, but we cannot hold your wedding breakfast here.' He saw the anger and disappointment on Frankie's face and fought to keep a smile off his face. 'If she had only reminded me earlier I could have told her that plans were already in place for that weekend. I had completely forgotten about our conversation after Christmas when we came to an arrangement over payment.'

Frankie was silent for a moment, trying to keep his temper under control. 'I understand,' he said finally. 'But that will come as a huge disappointment to my intended. We were both looking forward so much to holding our breakfast here. I don't know where will be able to cater to our needs at such short notice – after all, it is only just under three weeks away, and with it being Easter, some places will be closed or too busy to fit us in.'

Frankie felt his stomach churning. He should have known that something was amiss, after not seeing Bea for so long.

'I'm sorry, my good man, but that is not my concern.' Richard looked up from his desk and blotted the cheque that he had just written out begrudgingly to Frankie Pearson. 'This I'm sure will cover what I owe you and the expense of finding somewhere at such a short notice.' He offered the cheque to Frankie.

'Surely you could have let me know sooner? What would you have done if I had not decided to call by?' Frankie asked. He took the cheque and looked at it. The sum was for nearly double of that of the baking that Benson had originally owed from December and would be a welcome payment into his bank balance.

'Oh, we'd have told you eventually. Day before or some such,' Benson said airily. 'Bea says that she will be placing an order with you soon, to feed these guests that we are expecting, so you are not too much out of pocket. In fact, I think that I have paid you more than enough. Now, if you'll excuse me, I have things to do. My butler will show you out.'

Frankie shook his head in disbelief. 'So, that it then? I've to accept this and be on my way. Is your wife available? I want to know what she thinks about this,' he said standing his ground.

Richard went over to the bell-pull to summon the butler and then turned and stared at Frankie, any pretence at civility gone completely from his face. 'Now look, you. Go on your way and you don't pester either me or my wife again. She should never have promised you the hall for your pathetic wedding. If you are not careful I will break your business, Pearson. I know what you are up to, charming my wife and her friends with your posh ways. Now, go, leave my house and leave me in peace.'

Before the situation could escalate further, the butler walked in.

'Ah, Parks, show Mr Pearson out please. We have concluded our business and I am retiring to the drawing-room,' Richard Benson said sharply and turned his back on Frankie.

'I'll not forget this, Lord Benson. Someday you'll regret the way you have treated me and have broken my fiancée's heart. You are wrong about me, I'm just going about my business,' Frankie said and picked up his hat from Parks as the butler gestured him to leave the room.

'Good day, Mr Pearson,' Lord Benson spat. 'If you want my wife's further trade, I suggest that you say no more. Believe me, if it was not for her, I would never have given you the time of day.'

Frankie walked out of Langroyd Hall, not even stopping to thank Parks, before he marched down the steps. What was he going to tell Meg and where was their wedding breakfast to be held now? Why had Richard Benson thought he was nothing more than a gigolo after his wife's money? He might be after her custom, that much was true, but it was she who deserved the bad reputation. He felt the cheque that he had put into his breast pocket. At least he was better off now with the payment he had received, but Richard Benson's thoughts about him were wrong. Thinking of that made the two miles walk back soon disappear and he arrived back home, flustered and upset by his visit.

'Whatever is wrong, Frankie?' Meg asked as she heard the front door slam shut and Frankie enter the drawing-room, a look of thunder on his face, going straight to the whisky decanter on the sideboard and pouring himself a drink.

'Bloody snobs, they are nothing but bloody snobs, that play with us that are trying to better our lives,' Frankie muttered. 'Lord help us if we forget where our place is in life!' He swigged his drink down quickly.

'What are you on about, my love?' Meg said and went to sit on the armchair and stroked his hair. She had never seen him in such a mood.

'That bloody Lord Benson has just had the gall to tell me or just as good as tell me that he does not want us to have our wedding breakfast at Langroyd Hall, that Bea should never have promised us the use. He'd been happy to take my baking in payment and now he's throwing it all back in my face.' Frankie told Meg. 'I'm sorry my love. I tried my best, but our wedding is not going to be the grand affair that I had so much wanted for you, at least not the breakfast.'

'Oh, Frankie, the hall was your idea, and I know you meant well. However, it's like music to my ears to hear that we are not to celebrate there,' Meg told him. 'I'd not have felt comfortable there, with all the posh folk that would look down their noses at us. Just think how Daisy and Betsy and her family would feel like sitting in a grand hall. Not one of my guests would enjoy their day for one minute. They are not used to grand ways and neither am I.'

She couldn't help but feel relief, but she knew Frankie had been hurt by his rejection from high society.

'The man thought that I was after his wife!' Frankie exclaimed. 'Yes, Bea is a very attractive woman, but how could I show any interest in her when I have you and am to be married to you? My dear, you are my life and have been ever since I met you.' Frankie calmed down a little. 'There is some good news. The upside is that he has paid me for my troubles, clearing the bill and more besides that he owed me from December, so that is a saving. However, that doesn't solve our wedding breakfast problems. Where are we going to go at such short notice?'

Meg smiled. 'I can't believe that you have just asked that when you own the perfect place and could do right by everyone we know.'

'What, do you mean ... You can't mean the tea room? That's not large enough. And what about all those that I've asked, the ones that are friends with the Bensons? We will be the laughing stock of that society once they hear our venue change.'

'One minute,' Meg said and walked into the morning room returning directly with a handful of envelopes with returned invitations within them. 'I wouldn't worry about that lot. It seems that Lord Benson has already influenced his friends. These have been returned over the last few days but I didn't have the heart to tell you. These are not true friends, Frankie, or at least some of them are not – they have given every possible excuse under the sun for not attending.'

'Lord, I'm a fool, but I so wanted my business to be recognized by these people,' Frankie said as he looked through the replies and their various excuses given for their recipients' non-attendance.

'I think it is best that a business and friends are kept separate, Frankie, or at least stick to people that you know that you can trust and that want to help you out more than keep you in your place,' Meg counselled. 'Even I thought that you were smitten by Bea Benson, so you can't blame her husband for treating you like he did. He'll also know that she's nothing but an upper-class floozy like everyone has been telling you. I'm sure you will not be the first man that he's spoken to in such a way.' Meg sat down on the chair arm next to a crestfallen Frankie and put her arm around his shoulder. 'Don't worry, we all make mistakes and want to be better than we are, but I think in the future we will be better at keeping the likes of Bea Benson at arm's length. Take her money if she returns to the patisserie and keep her happy, but perhaps not move in the same circle? You can only move so far up in society and then they close ranks.'

'All I want is for you and me to better ourselves,' Frankie said and held Meg close.

'Being wealthy does not make you a better person, as you have found to your cost. We will succeed, Frankie, and they will want to know us then. You can bet your last penny on that.'

Chapter 20

Florence Pearson sat back in her chair in her new Paris apartment and looked at the silver gilded invitation, engraved with lilies in each corner. It must have been chosen by that girl, not her Frankie. He would have had more taste. Lilies were for funerals, she thought as she read the wording, then smiled bleakly. He might as well be going to his funeral if he was going to go ahead with marrying the shrinking, back street wallflower that she had met a few years earlier. Perhaps she had not been after his money after all, because he must have spent what he had by now, knowing Frankie.

'Pass me my writing slope, my darling boy,' Florence said to her latest muse. He was a young model who she had found lying naked on a chaise longue posing for a painting in a back street studio and had immediately decided to take him under her wing. She smiled as he picked up her mahogany writing slope and opened it for her, placing a piece of best-watermarked paper under her nose and handing her a pen. He really was the fittest and most handsome man she had ever seen, she thought as she smiled and decided what to write to her beloved, wayward son.

Apartment 10
The Rue de Lyon
Paris

My dearest Frankie,
So, you have decided to finally get married to the girl from the back streets, well you know how I feel about that. However, I concede that you must truly love her and she you, or else she would still not be by your side.
All I ever wanted for you was to be happy and to know that you were loved and cared for no matter what you thought my intentions towards you were. As I am still your loving mother, I will of course be joining in your celebrations and will be delighted to join you both on your wedding day. I see the breakfast is to be held at Langroyd Hall. I'm afraid I will not attend that. Lord Benson is an absolutely, terrible snob, from what I remember, and his wife is rather decadent. She has or did have a terrible reputation, although I know that is the kettle calling the pan black in my case.
I will catch the train and will make my way to your home on the night before your wedding. Please ensure my usual bedroom is aired and ready for two guests. I will be bringing Rupert with me. I'm sure that you will make him welcome.
Your loving mother
Florence

She sat back and smiled. It was time to make her peace with her son and the timing was just perfect for righting a wrong that had caused heartache for them both. She hoped to make his wedding day more than special.

Frankie looked across the dining table at Meg after laughing out loud at the letter he had just opened. 'It seems my mother is to join the wedding party – and the timing of this will make you laugh! She has declined the wedding breakfast because she says Lord Benson is a snob and that Bea is too decadent.'

'Well, I'm glad that she will be joining us and you must admit that she's not wrong when it comes to the Bensons. You will try to be right with her, won't you? Is she coming on her own or has she got that terrible man with her?'

Frankie sniggered. 'Oh, that one's well gone,' he told her. 'We have a Rupert in tow now. She's asked for the double bed to be aired for her arrival.'

'Now, who's decadent? I wouldn't dare live my life like your mother,' Meg replied, looking serious. 'Surely she has been talked about just as much as Bea Benson . . . in fact, I'd think even more.'

Meg patted her lips with a napkin after finishing her portion of jam roly-poly. She had loved every mouthful and had to admit that keeping Cook on had been one of Frankie's better decisions.

'She was always like that,' Frankie pointed out. 'I don't know why my father married her. She used to say it was the artist in her, that she was a Bohemian. Not that she had ever anyone interested in her paintings, they were terrible but nobody dare tell her that. She just attracted men because she was beautiful in her day.'

'He must have loved her, else he wouldn't have stayed by her side.'

'Yes, he did. He treated her like a queen, and looking back she must have broken his heart many a time. I promise I will never be like my mother, it caused too many rows and too much heartache. My father used to put me to bed most nights because my mother was at a new exhibition or a gallery showing, talking and laughing loudly with one or other of the artists that had caught her eye. And that always had the neighbours gossiping when she came back. I know all too well what an unfaithful wife can do to a man.' Frankie stared into the distance. 'You'd think I'd have a bit of sympathy with Lord Benson. Although I still don't believe that Bea Benson is as bad as everyone says, but she does remind me a little of my mother, now I think about it.'

'Oh, Frankie, you really do not have a lot of time for your mother. Did you not think that she might want a life of her own and be a little frustrated with being married to your father? Who by all accounts was a good man, but perhaps a little predictable. Sometimes a little excitement is all that's lacking instead of monotony. You know yourself that you like a challenge – after all, you have taken on not one but three properties and made two of them a success, which must tell you something about yourself.'

'Yes, but you've saved my skin more times than I can count now. Headingley bakery is doing well now with you and Rosie running it. Your jam is even being asked for in my patisserie, so if you can supply me with some, I'd be grateful.'

'Of course I will. Have you thought any more about holding our wedding breakfast in the tea room above the patisserie? I think it will be ideal and we will be able to supply everything ourselves – and we have the staff to serve everyone, plus they can join us once the work has been done. I'd like that because without them we would have nothing between us.' Meg held her breath and hoped that he was now in agreement. She had never wanted anything fancy, just a nice homely lunch with friends and what family they had between them.

'I looked around the tearoom today,' he said. 'We can fit fifty people in there and we would be able to serve them with a menu that I have put together in my spare time this afternoon.' Frankie stood up. 'Come through to the drawing-room and I'll show you my suggested menu and see what you think. I've tried to make things that can be served cold and take the least organizing, but I've not skimped on the cost, which you might be a little annoyed with, but after all, it is our wedding day.'

Meg smiled. 'I'm glad that you are in agreement with the idea of the tearoom, and if we can save on the cost of hiring somewhere there is no need to skimp on the food, and if we have a say in making it, we know that our guests will be fed well.' She rose from the table and thanked the maid and asked her to bring the tea tray she was laying into the drawing-room.

'This is my menu. What do you think?' Frankie said and held out a handwritten menu to Meg as they sat on the sofa together. Both were excited over the breakfast that they now had to plan and both realizing that it could have their personal touch for their guests.

Oyster Patties	Petites Pates aux Huîtres
Lobster Salad	Salade de Homard
Pigeon Pie	Pate de Pigeon à l'Anglaise
Meringues with Cream	Meringue à la Crème

'That's better than any menu that those at the big house could put together for us, Frankie,' Meg said once she'd thought it through. 'A lot of this can be made the day before and just cooked and served on the day. Norah and the other girls can serve it at the breakfast as well as joining us in our celebrations. It is perfect, it's better than I could ever have imagined and it will not be that expensive.' Meg hesitated. 'I take it this writing on the right is French, because I can't read it?'

'It is. I thought it shows that we are eating in a patisserie and carries my love of the French cuisine over,' Frankie said and looked lovingly at his handwritten menu.

'Then we will keep it that way. It shows both sides of our love, which is only fair. I'm glad that Lord Benson would not let us have our breakfast at his hall. This is more personal and will be made with love and our down-to-earth guests will enjoy it more than any posh do.'

'My mother will turn her nose up at it!' Frankie said.

'Then let her! It's not her wedding and we don't owe her anything. It's our day, Frankie Pearson, and she will she just have to lump it.' Meg kissed him lovingly on the lips. 'I love you and always will, without money or with. It's not your bank balance I'm marrying. It is you.'

Florence sat in the Salon des Independents art gallery, her heart in her mouth.

She watched buyers and investors view and discuss the two Toulouse-Lautrec paintings in the impressionist style, one of Can Can Girls and the other of his friend Jane Avril. They were the two paintings that she had bought from the artist with Frankie's inheritance money.

Toulouse was getting more and more famous but he was also getting increasingly more unstable. His drinking and insecurities had him on course for an asylum, all of which made his paintings more attractive to the ones who knew that his work was unique.

Now was the time to sell his work, she had decided. Now was the time to pay Frankie his inheritance back. He'd proved that he could stand on his own two feet and not sink into despair. He also had proved that his love for his bride to be was true and hers for him, so it was time for her to undo what he thought was the wrong she had done to him.

She watched the salon manager shake a buyer's hand. One

sold, she thought, for at least four times the price that she had paid for it, and the other would soon be gone, by the looks of the interest it was attracting. She would be returning to Yorkshire with enough money to start her son – and hopefully soon his family – in a good lifestyle and make a name for herself as an art dealer.

Hopefully, Frankie would forgive her and welcome her back. She had missed him.

Chapter 21

Sarah felt sick, her stomach was churning and her heart wouldn't stop fluttering as she walked down the centre of Dorset Street next to Sam. His hands were bound in bandages and he only wore just a vest along with his belted trousers. She could see the muscles that he had built up over the last few months tensing in his upper arms as he fisted the air in an order to look tough and hard.

Crowds packed around them and urged him on, patting his back and shouting his name as he made his way to the backyard of the Ten Bells Inn, the heart of gangland where the fight with the boxer from the Odessian gang was to be held. The yard was packed with gang members, their faces hard, their voices still betraying their roots in Eastern Europe as they laughed and joked and took bets, running books at extortionate odds on both men.

Before going into the main yard, Sam stopped and pulled Sarah into a doorway, trying to block the crowd out to try to give her some last minute advice.

'Listen my gal, you know what to do, and you know where the money is. If it looks bad for me, you flee before the end of the bout. Don't wait for it to finish. You get the hell out of here. You take the money and the things that I told you to pack this morning and you leave the area. This fella I'm against, I don't think I can win. No, I know I won't. My ribs still ache and I'm not fit. I shouldn't be fighting but you know I've no option.' Sam looked worried as he held her at arm's length. He shook her gently as she sobbed. 'Please, go home, I don't want you watching. If I lose I've arranged for someone to come tell you.'

'I'm staying Sam, you'll need me. I'm not going home until it is finished and you are by my side,' Sarah said and wiped her running nose and the tears from her eyes. 'I don't want you to get hurt. Come on, we'll both run away now. We'll disappear into the crowd and both leave London.'

'Nay, I've given my word to fight. Hopefully, the brute that's fighting for the Odessians will know when to stop or I'll win him,' Sam said, trying to hold his own fear inside. 'But, if you see me fall to the ground and there looks like no hope, you flee, gal, before they come and oust you out of our home and make you walk the streets. Go and get a train from King's Cross back up north. You hear?' Sam said and then grabbed her close to him. 'Another year on and I'd have wed you, lass, you know that, don't you?' He looked down into Sarah's frightened face and smiled and kissed her on the brow. 'Now, do as I say and promise me that you won't stop and see if I'm alright if I'm down and that you'll leg it. If I survive, I'll find you, and if I don't, well somebody will bury me. Promise me, Sarah.'

'I promise, Sam, but you'll win, won't you, I know you will,' Sarah replied in a small voice and looked at the crowd urging him to go to the centre of the yard to where a ring had been formed by both gangs' heavies.

'I'll try, my gal, but you keep your promise to me. I want you safe. Now, go and stand with Scabby Mary. It was her who was going to come and tell you, and she's promised me to look after you, no matter what.' Sam smiled weakly and looked at the lass whom he had started to love. He knew he had to protect her from one or other of the gangs if at all possible. 'I'll be right, gal, don't worry.'

Sarah clung onto his arm as he walked out into the crowd. Sam was picked up above his gang's heads and carried into the ring by an excited crowd, all jeering as the rival boxers looked at one another and eyed one another up for weaknesses. It was to be a bare-knuckle fight with no nonsense about Queensberry rules or such la-di-da ideas. Their job was to defeat their opponent through fair means or foul, almost certainly foul. The only winners were the gang leaders that took a cut of all bets laid and got the prowess of knowing their man had won in the name of their gang.

'Come on, I promised Sam, I'd take care of ya,' Scabby Mary said in Sarah's ear. 'I told him you shouldn't be here, that ya should have stopped at home. It's not right for you to be here.' Mary linked her arm through Sarah's and pulled her to the edge of the crowd.

'I wanted to come, I should have been with him last time,' Sarah sniffled.

'Last time was nowt compared to this fight, gal. There's half the Bank of England being bet on this fight, not to mention the pride of the gangs, and they are a proud lot. Neither will forgive their boxer if he loses, and that's why Sam says I've to look after you if the worst comes to the worst. The Odessians haven't forgotten that they lost a load of streets because of your man. They'll show him no mercy if he loses.'

Mary pulled Sarah up beside her, both standing on a row of crates to look over the mobbing crowd at the pair of boxers in the ring and at Stephos, head of the Bessarabians, holding them apart as they postured and threatened one another. 'That's Bruno the Bear they call him. He's a big bastard – rather your Sam than me, fighting him,' Mary said under her breath.

The crowd roared and Stephos stepped aside, leaving the two men at the mercy of one another. Sarah looked at Sam's opponent: he was a lot larger than Sam, his nose broken from several previous fights and his muscles rippled as he stepped forward – only for Sam to land the first punch on his chin. Bruno smiled coldly and continued to step forward as if he had not felt a thing. He lifted his fist and slammed into Sam, but the smaller man had seen it coming and dodged the blow.

Sarah held onto Mary's arm tight and shut her eyes as another round of blows followed. It was almost worse just hearing it. This time Sam was not so lucky and Sarah winced she heard the distinct crack of a punch hitting his ribs. Sam's opponent obviously knew his weak spot as he lifted his fist again and hit him in the same place again. And again.

'Stop them! Stop them! This isn't fair, the other man is ten times bigger than Sam and he knows his ribs are damaged from the last fight!' Sarah screamed at the top of her voice, but nobody cared. No one could hear her pleas above the surge and the noise of the crowd as the boxers hugged one another from exhaustion and then parted again to swing another punch.

Time and time again the boxers hit one another. Blood was dripping from both faces as Sam landed a punch that caught Bruno fair and square on his jaw. This time he obviously made contact as the huge man stepped back for a second and shook his head, as if to clear it after losing his senses. The Bessarabians in the crowd cheered. This was what they had come to see, the lad that had saved their streets for them slaughtering the big bastard that had won against nearly every man he had fought that side of London.

'Yes, you cockney lad, give him some of his own medicine!' Mary yelled and jumped up and down as Bruno gathered his senses.

The huge mauler knew it was now or never. He couldn't show it, didn't dare show it for fear of what his own supporters would do to him, but he knew he had to rid himself of Sam. He'd have to show the upstart that was new on the patch just what he could do.

Anger raging, he stepped forward and pummelled his

fists first against Sam's body and then his face, time and time again hitting him without hesitation. Sam reeled around the ring.

Sam glanced up at Mary and Sarah through swollen eyes as his assailant hit him again and again, breaking his teeth and making his head spin as no mercy was shown him. The last thing he saw before an uppercut smashed him six inches into the air was Mary pulling on Sarah's arm, hopefully telling her to go with her and leave the match.

Then all was darkness.

Sam lay on the ground as the Odessians kicked and spat on him. Other fights started to break out between gang members all around him.

Sarah's fight was only just starting. She begged Mary to let her go and rescue Sam from the crowd, shoving her way through the fighting men, trying to get to the centre of the ring and tend to her Sam. She ducked and dived while all the time Mary was pulling her the other way. She had to save Sam.

Finally, she got within reaching distance only to find Stephos ordering his men to lift Sam's body out of the ring after feeling for a pulse and before the Odessans kicked him into pulp. Sam was dead, she knew he was, but Sarah still wanted to see him to make sure.

She scrambled out from within the crowd and pulled on Stephos's long coat.

'Let me see him. Please let me see him!' She looked down at the blood that had been spilled in the ring and Bruno

still parading around showing his muscles and roaring
with rage.

Stephos turned around and pushed her backward and
snarled, 'He's dead and you are now mine. I'll find you later.
He let me down, he owes me. You pay.'

Sarah gasped and fell back into the crowd. The leader of
the Bessarabians glared at her before following his men to
the side of the yard.

'Sarah, come on there's nothing you can do now,' Mary
said desperately pulling at her arm. 'Come on you know
what you've got to do now, to save your own skin. Come
on gal, I promised him I'd look after you if this happened
and I'm not going to let him down.'

'I need to see him, I need to know if he's still alive,' Sarah
wailed and got up on her feet and tried to fight through the
men in her way.

'Sarah, he's dead. Dead as Prince Bloody Albert. He had
no chance and he knew it. They'll see to his burial. Now
you come with me, while everybody's still scrapping. Come
and get your things and get away back home as he wanted
you to. I promised him, please, before Stephos or the
Odessians claim your house and you . . . and you end up like
me.' Mary knew if she was seen helping the loser's woman
she'd be up for as much punishment as Stephos felt like
doling out. She tugged on Sarah's arm. 'Come, come now,
else Lord knows what life you'll have once these lot calm
down and start claiming what they will think is theirs.'

'I don't want to, I want to see that they are doing right to

Sam,' Sarah cried and turned around and looked at Mary. She didn't want him to be like the little baby she'd found all those weeks ago, just dumped on the side of the river.

'You'll do right by Sam if you come with me. You know you will, it's what we both promised him,' Mary gabbled at her. 'Now *move*. Nothing more can be done for Sam. I'll see his body gets a decent burial. Stephos Stefani owes him that, he knew your Sam didn't stand a chance. I think he was just a pawn in the gang games. I've heard that both the Odessans and the Bessarabians are going to rule these streets together. That's why Sam wanted you on your way back home. Now come on, run for it while you can.'

Mary saw the panic and grief rise on Sarah's face as she suddenly realized there was nothing she could do for her Sam, and that yes, it was time for her to make good her escape and flee.

'I'm coming, but I don't want to leave him. I should stay, stay and see if I can help him, just in case they are lying and he's still alive,' Sarah cried as she followed Mary out of the hell pit of the Ten Bells Inn. But she knew Mary was right and she must go now else she'd never escape the claws of the London gangs and would be made to earn a living just like Mary or even worse.

She ran up Dorset Street for her life, as if the hounds of hell were following her. Ducking and diving through back alley-ways, she and Mary reached their own street. Turning the key in the lock of the house she had first thought would be the perfect home, she made straight for the hidden cash box up the chimney. Its contents had grown since the last time she had seen it. Sam had got a good pay-out from Stephos for his first fight and he had stashed it away knowing that it would be needed by Sarah if anything befell him.

'That's it, gal, you put that in your bag and pick it up and *run*. Run for your life and catch the first train up north that you can.'

Mary stood guard by the open door and watched Sarah pick up the readily packed carpet bag with things that she thought she wanted to take with her. She'd not a lot but of late Sam had brought her home clothes from houses that his gang had plundered, so at least she was better dressed than she had been a few months ago. She glanced wildly around her home and thought of Sam and the life she had been living with him. It had been hard, she knew that sometimes the drink had got the better of him and it had taken her a long time to regain trust in him after the time he had hit her and abused her. But on the whole, he had been a good man and looked after her well, for little or no reward. She wiped the tears from her eyes.

'Sarah, come on! I can hear them coming up the street. They will parade the bastard of a man that won against your Sam all round the area, and they are bound to knock your door down and make sure that everyone here knows there's a new force on the street. Hurry, just save your life, you don't need nothing else!' Mary shouted.

Sarah glanced around the room and noticed the wedding invitation that had just arrived earlier that week and she ran over to grab it. She couldn't have the gang following her to Leeds and knowing where her sister lived. She folded it and put it in her pocket and then grabbed her bag and swept past Mary.

'You know where to go, don't you, gal? You know your way to King's Cross?' Mary said.

'Yes, I know, don't worry. Take care of yourself Mary, thank you for your help,' Sarah said and gave her a quick hug.

'Go, then go! They are coming. I need to make myself scarce and you need to go.' Mary watched as Sarah turned on her heels. 'Take care, gal,' Mary thought as Sarah ran down the streets, not wanting to draw any attention to her.

Sarah weaved her way through street after street, her heart beating fast and a pain that hurt so badly as she thought of Sam being carried out of the boxing ring unloved and uncared for. She was relieved when she came to the Gothic building of Saint Pancras, its architecture more in keeping with a cathedral than a railway station and next to it the more sedate building of King's Cross station and her way back home.

Outside the station, carriages and people queued, passengers coming to and from London and all going about their own business. She caught her breath and mingled into the crowds. She slowly walked into the station. Neither of the gangs would follow her this far – they had no reason to know this was where she'd head for, and it was too far off their own patch. They'd as likely be attacked by one of the Cross gangs, and Sarah wasn't worth that much to them.

Sarah caught her breath and sat down on the first empty

bench that she came to. She needed to calm herself, get her breath and think through her options. The station was filled with the smell of soot and coal, and steam engines blew their whistles and carriage doors were slammed as people went on their way.

She sat back, trying to make sense of the death of Sam and her life since she had left the security of Meg's love and Leeds – a place that she had once hated. The last time she had been in King's Cross station she had been full of hope and joy at the thought of the job on the stage that Larry Hopkirk had promised her. That had come to nothing and had just worsened her lot.

If she was truthful with herself, nothing had gone right since she moved down to London. It was time to go home and beg forgiveness from Meg and hope that she still loved her, even after she told her all that had happened to her. She now knew that Frankie Pearson was a good man and that Meg had done well to find him. It was time to go home and to grow up, show her loyalty and love to her sister.

She knew she couldn't make herself a target for thieves, so went down to the public conveniences, cleaned her face, and then, in private, took some money out of the box. She then made her way to the ticket office and bought a ticket for Leeds. She looked down at the hem of her skirts as she climbed into the train carriage and realized that they were stained with Sam's blood from the Ten Bells yard. It wasn't only her skirt that was stained with Sam's blood, she thought. Her heart was as well.

A few tears ran down her cheeks as the train slowly made its way out of the station carrying her and her pain back home to Leeds.

In the middle of the night, three men flung the body of Sam Waites into the Thames from the edge of Old Swan Pier. Just another unwanted body to be embraced by the flowing waters of the mighty river. Nobody would miss him, nobody would cry over him. Nobody, that is, except Sarah with her broken heart.

Chapter 22

Sarah sat back in her seat and watched people join and leave the train, wondering if they had experienced anything like what she had in the few years she had been on Earth.

You couldn't tell from the outside. Nobody knew what was going on in other people's lives and what home or work they were returning to once they closed the train door behind them and made their way out of the station.

She herself felt dead inside and tried to stem the tears that she refused to show to the outside world and particularly the people in the carriage with her. She was conscious of the stained hem of her skirt and tried to hide it, wrapping it around her legs and tucking it behind her boots as she looked out of the windows of the train at the scenery outside changing from a smoky industrial town to open fields and hedgerows that were bursting with new spring greens and the white of blossom.

Pulling into Sheffield station she started to worry about what she was going to tell Meg about her life in London. Meg at least knew that she was no longer working for Larry Hopkirk and that she was now living in Spitalfields. But what her sister didn't know was that she had been living on one of the worst streets in London and about the life she had lived there.

Did she need to? Perhaps it was time to be truthful with her sister. She'd had enough of living in a fantasy world when she wrote to Meg and pretended that everything was alright and that she was doing well. She'd never done well since she had left Leeds and now she knew that the other man's grass was not always greener.

She shuffled back in her seat and held her bag close to her as her carriage filled up with new passengers and tried to keep her gaze to herself.

A lad her age came and sat across from her and to her surprise he spoke her name. 'Sarah . . . Sarah Fairfax, is that you? It is, isn't it? Well, who would have thought it?'

Sarah looked up at him and recognized him as Harry the lad that had for years been her next-door neighbour and whom she would have run away with if he had only asked her properly.

'Harry, I never thought that I'd see you on this train. Are you going home? What have you been doing in Sheffield?' Sarah felt herself panic. She knew she looked a mess and there was Harry sitting across from her in a good tweed suit and matching cap with polished brogue shoes on his feet, a gentleman in the making. He had changed. Three years on, he was now a handsome young man. He smiled and leaned forward.

'Well, I never, fancy me and you being on the same

train. I'm in Sheffield because I missed my connection from Hull, so I had to come this way round to get home. I was late leaving the office so it was my own fault, I could have cursed when I missed the direct Leeds train by seconds.' Harry looked at Sarah and saw that she looked pale and thin underneath her clothes.

'You've come on a long way from jumping about on loads in the tom puds on the cut.' Sarah smiled and remembered the good and the bad times with Harry. Sam had been a lot like him, she thought as she saw him look at the bottom of her skirts, noticing the stain of blood and quickly trying to hide it. 'Don't look at my skirt, I was walking through the market when a barrow boy spilled a pig's carcass and its offal right at my feet. I could have lost my temper with him and I really should have changed my skirt but I hadn't time, I'd to catch this train too,' Sarah lied.

'I couldn't help but notice, but it's only because I'm eyeing you over because it is so good to see you,' Harry admitted. 'Meg told me that you had gone to London, but I didn't know where you were, else I would have hunted you out. I've been down there a lot of late. I work in an office now. I'm not a labourer anymore,' he said proudly. 'I was lucky enough to be listened to with a new idea for Hull docks and then they that were in charge placed me into the planning office. I've been going back and forward to the new docks being added on down at Tilbury at the mouth of the Thames.' Harry smiled. 'We always said that we'd run away to London, but we did it on our own in the end.'

'That seems like a lifetime ago, Harry, so much has happened since then.' Sarah summoned up a small grin. 'Have you a beau or even a wife nowadays?'

'No, nobody has managed to catch me yet. Still single and that's how I like it. And you? Have you got a fella?' Harry asked as the train pulled into Wakefield station and they both watched the passengers alight and embark. The train let off steam, wisps of it curling around the window that Sarah looked out of to try to hide the tears that threatened to overwhelm her.

'I've just lost him, consumption, that's why I'm coming home. I've nobody down there now. Besides, it is our Meg's wedding and I decided to return home for it now I'm on my own.' Sarah hung her head. She'd vowed that she would tell the truth to anybody who asked her, but she found herself so embarrassed at what she had been part of.

'I'm sorry, my condolences. Were you married? He must only have been young?' Harry asked with concern as the train pulled out of the station to the guard's shriek of his whistle and the carriage doors slammed.

'No, we weren't married, but we were about to be. It was the thick London smog, it didn't agree with his lungs.' Sarah lied and hoped that Harry would ask no more of her life. 'Where's your mam and the rest of the family?'

'I'm going back to see my mam, she's got a new fella in her life. My father buggered off and left her. We think he's in America, living under another name. Wherever he is, good riddance to him, he wasn't good with my mam and we never had any money. She's living with a butcher from Middleton, happy as Larry. Thankfully I've no more brothers and sisters and I hope none on the way. We are a big enough family.'

Harry looked at Sarah. The flush of her younger years had left her cheeks and he couldn't help but think that she had been living a hard life down in London. 'I bet Meg will be glad to see you coming home for her wedding. She's asked all of us. I don't know about the fancy wedding breakfast at Langroyd Hall, though, it is not up my lot's street. Although I know my mam will tell them all to fill their boots and not hold back to eating anything that's on the offing. Old habits die hard.' Harry laughed.

'I bet that's Frankie's choice, he always did think himself a bit better than anyone else,' Sarah said. 'I still don't know what he sees in our Meg, she's not in the same league as him with his posh ways.'

Sarah looked at the first wild boy that had captured her heart even though she had been too young to know it back then. But all she could see and think of was Sam and wondered what had become of his body.

'You can tell you haven't seen much of your Meg of late and you must not have heard much from her,' Harry said. 'Mam says the bakery that old Lund had is making money hand over fist and that now she's running one for Frankie in Headingley. Between them they must be worth a bob or two.' He stood up as the train slowed down. 'We are nearly in Leeds. I need to get out quick and catch my connection on the Middleton line to get me back to my mam's. I'll no doubt see you at your Meg's wedding and we can have a good catch up then. Perhaps we could share a tea sometime if you are back in Leeds to stay and I'm not travelling about?'

'That would be good, I'd like that.' Sarah looked up and smiled at Harry. She was in no mind to flirt but she still felt something for her first love.

'Meg has my mam's address and here, I'm swanky, I've even got my own business card now.' Harry pulled out a small white card from his inside pocket and gave it to Sarah and winked. 'That's me Harry Hedges, planner and surveyor. Gone up in the world, I have, lass. You can't hold good stuff down. Now, I've got to rush, but keep in touch.'

Sarah looked at the card and watched Harry make his way quickly down the carriage. She put the card into her bag before standing up and collecting her things as she joined the passengers alighting at Leeds station. She held onto the carriage sides as the train jerked as the brakes were put on.

Her legs felt like jelly and her stomach churned. She was back in her home city of Leeds. Back home with a broken heart, down on her luck, and with a past that she really could tell nobody respectable about.

Even Harry Hedges had made more of his life than her, Harry whose bum always hung out of his trousers and swore like a trooper. She had ruined her life and it was time to turn it around and grow up – ironically, just as Harry had told her to do all those years ago.

She stepped down from the train and looked around her. The last time she had stood on that platform she was leaving for what she thought was a better life down in London. How wrong she had been, and now she was returning home like the prodigal son.

Would Meg be glad to see her or would she disown her once she found out the real truth about her young sister's life? She would soon find out, she thought as she handed in her ticket and walked out onto Aire Street and headed in the direction of Meg's bakery on York Street.

She knew these streets like the back of her hand. It was good to be home and recognize the shops and the market that she and Meg had scrounged for food around in years past. She passed the opening of the lane to the Music Hall and shook her head. She should never have been so vulnerable. How stupid she had been believing every word that Larry Hopkirk had said to her. You got nothing without having to pay for it, and that was a lesson she had learned from being headstrong and stupid.

Her a music-hall star? How gullible had she been! She couldn't dance, she couldn't sing and at the moment she certainly didn't have the looks. It was time to eat humble pie, face Meg and tell her, if nobody else, about everything that had happened in her life and hope that she would forgive her.

Sarah stood outside the bakery on York Street and peered in through the window.

She couldn't see anybody behind the counter but she noticed how much the shop had changed. It was no longer a dirty looking bakery that sold bad-quality bread and looked unloved. The glass shelves were piled high with tasty savouries and scrumptious cakes and scones, just asking to be bought and eaten. Above the showy window was a brightly painted sign with Meg's name upon it. Her sister had done what she had always wanted to do and now hopefully she was happy in her life.

Sarah peered in through the window again and felt apprehensive about walking into the bakery and taking her sister by surprise. It was late afternoon. She heard her stomach rumble and found her mouth dribbling as she looked at the baking and suddenly realized how hungry she was. She'd not eaten since before the fight first thing that morning and now her legs started to feel faint beneath her, partly with hunger and partly with the relief of reaching home and the safety that it would bring.

Suddenly she noticed Daisy come into the shop and reach down into the window to start clearing the shelves for the end of the day. She smiled as she saw the look of surprise then horror as Daisy suddenly recognized who it was staring into the bakery. Memories of her and Meg sitting around the table in their home in Sykes Yard flooded back as Daisy waved and rushed around the counter to open the bakery door and greet her.

'I had to look twice,' she said as she ran out and hugged Sarah. 'I couldn't believe it was you. You have grown, just look at yourself. Aye, lass, your Meg will be glad to see you. Does she know you are coming? She never said anything last week about you coming back home.'

'It's good to see you, Daisy.' Sarah fought back her tears and hugged her in return. 'No, she doesn't know I'm here. I just decided to come home this morning. Is she in the back baking? How long have you worked for her? She's never said.' Sarah looked at Daisy, she too was looking older and more vulnerable. Perhaps her life had not been so good either.

'No, Meg's not here, but come through to the bakery and Janet will make you welcome. Your sister doesn't work here most of the time – she's running the shop down at Headingley for Frankie, when she's not making jam that is.' Daisy grinned.

'Making jam? Is that what she is up to? She never stops, does she. If Meg's not here, I'll wait upstairs in her rooms. She must return in an evening, doesn't she?' Sarah said and felt weariness descend.

'No, she's living in the guest room with Frankie at the moment and letting Janet stay in her rooms for the time being because it is easier that way for Janet. But come in and we'll send word to her. Timmy on the corner will take her a message for a farthing or a ha'penny if you don't want to walk there or take a carriage.'

Daisy saw the disappointment on Sarah's face.

'Who's Janet? She's never told me about her either. To be honest, we have only just started writing to one another and that was partly my fault for not giving her my address as I moved around London,' Sarah replied and looked sheepishly at Daisy. The fewer people she talked to the better, she thought. She had been surprised by Daisy working in the bakery, but she knew she needed to tell the same story to everyone if she was to be believed.

'Janet Campbell – her mother and family live on Albert Street. You'll remember her if you see her. She comes from a big family, but like your Meg she can bake with her eyes closed. She'll make you more than welcome when I tell her who you are.' Daisy looked at the worry on Sarah's face. 'Come on, come on in, you look so tired after your long ride up on the train. I still think that it's a miracle that you can get to London in a day. Who would have thought it when we were children!' Daisy said kindly and urged Sarah inside the bakery.

'No, I'll walk down to Frankie's house. By the time I get there, Meg will definitely be at home,' Sarah said although she felt as if she could walk not another step forward into the bakery, let alone the mile and a half to Frankie Pearson's house. 'I'll surprise her by turning up on the doorstep.'

Sarah started to walk away but as she did so her legs went weak and she felt herself stumble.

'Sarah, Sarah, I'll get you a cab,' she heard Daisy say. She turned and looked at her only to find her words coming out in a jumble and the sight of Daisy went hazy as a terrible heat came over her and she felt dizzy and fell to the ground clutching her bag and worrying about the state of her dress as she closed her eyes.

Sarah fainted, exhausted, outside her sister's bakery.

*

'Just look at her, Daisy, she's not got an ounce of fat on her, and her clothes, well, we wore better when we were penniless and at Sykes Yard.'

Meg looked down at her sister and stroked her long, matted ginger hair. 'What's she been living like, I wonder, to get into this state? Aye, Sarah, you should have come home sooner, it wouldn't have mattered to me what you were up to,' she said quietly, with love.

'I don't know, Meg, she looked ill when I was talking to her persuading her to wait here for you to turn up,' Daisy said, 'and then she just fainted in front of my very eyes. Janet helped me up the stairs with her and now she's gone home to her mother's for the night so that you and I can sit with her. Sarah looks as if she's been through the mill, Meg. Have you seen the blood on the bottom of her skirts? I dread to think where that has come from. She should have never gone down to London, she would have been a lot better off staying with you and Frankie.'

'We both know that, but did you listen when folk were telling you not to bed Tom Askew and did I take any notice of what folk thought of Frankie and his false friends and French mannerisms? We only hear what we want to hear sometimes.'

Meg patted Sarah's head with a face towel from a bowl of warm water by her bedside and looked with concern as her sister moaned under her breath and muttered 'no, no don't kill him, please don't,' making both friends look at one another in horror.

'Shush, shush, you are safe now Sarah, you are back home with us. No one's going to kill anyone and no one is going to get you here,' Meg said gently and looked at her young sister with tears in her eyes.

'Where and what the hell has the lass been doing?' Daisy said. 'I bet our lives here have been nothing compared to hers by the look of it.'

Meg wiped a tear away. 'Oh, Sarah, you pig-headed girl. I'm not letting you from my sight once we have you back in health. You never should have left home and I'm not letting you go away again, do you hear?' she whispered to the semi-conscious lass that she loved with every beat of her heart. She vowed that now she was back home at long last, she would be staying there.

'How long have I been lying here?' Sarah asked weakly and propped herself up in the bed above the bakery.

'Only overnight. I think you were exhausted and hungered by the looks of you.' Meg said and kissed her forehead. 'It's so good to see you, my Sarah. I worried all the time you were away. I'd have worried even more if I'd have been able to see the state of you, but never mind with that now, we have plenty of time to catch up. Here, take a sip of tea and there is some porridge here if you can manage to eat it.' Meg passed her a bowl of porridge that Daisy had made at home and had kept warm on the stove down in the bakery.

Sarah looked at the breakfast and realized how much she had missed the love shown to her each morning without knowing it. A tear trickled down her cheek as she sat up and balanced the dish of porridge on the bedspread over her knees. The smell made her mouth water and she quickly took the spoon and started to eat.

'That's it, eat up, there's more if you want it,' Meg said. Her young sister had grown into a woman while she had been away and she realized that they were not dissimilar in looks if not in mannerisms. 'Oh, Sarah, you look so frail, we have so much to catch up with once you are able to.'

'I know and it is all my fault. I've been stupid and selfish, but I'll not be that anymore, Meg. I've learned my lesson,' Sarah said between mouthfuls of the creamy milk porridge that tasted like a little piece of heaven as she swallowed each mouthful along with her tea.

'No, I should have listened more to you and been there for you. I was too busy wrapped up in my own life,' Meg replied, and sat down beside her on the bed and put her arm around her. 'Anyway you are back now and I'm not letting you leave my side again.'

'You haven't heard how I've been living. You'll perhaps not want me once you know,' Sarah said quietly and looked at Meg with hurt in her eyes.

'You can tell me as little or as much as you want, it is up to you. And if you worry about what Frankie will think, don't! He is just happy that you have returned to us.'

'Oh, Frankie, I wasn't very kind to him either. I realize now that he was only helping our mother. I was a fool.' Sarah sighed and suddenly looked around her for the dress that she had been wearing on her arrival at Leeds and Meg's bakery. 'Where's my clothes?' Sarah looked down at the nightdress that somebody had put her into and wondered what had been said about her blood-covered skirts.

'I undressed you and your clothes are in the wash. Don't worry, no one is going to ask you about how they got into that state. There was only Daisy and myself saw them and Daisy won't say anything.' Meg hesitated. 'Once Janet realized who you were, and how exhausted you were, she did not argue for one minute about you staying in my old bedroom. After all, it was only for the night. Today I'll take you back home with me, where we can talk freely and you can tell me what you want to about your life in London. I take it that it has not been a bed of roses, like the picture that you were trying to describe to me?'

'No it hasn't, Meg, and I'm sorry I lied to you. I didn't know what else to do!' Sarah bowed her head and sobbed. 'I was headstrong and I thought I knew everything when really I knew nothing. I'm sorry, forgive me.'

Meg placed the empty dish to one side and hugged her sister tightly. 'We are both to blame. But, you must promise me to never get in this state again and to know that I'm always there for you no matter what. I love you, our Sarah, you are my sister, my precious sister.'

'So, she's back in our lives, and seems a lot less fiery than she was the last time I saw her. I hope that she stays that way.'

Frankie poured himself a brandy and sat down next to

the fire in the parlour of his home. It was later that evening. Sarah had retired to her bedroom in Frankie's house, quieter than Frankie had ever seen her and clearly just thankful that she was back in arms that loved her.

Meg looked with slight disdain at her beau and replied, 'Frankie, by the looks of her she's been through hell, so please be kind to her.'

'I always have been kind to her, unlike her to me. However, I must admit she does look as if she has learned her lesson the hard way. I know that you have been worrying about her, so I am happy for her to stay here under my roof.'

'*Our* roof Frankie. Or very soon to be our roof once we are married,' Meg said sharply, implicitly reminding Frankie that she worked just as hard to keep the roof over their heads. 'Anyway, keep your voice low, she's only just in the bedroom above us, she will hear you. Although she seems exhausted, Lord only knows what she's been doing. She has told me a little today and I expect that she will tell us more over the coming weeks. She thinks the lad that she has been living with is dead – it was his blood that was on her skirts after he got involved in a gang fight. She had to flee for her life.'

Frankie slumped in his favourite chair. 'Lord, I don't know if I want to hear any more. As long as her new associates have not returned with her, I don't want any ruffians knocking on our door.' Frankie looked at Meg, who looked a little wan. 'I'm just glad that it is not her body that had been found on the streets of London and that she is back in time for our wedding. Even I must admit it wouldn't have felt right without her there.'

'I asked if she wanted to be a bridesmaid, but she said no. I think she wants to keep a low profile at the moment and get back on her feet. Although I was surprised to hear her volunteer help in the bakery with me tomorrow once she has caught up with sleep. She must have been living on her nerves for so long. She looked instantly better once she had taken a bath and changed her clothes.'

'She's actually volunteered to help you? Lord, she must have grown up.' Frankie sipped his brandy. Meg sat down on the chair arm next to him and kissed him on his brow.

'Yes, and I must admit, I could do with all the help I could get, both bakeries are busy. Easter and our wedding is nearly upon us. Have you finished icing our wedding cake yet? At least if that's done it is out from under your feet.'

'Yes, I've just the intricate details to place on it next week, but it is royal iced now and looks wonderful. I've ordered the ingredients that we need for our wedding breakfast. Joe Dinsdale gave me a good discount and I've also employed a cook that used to work at the Queens Hotel, to see to the actual meal on the day. He came and looked around the bakery's kitchen today and was quite happy with it. He's also bringing some girls to serve the meal so that our staff can enjoy our day with us.'

'The bakery's kitchen, Frankie? Surely you mean the patisserie's?' Meg smiled and joked at the slip up in Frankie's wording.

'No, I do mean bakery. It is not only Sarah that has grown up, it is also me. After our wedding day, I'm renaming it a bakery. Your baking sells ten times better than mine, and the ordinary people of Leeds are a lot better payers than the upper classes.' Frankie couldn't help but give a little sigh at such a clear sign of the end of his dreams.

'Oh, Frankie, that's a shame, you love your French pastries, but it does make more sense. You could still make eclairs and macaroons and the things that you know that sell well for you.' Meg slipped down onto his knee and placed her arms around his neck. 'Am I losing my French man, on the quiet?'

'Yes,' he replied resolutely. 'I'm Frankie Pearson from Headingley, Leeds, as Yorkshire as they come.'

Chapter 23

'So, Sarah, you are to help Meg in the bakery today?' Frankie asked the lass who previously had made it quite plain how much she hated him. He pulled his gloves on and tapped his hat onto his head and checked his look in the hallway mirror preparing to go out into the fresh April morning.

'I am, I can wash up and tidy if nothing else,' Sarah said and looked down at her feet, remembering the way she used to talk to Frankie in the past.

'You will be a welcome hand no matter what you do,' Meg told her. 'Poor Rosie and I are run off our feet with orders for Easter and I'll have to visit my own bakery on York Street twice this week. I'll be glad when it is Good Friday and we can close all the bakeries to celebrate Easter and our wedding. Oh! Lord, our wedding has come so fast with one thing and the other happening.' Meg put her arm through Sarah's and smiled at Frankie. 'You'll check everything is in hand again, won't you Frankie, that Joe Dinsdale can deliver everything he's promised and the girls know how to set the tea room for our big day? I'm leaving that all with you as I've enough on my hands this week.'

'Yes dear, all's in hand, don't worry. Now, I'll see you both this evening and stop worrying, Meg, you looked decidedly peaky this morning. All is organized and will go to plan.' Frankie stepped out and got into his waiting carriage as he did every morning at five to bake and open his bakery, with Meg following him not far behind to the bakery at Headingley but with this time with Sarah by her side.

Sarah hid a smile. The tables had definitely turned since she had been in London. Her sister Meg was now as bossy and in charge of her life and Frankie's as much as he was, if not more. 'I thought you were having your wedding breakfast at Langroyd Hall? That's what was on my invitation,' Sarah said as she tried to keep up with her sister as they walked quickly down the streets in a bid to get to open the bakery on time.

'We were, but things have had to be re-planned. There's been a little misunderstanding with the Bensons that own it and we have had to rearrange at the last minute. To be honest, I was glad. I'd have felt out of place having my reception there.'

'I guessed it was Frankie's doing having your do there. It's just like him to think himself a bit better class and have a posh do. Although, from what I've seen of him since I came back, he's not as hoity-toity as he used to be.'

Meg got the key out for the bakery and turned to her sister. 'He's had it tough as well, Sarah. Perhaps we have all changed these last few years. I think we all have had to, whether we wanted to or not. He's a good man: give him a chance Sarah, he deserves that as he's willing to forget the past and for you to stay with us as long as you wish.' She opened the door to and stepped into the smell of bread and flour that greeted her every morning and made her feel welcome and secure in an environment that she loved.

'I'm sorry, I can't judge anybody now, can I? Not after what I told you of what my life has been like since I left home. I'll be right with Frankie, don't worry.' Sarah bowed her head. 'Now, what can I do for you this morning? You do know that I don't have the knack like you with baking? I don't know what went wrong when our mother had me. I'm not much use to anyone.'

'Of course, you are. Stop feeling like that,' Meg said and turned and hugged her. 'Now, how about you look after the jam pan this morning? I had no idea when I stupidly said to Rosie that it might be a good idea if we made some, how well it would do, and now it is selling as well as my baking. In fact, I haven't said anything to Frankie, but I think I could set it up as a separate business, it is doing that well. At the moment I'm only making rhubarb jam and lemon curd, but it is nearly strawberry and raspberry time, so I'll be adding that to my list.'

'You never stop thinking and looking forward to the future, do you?' Sarah asked. 'Just look at this bakery, it is all so modern and spick and span, with a gas oven and hob and everything smells so lovely. Are you sure you want me let loose in here?'

'This is Frankie's bakery. I came into it because it was losing money and his baker was not pulling his weight. It's working now because I've spent a lot of time here and Rosie my assistant is a Godsend.' Meg looked at Sarah. 'So, you see not everything has gone well in our lives either. Now, how are you at peeling rhubarb and chopping it up? There are nearly twenty pounds of it to be peeled and chopped and then made into the jam with some ginger added. Rosie's uncle delivered me the last batch of his forced stock on Saturday, so that needs dealing with. You'll find everything to hand and I'll give you the quantities you need as I make the bread that we will be selling today and then the fancies. Rosie will be here by seven, she's a nice lass, you'll like her.'

Meg tied an apron around her waist and passed Sarah one, once the oven had been lit, and went about her work. Meg had always been the worker, Sarah thought, and it was time that she too pulled her weight as she looked around the kitchen and carried the many stalks of pink rhubarb onto the table and started peeling and chopping.

Meg looked over at her young sister as she did as she was told. She was back where she belonged, for now, and she hoped that she would enjoy working alongside her. It would be so wonderful if Sarah could become part of her business as well as return to the family. The old Sarah had definitely gone and had been replaced with a more humble one.

Kneading the dough, Meg watched Sarah measuring the sugar out to be added to the rhubarb. She couldn't help but think that Sarah had arrived home just at the right time; an extra pair of hands would be more than welcome in the bakery in the run-up to Easter. There were hot cross buns to make for

Friday, Simmel cakes to ice, as well as the everyday baking, and on top of that, it was the last few days of her being single before the wedding at the weekend. Sometime before Saturday, she would have to visit the market and see what flowers she could buy to decorate the church for her wedding. Yes, it would be good to have Sarah back not just to help, but also to be by her side, like a sister should be, now to share the good times with.

Soon after they started, Rosie arrived, and started on her daily work. Meg explained that Sarah would be helping them, and once it was time for a break, and they all sat with a cup of tea, the young farm girl was full of questions about London.

'So it's not as good as it's all made out to be then?' Rosie said in her matter-of-fact way.

'No, I always believed that the streets were paved with gold, but believe me, they aren't. It's just like Leeds but there are ten times more older buildings in it and ten times the amount of poor people in it as well. The poor are poorer and the rich are richer and the ones in between are just trying to make a living.'

'Well, I never fancied going anyway. I'd rather have my open fields and my own home. There's nowhere better than home, I'm content with my lot,' Rosie said and looked across at the jars of jam that Sarah had made and smiled. 'So you are going to be our jam-maker, are you? That'll be grand, keep it in the family. I wish I'd never told your sister about it on the quiet,' Rosie added softly to Sarah.

'Hey, I heard that, you monkey. But yes, Sarah's made a good job of that. She can make some curd this afternoon while I finish these Simmel cakes. We've had more orders than I like for the run-up to Friday. I don't know how Frankie will be managing – he's been making chocolate eggs, icing our wedding cake, and making the same as us. No wonder he was drinking brandy last night.'

'Brandy, now that's posh.' Rosie winked at Sarah and smiled.

'He's not that posh, he deserves his brandy,' Sarah retorted. 'Now, who's going to show me how to make this curd? I've never heard of it before, let alone made any. I hope it is not too complicated?'

She was enjoying her morning in the warmth and friendship of Meg's bakery. Had it always been this way and why hadn't she realized earlier? She should have been helping her sister all along instead of chasing her dreams, she thought as she cracked eggs over a bowl and looked across at her sister doing what she did best: baking her loved bread and taking care of everyone around her.

Frankie kept his hand slow and steady as he piped the thick royal icing delicately into flowers, leaves, and buds to place upon the cake that had been made with so much love between them. It was four in the afternoon and the bakery and tea room had closed for the day, so he was on his own to concentrate on the job at hand and think about the last few months – a rollercoaster of emotions that had not yet finished playing out. His mother was due to arrive to stay on Good Friday in time for the biggest day of his life, his and Meg's wedding. He was dreading seeing her – he could just hear her voice criticizing everything, especially the wedding breakfast now being held in the upstairs tea room. Oh, yes, she would have plenty to say, no doubt, she would never change. Unlike Sarah.

Her arrival back into their lives had also caught him by surprise, but it seemed to him that she had changed both in appearance and in her ways. She was no longer the cocky mouthy, young lass who had only shown resentment towards him. He just hoped that she was going to remain like that, especially if she was to live in the same house as them both.

He placed his icing tube down and looked at his work. The top tier of the cake was complete. It had a delicate hand-piped pair of doves, holding a ring made out of gold leaf in their beaks, surrounded by delicate roses and leaves which he was just finishing to be added to the bottom tier between the piped swags and ribbons that covered the cake. It was a work of art, even though he did say so himself. His heart and soul had gone into it.

He'd do anything for his Meg, he loved her so much. She had stuck by him through thick and thin and helped him with all his problems. He might not have liked being told some-times what she thought was wrong with his life and business but she was proving to be right with what she had done for him so far.

The bakery was full of Easter delights. The chocolate eggs that he had tempered chocolate for, poured into moulds and then decorated with roses like the ones on the wedding cake. Hot-cross buns ready-made for the coming morning and small iced cakes covered with marzipan with flowers adorn-ing those. In one corner were stacked the non-perishable goods ready for the wedding reception to be held above in the tea room.

There was just one thing missing that would make Meg's wedding day complete and he knew just what to do about it. As he untied his apron he thought he'd been good of late, but now it was time to spend money a little recklessly, as he knew it would complete Meg's perfect day.

'Well, that was a turn up for the books, your Sarah turning up like that out of the blue. She looked as if she had been through the mill. Is she alright now?' Daisy asked as Meg paid her usual Thursday visit to her own bakery.

'Yes, she's alright now. I think she had got mixed in with a bad bunch, so I'm glad that she's home now. I tell you what, Daisy, she's grown up, I can't believe it. She's as meek as a lamb and she is actually enjoying working in the bakery with me. She's made all the jam and curd this week for me and she and Frankie are hitting it off famously.'

'I bet you are glad she's home,' Janet said. 'I know you thought I didn't notice but that was blood on the bottom of her skirts. She'd not lost a baby, had she?'

Meg looked hard at Janet. 'No, she'd picked it up on the streets, that's all, she'd walked in something on her way through London.'

'I just wondered, what with her fainting and all. At least she's back for your wedding. That will suit you. Mentioning that, I'll go back to my mam's tomorrow night. You can't sleep under the same roof as your man, it would bring you bad luck. So you'd better have your room back,' Janet said bluntly.

'You needn't do that, I'm not superstitious and besides his mother is coming to stay tomorrow night. I'll have to be there,' Meg said.

'Meg Fairfax, you do not stop under the same roof as your fiancé tomorrow night, that's tempting fate. Besides your dress is still upstairs and you can't get that home without Frankie seeing it and that really would be bad luck!' Daisy interrupted. 'You've made him wait this long, now don't bring bad luck upon your day.'

'But there's Sarah. I can't leave her with Frankie and his mother. Lord knows what would happen,' Meg said.

'Then bring her with you, there's room in your bed for two,' Janet said without thinking and making Daisy laugh as she realized what she had said.

'Well, you'd know, I have noticed that George has been staying lately,' Daisy whispered and made Meg smile as she saw Janet blush for the first time ever.

'I suppose you are right,' Meg agreed. 'His mother is not keen on me, so the less I have to do with seeing her the better. It would give Frankie and his mother time to kiss and make up before our wedding, providing she doesn't upset the apple cart again. And it would be nice to spend my last night single with Sarah. It would be like old times.'

'There you go then, and we can both come here to be with you before you walk to the church. That is if you are walking to the church, it is after all only a few yards down the road and it's what everyone around here does,' Janet said and looked at Daisy and winked.

'Oh, yes, I'm walking there, it would be stupid to do anything other. I'm not that posh yet. I suppose you are both right, so I'll do that, but I bet Frankie will not be happy with the arrangement when I tell him.'

'He'll be fine. Now, what time are we closing today? It's after four and tomorrow is Good Friday. I take it we will just be open just till dinner time? A half-day and all the weekend to ourselves, now that's a treat. George says he's taking me to the boating lake on Sunday after the thrill of your wedding. What are you going to be doing, Daisy?' Janet asked as she took off her apron ready for going home.

'I'm off to Jimmy's mother's for dinner, Lord help me, and she looks at me as if I shouldn't be with her precious son,' Daisy said and then looked at Meg. 'And we will not ask what you'll be doing, because we both already know, Mrs Pearson. It's a good job that the bakeries are closed on Monday as well, you'll need the rest.'

'I don't know what you mean!' This time it was Meg's turn to blush. 'I'll see you both on Saturday at twelve when my legs will be like jelly and my stomach will be churning. Oh, Lord, my wedding day, it has come so quickly!'

Chapter 24

It was lunchtime on Good Friday. All the shops were closing for the Easter holidays, including the bakeries owned by Frankie and Meg, who welcomed the break from work especially as the coming days were going to be ones of celebration.

'Are you coming with me to the market, our Sarah? It would be nice if you could,' Meg asked her sister as they locked the bakery door and made their way home. 'I'm going to buy some flowers for the church for the wedding. There will be some already in there but I thought a few more would make it brighter. Come with me and we can put a bunch of daffs on our mam as well.'

'I don't know. That would mean I'd have to say hello to Roger and Mick and I don't know if I could face them,' Sarah said remembering how she had stolen from the two stall-holders on the market and given them cheek when younger.

'Well you need not worry about them. Roger went a few years ago, got married, and left with his wife, and Mick now has a vegetable and fruit shop in Ilkley, so you can save your blushes. Come on it will be like old times, but this time we will have more than a sixpence to do all our shopping with,' Meg encouraged as they walked up the main street of Headingley heading for Leeds central market.

Sarah decided to join her. It was better than going back to their home as she knew preparations were being made for Frankie's mother, arriving later that day.

'Leeds has really changed in the short time I've been away,' she pointed out. 'New houses have sprung up. I suppose our old one has been knocked down now, not that I want to go back and see what has become of it.'

'Yes, it has. Everything has people expect bigger and better. Soon there will be no slums left in Leeds. Even I have had to give in to it – I have just ordered a gas oven to be fitted into my bakery, now that gas is being piped down York Street due to people demanding it.'

'You and those gas ovens – it was all you talked about sometimes,' Sarah said with a laugh and then said quietly, hurt clear in her voice, 'There are plenty of slums in London. There are people sleeping on pavements, under boat hulls on the side of the Thames and anywhere they can lay their heads. It's not like you are told when you are at school. There are the castles and grand houses but there is also a lot of poverty and pain.'

'Oh, Sarah, you are away from it now, you are back where you are loved. Now, tonight it will just be me and you. If you don't mind we will share the bed over the bakery on

York Street where you slept the other night. Janet and Daisy will have me stay there, saying it is bad luck to be in the same house as Frankie on the night before our marriage and I didn't think you'd want to be in the house with him and his mother by yourself.'

'No, from what you've told me about Frankie's mother, I think they are best both left to one another. It will be a bit of a squeeze in that bed together, but I don't mind if you don't. It will be like old times.'

'That's what I thought. It will be the last time I suspect. I'm so glad that you are home, Sarah.' Meg squeezed her sister's hand as they walked down into the busy market. 'Look, some of the stallholders have now got permanent stands that they can lock up of a night and leave their wares in. Money has been spent on making the market a lot better than when you left. They are sheltered from the weather and some even have shops around the edges. Mr Marks' penny bazaar is now in one of those and he's even more successful than he and his partner have ever been,' Meg explained and watched as Sarah walked to the flower stall and picked up six bunches of narcissus. She herself picked some lilies that the saleswoman had advised for her to have in her bouquet, but thinking better of it as she spotted a ready-made bouquet that would be perfect for her day. It was filled with lily of the valley, apple blossom, and narcissus mixed in with green shoots of spring tied with a white lace ribbon. She smiled as she took it in her arms and passed the narcissus to Sarah once she had paid for them.

'You are going to be beautiful, our Meg. I couldn't help but notice your wedding dress hanging up in the bedroom. I'm sure your day will be perfect. Sam said he'd marry me, once I was a little older, but that's not going to happen now,' Sarah said and looked down at Meg's bouquet and held back the tears.

'Sam was the man you were living with? You mentioned him in your letter,' Meg prompted, hoping to gently tease a little bit more of her sister's life from out of her.

'Yes, but it's in the past now, I'd prefer not to talk about it,' Sarah said as she lifted her head high and followed her sister to the church, to decorate it with the narcissus and show their respects to their mother's grave.

'Mother, you are on your own! I thought that you said you were bringing a companion with you?' Frankie said as his mother entered her old family home with her usual disdain of the maid, who took her coat and curtsied.

'I thought that it would be more appropriate for me to arrive on my own this time. Besides I'm getting too old and I'm weary of the young men who try to flatter me because they need my backing. I'm not that stupid, even if it does the ego good.' She looked Frankie up and down. 'Well you look to have come down to Earth with a bang. Working hard, are we, and having to account for every penny? It will not do you any harm, to have had to survive in the real world for once.'

'Mother, don't start. It is my wedding day tomorrow,

please let us celebrate in peace and have no bad words,' Frankie begged as she made her way into the parlour.

'Are you on your own? Where is your intended? Will she be making an appearance this evening? It looks like she is already living here.' Florence pointed to Meg's embroidery ring that she had left on her footstool.

'Yes, she has been living in the guest bedroom, because she's been helping me with my bakery at Headingley, and no, she will not be joining us this evening. She is staying in her own room above her bakery with her sister. You'll not need to talk to Meg until after we are married.'

'You needn't say it like that, I have no qualms with the girl, now I know that she's not a gold hunter. She obviously loves you, so that's to be commended.'

Florence sat down on the sofa, put her bag on her knee and then delved within. 'Before you start on about me being an uncaring mother who stole your inheritance, let me get this out of the way.' Florence saw the anger rising on her son's face. 'I did it in your best interest and you should have had more faith in me. You are my only son and you mean the world to me. Sometimes you have to be cruel to be kind.' Florence fished an envelope out of her bag and passed it to Frankie. 'Go on, open it and then tell me what you think of me?'

'What's this then? An official letter of apology or is it a bill for your train journey here to join my wedding?' Frankie took the envelope suspiciously and looked at his mother's stern face. He opened it and took out an art gallery receipt with the cheque made out in his name. He looked at it, then at her, and then back at the cheque. 'This is made out to me. There must be some mistake. It is you that owns the paintings that are listed here, and surely the payment is yours?'

'No, they were bought with your inheritance money. The cheque is yours to keep. I made an investment . . . No, I took a gamble and thank heavens it paid off,' Florence admitted. 'There's enough money there to keep you and your wife-to-be quite comfortable for quite a few years. It is treble the amount I *borrowed* from you and that was only because I knew that at that time either you would fritter it away or your wife-to-be was after you for your money.' Florence sat back in her chair and smiled. 'Now, that is a wedding present, don't you think, and I hope that I am forgiven.'

'I can't take it all, surely? Won't you need some of it yourself?' Frankie looked at the cheque again. The sum flabbergasted him. That would clear all his debts and leave him still with money in the bank.

'I may look a vain, stupid old woman, but I have a keen eye when it comes to the art world. My own bank account is quite healthy because of my financial dealing. Now – am I forgiven?' Florence could see the relief on her son's face as he placed the cheque safely back in the envelope.

'I don't know if I can accept it. I'd rather earn my own money and make my own way in the world. I've learned a lot since Meg and I have worked together,' Frankie said softly.

'Of course, you can, it's your wedding present! Put it into the bank and look forward to the knowledge that you are wealthy enough to support the children that will inevitably come along with marriage. I don't want to hear of my grandchildren being dragged up like urchins with no shoes on their feet. This Meg that you are to marry, she obviously loves you else she would have left you long before now, even though it's taken you three years to get a ring upon her finger. Now say no more, put the past behind us, and let us celebrate in fashion.'

After a moment, Frankie's face broke into a relieved smile. 'Thank you, Mother, I don't know what to say.' He folded the envelope into his jacket pocket.

'Don't say anything although a glass of sweet sherry would not go amiss and then you can tell me just why you are holding your wedding reception at Langroyd Hall?' Florence said in a most disapproving tone.

'I'm not anymore. I'm afraid it is to be held above my bakery, in the tea rooms,' Frankie said humbly as he passed his mother a glass of sherry.

'Your bakery? Oh, your *patisserie*. Thank the Lord for that. I cannot stand those Bensons, she is a lady of the loosest kind.' Florence sipped her sherry. 'Those sorts cannot be trusted you know. She always was such a one for the men and him, well he's just a buffoon!'

Frankie smiled. 'You could be right there, Mother.'

'I know I'm right. Too much money and not enough brains. Now don't you ever be like that, Frankie, else I will disown you.'

'I don't think there will be any chance of that, Mother.'

Frankie felt a wave of relief come over him as he felt the cheque in his jacket pocket. Now he could truly enjoy his wedding in the morning.

Meg and Sarah nestled in bed together.

'I do love you, our Meg. I didn't know how much until I was down there in London and it was a fight for survival every day,' Sarah said softly as she closed her eyes and felt safe in her big sister's arms.

'And I love you. I might have been hard on you when you were younger but life was hard for me, especially when our mam was dying. I've worried about you so much. You'll still live with Frankie and me, won't you? I'll not lose you again will I?' Meg said quietly, as she ran her fingers through Sarah's auburn locks.

'I'm not going anywhere, but one day I'll have to find somewhere of my own . . . but perhaps just not yet, if you and Frankie can put up with me for a while,' Sarah said sleepily.

'Of course, we will my love. I'm never going to let you out of my sight again, that I promise you.'

Chapter 25

'We aren't open today, come back Tuesday!' Sarah shouted out of the bedroom window above the bakery at the person down below as Meg pulled her overnight rags out of her hair and looked at herself in the mirror, surveying every line on her face and hoping that Frankie would not notice them on this their wedding day.

'It's an urgent delivery for Miss Sarah Fairfax from Hopkin's. I was told strictly to deliver it before ten o'clock and to make sure that it was not returned!' the young delivery boy yelled up at Sarah and swore under his breath as her head disappeared from the window and he was left holding the box that he'd been told was so important. He straightened his face as he heard the bolt being drawn on the shop's door and the bell tinkle as Sarah came to the door.

'It can't be for me, no one knows I'm here!' Sarah said and looked at the box tied with ribbon.

'Well if you are Sarah Fairfax and this is the bakery on York Street, then I've done my job. Now, just take it and let me be on my way.' The lad thrust the box into Sarah's hands and trundled off down the street, leaving Sarah looking at the box tied up with white ribbon and with her name and address upon it, making it indeed hers. She carried it upstairs and showed Meg.

Sarah gasped. 'It is from Hopkin's – look at the label.'

'Well, what is it? Somebody obviously knows you are here with me and thinks that you are worthy of a surprise present.' Meg pulled her underskirts up and smoothed her stomach down.

Sarah placed the box on their unmade bed and pulled on the ribbon ties before lifting the lid. 'Oh, Lord, just look at that, it is the most beautiful dress I've ever seen. It's emerald green, my favourite colour, and it shines in the light.'

Sarah pulled it up out of the box and held it against her, looking at her reflection in the mirror and smiling.

'There's a note in the box and a comb for your hair. By the looks, you must have an admirer.' Meg smiled. She knew exactly who the gift was from because it had been hinted as she kissed Frankie and had left his house.

Sarah quickly put the dress to one side and reached for the note, and read it. '*Meg would really like you to be one of our bridesmaids today and so would I. I hope that the dress fits and that I have chosen it well. Your loving brother-in-law, Frankie.*'

'It's from Frankie, he says that you would both like me to be one of your bridesmaids today. The dress is beautiful, but I don't know if I want everyone's eyes on me and they will all be talking about me.' Just for a moment, when she had seen her name on the box, Sarah had hoped and prayed that the box had been sent from Sam and that he was still alive but then her hopes had been dashed once she read the enclosed note.

'What, that you have returned to be a bridesmaid at your sister's wedding because of course that is all there is to talk about *at my wedding*. Now try your dress on and yes, please, I would love you to be my main bridesmaid. It would mean the world to me.' Meg put her arms around her sister. 'It's where you should be.'

'Alright, I can't put up a stronger fight against it as I want to look at myself and preen like a peacock. I truly have never seen dresses like the ones we are to wear today. I keep looking at yours with all the embroidery and lace upon it. You are going to look so beautiful. Frankie is such a lucky man, you've got brains and beauty.' Sarah laughed, the first true laugh that she had given since returning home.

'That's good to hear. Now, where are Daisy and Janet? They said they would be here by ten-thirty so that we would get to the church on time? I know it is fashionable for the bride to be slightly late, but I really don't want to keep Frankie waiting.'

Meg pulled her dress on and asked Sarah to button the small silk-covered buttons up her back before pulling on her cream laced boots onto her feet and placing her garland of lilies on her head. Looking at herself in the mirror and not believing the reflection that was looking back at her, she smiled. She was worthy to be walking down the aisle next to her fine French Yorkshireman.

'Mam would have been so proud of you, our Meg. You are beautiful,' Sarah said and looked at her sister whom she now appreciated and would always be there for.

'Go on, your turn now. Let's hope Frankie has got the size right. I told him to hunt the old receipt out for the blouse that you once had and then go up an inch or so. It looked about right when you held it to yourself.' Meg watched as Sarah pulled the dress over her head. Her sister turned to be buttoned up then she arranged her hair over her shoulders before placing the shining emerald comb into her hair.

'Now, don't we look like two ladies. We've come a long way since we both lived in Sykes Yard. Mam will be looking down and smiling at us,' Meg said and kissed her sister.

'She might be smiling at you but she won't at me,' Sarah said quietly.

'Oh, yes she will. She'll be smiling because you have at long last come home and hopefully have realized that the other man's grass is not always greener no matter where you go. Now, where are those two girls? We are going to be late.'

Meg peered out of the window and was taken completely by surprise. Outside down on the street was an open coach pulled by a team of white horses and sitting in the coach surrounded by flowers were Daisy and Janet beaming up at her. 'Oh Lord, please tell me he hasn't! It's only a few yards to the church.'

'It looks like he has. He's full of surprises is your Frankie and just look at the folk standing in their doorways waiting to see you. I thought you said it was going to be a quiet wedding?' Sarah teased. She and Meg peered at the people waiting to see the bride off to the church in her coach: the baker whose food kept them fed, but more importantly, the lass whom they had all come to love.

'It was, it is! We have only got people that mean a lot to us at the wedding and definitely at the wedding breakfast above Frankie's patisserie.' Meg pulled on her gloves and smiled. 'Well, here goes, let's face the day. Frankie will be waiting and will be a bag of nerves especially after staying with his mother on his own a night.'

'I'll get your bouquet from the kitchen. You go and meet your well-wishers, I'm right behind you.' Sarah said and felt like crying. She'd gained her sister but in a way had also immediately lost her. She was to marry Frankie and probably have a family of her own to look after.

'Thank you, Sarah, I love you,' Meg said and kissed her delicately on her cheek.

'And I love you, my sister,' Sarah whispered, words that neither of them had hardly ever shared before.

'Oh, Lord, what has he spent good money on a carriage for?' Meg muttered as she stepped out onto the street. The neighbours and customers waved and cheered as the two sisters climbed into the carriage and sat down next to Janet and Daisy. They were on their way to the wedding, the wedding that had taken so long to take place.

'It may be because he loves you, Meg Fairfax. Now for once enjoy your day and stop worrying,' Janet said bluntly then smiled. 'You both look absolutely beautiful and the weather is just right for a wedding.'

Meg felt that her stomach was full of butterflies as she alighted from the carriage and smiled at Joe Dinsdale, who was waiting for her at the church gate.

'Well, lass, it's your big day, and don't you look the part. Not a bonnier lass in Leeds, I'm willing to bet,' he said and took her arm, followed by Sarah, Janet and Daisy.

They walked down the church path, with apple and cherry blossoms in full bloom over their heads as the organ played the bridal march. They processed into the darkness of the church, with the light beaming through the stained glass window shining directly onto the vicar and Frankie. Her shining French knight stood smiling waiting for her as the guests stood and looked at the bonniest bride they had ever seen. It looked like the perfect wedding to the vicar as he asked the congregation to rise and saw the love in the eyes of the betrothed.

'You look beautiful,' Frankie whispered and took Meg's hand, 'and I'm the luckiest man on Earth.'

'And I'm the luckiest woman,' Meg whispered as he took her hand and the ceremony began.

With a ring upon her finger and Frankie on her arm, Meg walked proudly out of the church. Life was perfect. She had everything that she had ever wanted and more besides.

Betsy's children yelled and whooped as they held the church gates tight shut with string, not opening them until a handful of coins were thrown into the road by Frankie's best man to pay the ransom. They scurried to pick the coins up as Meg and Frankie climbed into their carriage along with Sarah, Janet and Daisy, to get on their way to their wedding breakfast at the tea room.

'Well, Mrs Pearson, that, I think I can happily say, was the perfect wedding and I have the most perfect wife by my side,' Frankie said and leaned over and kissed her.

Daisy said in her usual outspoken way. 'Now then, wait until you are on your own. Don't make us three ladies blush.'

'I can't believe today – everyone has made it so special,' Meg said and looked across at her two best friends and Sarah. 'George looked very handsome and so did your Jimmy.' Meg looked at her sister. 'And I don't think Harry could take his eyes off you, my darling sister. Perhaps your friendship could be rekindled?'

'Perhaps. I did speak to him briefly on my way back when I met him on the train. He's done well for himself, he's management.' Sarah smiled. She too had seen how he looked at her, and even though she was still grieving Sam, she had felt something for him.

'There you go, we should be all thankful for the men we have got in our lives,' Meg said and squeezed Frankie's hand tightly as the carriage pulled up outside the patisserie on the Headrow on a busy Holy Saturday. The Leeds shoppers gasped as the wedding party in all its glory walked into the bakery and climbed the stairs to where the breakfast tables were spread out before them. White table cloths were on every table and a swag of lilies was on the main table as Frankie showed Meg the way to her seat.

'My staff . . . *our* staff has done us proud, my love. I'm not worried that we are not dining in the hall. This is more our style and we can talk to our true friends. The smell that is coming from the bakery is unbelievable. My choice of a chef was a wise one.' Frankie smiled as the guests that had walked from the church arrived, Frankie's mother being one of the first as she sat down beside her son.

'You look lovely, my dear, welcome to the family. I am so happy for you both,' Florence said with true sentiment.

'Thank you, and thank you for attending, I know it means a lot to Frankie to have you at our wedding,' Meg said.

'Mother has given us the most wonderful wedding present, her investment of my money has been trebled and is now back in my hands,' Frankie told her, turning to Meg and whispering, 'All our troubles are over.'

Meg couldn't believe it. She was thinking of scolding Frankie for being so reckless with bridesmaid's dresses and carriages, even though they had made the day more than special. Now their troubles were indeed over, all the businesses were making good money, the family was back together and they were both united.

She smiled. All she had and ever wanted was around the tables,

'To my wonderful wife, who has just made my life perfect. Please raise your glasses to the Pearson and Fairfax family union. Bakers of perfection.'

'Oh, Frankie, it's taken us a while to get married, but now we can be truly happy,' Meg said as she saw the beautifully iced wedding cake. She knew everything would work out just fine. Sarah was talking to Harry and looking happier than she had ever seen her.

Family and baking were everything, she thought as Frankie looked at her with love in his eyes, and she was indeed lucky enough to have both in her life.